THE KING'S STOLEN JEWELS

Shadow Cutpurses Thrillers Book Four

Adele Jordan

SAPERE BOOKS

Also in the Shadow Cutpurses Series

Murder at Greenwich Palace

Death At The Tower

The Body in the Chamber

The Tudor Vanishing

THE KING'S STOLEN JEWELS

Published by Sapere Books.

24 Trafalgar Road, Ilkley, LS29 8HH

saperebooks.com

ISBN: 978-0-85495-825-2

ACKNOWLEDGEMENTS

I wish to thank the whole team at Sapere Books for publishing this book, including Amy, Caoimhe, Natalie and Matilda. If it had not been for their diligent work and their devotion to the written word, I would not have had the opportunity to finally write some stories in my own name.

I'd also like to thank the team of other Sapere writers, including C. V. Chauhan, Michael Fowler and Ros Rendle. These fellow writers in particular have helped to inspire this story, and I am grateful for the kind feedback they have offered in the past.

I'd also like to thank the late Elizabeth Bailey. This wonderful mystery writer had a significant impact on my writing. I'm delighted to be working as co-author on her latest book, which is due to be finished this year. In Liz's memory, I'd like it to be known what an influence and an inspiration she was to my career, from the first time I met her at a Sapere Books writing retreat. She will be missed greatly.

CHAPTER 1

Greenwich, London, Christmas Eve 1536

"Good evening, miting."

Gwynnie Wightham spun round so fast that she knocked one of the three candles off the desk in the office. It was snuffed out on the wooden floorboards. A tall shadow hovered in the corner of the room, both familiar and foreign.

This shadow couldn't be her mother. It was impossible. Emlyn was far away in Bristol, and yet Gwynnie knew at once by the voice and that name, *miting*. It was her mother's pet name for her, even though Gwynnie had always detested it — a constant reminder of her short stature.

"Ma?" Gwynnie whispered, her heart thumping.

The shadow stepped forward.

In the light of the two remaining candles, Gwynnie glimpsed Emlyn's face. The skin, once smooth and pale, was lined with scratches. Her dark eyes were tired, heavy shadows weighing on the skin. She was dressed as a clerk, in a thick doublet and rather fussy shirt, with tall boots reaching up to her knees. Her dark curly hair had been stuffed tightly under a felt bonnet, which Emlyn now readjusted on her brow, revealing more of her face.

"At least you recognise me, miting."

Gwynnie felt as if the breath had been stolen from her body. It had been nearly a year since she had last seen her mother.

Before that, they had scarcely spent a day apart. Gwynnie had grown up at her mother's side, learning to steal in order to survive. Together, she and Emlyn had been known as the

Shadow Cutpurses, the infamous jewellery thieves. It was what had brought them to Greenwich Palace. Emlyn had convinced Gwynnie that one last theft — that of Queen Anne Boleyn's jewels — would set them up forever. They had talked of running away to France and forging a new life.

Such memories seemed like a lifetime ago. Their plans had disappeared like water through cupped hands when Gwynnie had observed a murder in the palace, and Emlyn had then fallen under suspicion. After days of turmoil, during which Gwynnie had proved her own innocence, it had become necessary for Emlyn to go on the run to keep her own freedom. She was suspected of another murder, which had taken place many years before in the streets of London. Seen fleetingly at night, all that was known was that one of the Shadow Cutpurse thieves had killed a man in cold blood. It had taken place too long ago for Gwynnie, a child at the time, to be suspected of such a crime. No one had doubted Emlyn's guilt, nor had she denied it to Gwynnie. The night Emlyn had left, Gwynnie had agreed to become an informer to Lord Thomas Cromwell's clerk, a lawyer named Elric Tombstone. In return for her work, Tombstone had made a vow. He would not search for Emlyn, nor make her pay the price for her crime.

Desperate to keep her mother safe, Gwynnie had helped Emlyn escape the palace. Since then, she had devoured the ballad sheets and pamphlets that Tombstone kept in a leather chest in his office. Some mentioned a tall thief in Bristol. Others bore secrets — secrets that Emlyn had never shared with her.

"What are you doing here?" Gwynnie's voice shook as she stepped away from the desk, where the pamphlets lay scattered.

Emlyn chuckled. “Quite a way to greet your mother, eh?”

She limped forward. One arm was strapped up in a makeshift sling, and now Gwynnie caught sight of a smear of blood on Emlyn’s neck.

“What has happened to you?” Gwynnie reached for her mother’s hand.

“Much.” Emlyn gave a weary smile and the tension in the room evaporated. Gwynnie pulled her mother into a tight embrace, careful not to hurt the arm strapped in its sling. “Oh, my child,” whispered Emlyn. “It has been too long. Too long indeed. You do not know how often I have thought of you these last twelve months.”

Gwynnie screwed her eyes shut as she buried her head in Emlyn’s shoulder. For a fleeting moment, she forgot all the fears that had plagued her during the last couple of weeks in the palace. She could think only of the joy of seeing her mother again.

“Well, you are in a better shape than I, at least,” Emlyn said with a warm smile as she stepped back and cupped Gwynnie’s cheek with her good hand. “Let me look at you properly. You’ve put on weight. They must be feeding you well here in the palace. That’s good.”

Gwynnie laughed with her as Emlyn took her hand and turned her in a circle.

“These clothes…” Emlyn murmured, dark eyes wandering up and down Gwynnie’s gown. “Tombstone must be paying you well.”

Shifting self-consciously from foot to foot, Gwynnie brushed a loose lock of hair back behind her ear. She was wearing a pale green kirtle, fitted tightly around the waist with laces, and a thick wool shawl across her shoulders that was dyed a rich dark blue. They were garments she had purchased with the money Tombstone had paid her for being his eyes and ears in the palace corridors.

"You are well looked-after," Emlyn's continued. "I thought you were quite beholden to him, his slave, if you will."

"Slave? Ma, I'm in his employment. That is a very different thing."

"Never mind." She forced a smile. "You are well? Tell me you are well, miting."

"I am well." Gwynnie nodded firmly. "I am better for seeing you, Ma." Her eyes darted between her mother's injuries. "But what has happened to you?" Hastily, she steered Emlyn toward one of the caquetoire chairs by the fireplace in Tombstone's office. "Sit. Tell me what has happened."

Hastening to a buffet cabinet in the corner of the room, she pulled out a small wooden casement which contained strips of muslin and various tonics she had seen Tombstone use for wounds. Fumbling between the tonic bottles, she found a honey-coloured liquid that Tombstone had labelled in black, spiky handwriting, *For open wounds*. Dabbing a little on a cloth, she reached for the cut on Emlyn's neck, wiping away the blood.

"Have you lost your tongue?"

"I was observing how at home you are in this chamber," Emlyn said with interest, looking around the room. "It is that clerk's study, is it not? Yet you treat it as your own."

"I've been here often enough." Gwynnie quickly dismissed the words. "Who did this?" She pressed harder on the cut and Emlyn winced.

"This one —" Emlyn pointed at the cut Gwynnie was attending to — "was from a particularly rambunctious lad who thought I was breaking into the palace tonight. I had to show him I was doing no such thing." She feigned an innocent look.

"This —" she nodded down at the arm in the sling — "is from a stab wound I received in Bristol. They aimed for my chest but got my arm."

Gwynnie hesitated with the cloth.

"I may have broken the bone. It was some months ago, yet I still wear this sling when it aches." Emlyn seemed unconcerned, though her eyes glazed over. "As for my leg, well, I fell from a rooftop. I am no great climber." She stretched out her long legs and sighed. " I cannot move as quickly these days, yet I'm well enough."

"Well?" Gwynnie huffed as she prepared a linen bandage. "You are a walking advertisement for a physician's care."

Emlyn ignored the comment. "What news do you have for me, Gwynnie? What has happened to you since I left the palace?"

Gwynnie paused. She could tell Emlyn about the hunt for the spy, Daundelyon, when Anne Boleyn was being held in the Tower. She could tell her about the killer who had left a body in Queen Jane Seymour's chamber. She could tell her about Connal Devlin, the man she had said goodbye to that very day, who had left her with tears in her eyes. Yet how could she speak of any of it when those pamphlets on the desk hinted at secrets Emlyn had kept from her?

In exchange for her help on Tombstone's latest mission, he had vowed to release to her all the information he had on the Shadow Cutpurses. Those pamphlets had revealed that the name went back years, to when Gwynnie was a child, long before she had ever started thieving. Someone else had had the name before them, and she longed to know *who.*

"Much has happened," she whispered, moving to sit in the chair opposite Emlyn. She watched the flames dance in the grate.

"Nothing you wish to share?" Emlyn asked as she toyed with the bandage now on her neck. "How interesting. There was a time when you never kept secrets from me, Gwynnie."

Gwynnie frowned. "It is certainly something, you accusing me of keeping secrets." She glanced toward the pamphlets on the desk, wondering what Emlyn would say if she brandished them now and demanded an answer. Despite wishing to do just that, something held Gwynnie back — something that made her palms sweat as she rubbed them on her skirt. It was fear. Fear of losing the closeness that had always existed between them.

"You wish to know my secrets? Very well, I shall share them." Emlyn sat back wearily in the chair. "First, do you have a drink to spare for your mother, miting? Something to wet my tongue after a long journey."

Gwynnie returned to the buffet cabinet and pulled out a small carafe of claret. She poured out two glasses, putting one in her mother's good hand. Emlyn raised it, gulped it back and smacked her lips together, as if it was the first taste of liquid she'd had in days. Wordlessly, she held out the glass for more, and Gwynnie obliged.

"Why are you here?" she asked, frustrated at the silence.

"I was in Bristol." Emlyn stared at the fire as Gwynnie returned to her own seat, not so interested in the wine she had poured for herself.

"I know. I saw you mentioned in pamphlets."

"They didn't mention me by name?"

"No, but I recognise my own mother, even in print," Gwynnie scoffed. "Why were you in Bristol? Was it just somewhere to run? Somewhere to hide?"

"Not exactly." Emlyn grimaced. "Oh, I thieved well enough. You may have always talked about me leaving such a life behind, Gwynnie, but there is only one way to survive on the streets when you have no position. You know it as well as I."

Gwynnie fidgeted in her seat but did not reply.

"So, yes, I thieved and I…" Emlyn hesitated, glancing at her injuries. "I got into a few scrapes."

"A few?" Gwynnie's scorn made Emlyn smile.

"Then I found what I've been looking for."

In spite of herself, Gwynnie leaned forward, the scent of ash and spiced wine filling the air as she hung on her mother's words.

"What? What were you looking for?"

"A woman. A widow. Her name is Marie Duffield."

Gwynnie sat back. There was something familiar about the name, as if she had heard it whispered once between friends but couldn't remember where or by whom.

"Do you remember her?" Emlyn asked, her dark eyes fixed on Gwynnie.

"No." Gwynnie shook her head. "Should I?"

"I didn't know if you would. You met her. We talked of her often enough, when you were a child. I needed to find her. It took many years, but I found her at last, and she was able to give me what I needed." Emlyn's excitement was palpable as she poured herself another glass of wine, pausing for long enough to take another large gulp. "She offered a hint as to where some loot is buried. A treasure I have been searching for, for a very long time."

Gwynnie stilled. "I should have expected this. That is why you're here. Not for me, but for some bounty —"

"We are thieves, Gwynnie," Emlyn reminded her. "Or have you forgotten who you are as you parade about this palace?"

"Parade?" she spluttered. "I do not parade."

"No?" Emlyn tutted. "I glimpsed you in that fancy hall, sitting next to the clerk. What was his name? Tomberoy?"

"Tombstone," Gwynnie corrected her harshly.

"Maybe you have forgotten."

"I have forgotten nothing," Gwynnie said abruptly. "So, what is it now that entices you? What is it that so eludes you, that you had to go all the way to Bristol to talk to some widow about it?"

"A king's treasure, Gwynnie."

Gwynnie's patience snapped. She stood sharply from her chair and marched across the room.

"Will you not even hear me out, miting?"

"Don't call me that!" Gwynnie growled as she reached the desk.

"You've always been my miting. My little mite, my small one." The softness in Emlyn's tone was short-lived. "This is loot unlike any other. I have been listening for a hint of it for years, for news of Marie Duffield. Now I have some information, I can act at last. Would you turn your back on a treasure that belongs to a king, Gwynnie? And for what? A few half-decent clothes and a meal or two in the palace kitchens?"

"Yes, because being able to eat a decent meal is something to scoff at, isn't it?" Gwynnie retorted sarcastically. "How many nights did we go without a meal when I was a child?"

Emlyn's voice faltered. "I looked after you as best I could. You never wanted for anything."

"Because I learned not to ask!" Gwynnie barked as she stared down at the pamphlets on the desk. Her eyes flitted across the dates she had been reading just minutes before: 1518, 1520 … all before Gwynnie had made her first theft.

She snatched up the papers and marched across the room, thrusting them toward Emlyn.

"What is this?" Emlyn scrambled to put down her glass and take the pamphlets.

"This is what I want to know." Gwynnie stood over her. "I want to know who the real Shadow Cutpurses were, Ma. Before we took their name. It's all here, printed in ink and dated from so long ago. Who were they? Who were these men?"

Emlyn had frozen.

"Ma!"

"Miting … can you really not guess who they are?"

"I want you to tell me!" Gwynnie was breathing heavily as she faced Emlyn. "What does it all mean?"

"Gwynnie, the *real* Shadow Cutpurses are why I'm here in the first place," Emlyn replied.

Before she could say any more the sound of heavy footsteps echoed down the corridor, beyond the study door.

"We're no longer alone, miting," Emlyn muttered.

CHAPTER 2

Gwynnie raced to the door and opened it a fraction. Pressing her face to the gap, she peered out into the dark corridor and saw that a yellow flame bobbed at the end. It was coming closer.

"It's Tombstone," she hissed, shutting the door fast. Scrambling around, she looked for the key to the door, sifting through papers on the desk with such haste that she made a mess of his neat arrangements.

"Are you going to tell me your plan?" Emlyn asked. She now stood, with another full glass of claret in her hand, clearly unfazed by the approaching footsteps.

Gwynnie's heart was in her mouth.

She and Tombstone may have developed a grudging friendship over the last few months, but he had made it plain that his hands were tied if Emlyn were ever to reappear at the palace. She still remembered his words: *I'd have no choice but to arrest her. She is guilty of murder, Gwynnie. The law demands she hangs from a noose, and I am simply a servant of that law.*

"No key," Gwynnie whispered.

"Well, shall I adopt the guise of a clerk?" Emlyn suggested, perhaps the worse for wear due to all the wine she had downed.

Knowing the disguise wouldn't fool Tombstone for a moment, Gwynnie leapt across the room and grabbed the glass out of Emlyn's hand. Hastening to put it down, she then dragged her mother toward the window.

"Get out."

"That's not very kind, dearest."

"Get out, please. There, how's that?" Thrusting open the lead-lined window, Gwynnie peered out into the darkness. It was quite a drop to the grass below, but nothing too difficult. Taking Emlyn's good arm, she thrust her into the gap.

"This isn't quite the warm welcome I was hoping for, Gwynnie, being manhandled out of a window."

"It could be much worse, believe me. I once hid in the fireplace in this chamber."

Emlyn glanced across at the roaring fire and gave a reluctant nod. "Window it is." She clambered out just as the door handle was starting to turn. They were out of time.

"Go!" Gwynnie hissed. "I shall meet you on the other side of the tiltyard in two minutes." She shut the window fast, glimpsing Emlyn's startled face behind the glass.

The door opened.

Gwynnie spun around, planting herself in front of the window so that Tombstone would not catch sight of Emlyn.

He halted as soon as he entered the room, staring at the papers discarded on the floor and the mess on his desk.

"I thought you would have learned that I like things orderly by now." He sighed, bending down to pick up the papers. "Well? What did you make of these pamphlets, Gwynnie?"

From the corner of her eye, she saw Emlyn loping off into the darkness. "I … yes, very interesting."

"Interesting?" Tombstone lifted his head, his copper hair flashing red in the firelight. Unlike many of the courtiers attending the Christmas Eve feast that night, who had opted for grand doublets, Tombstone had dressed demurely — head to toe in black. He stood up, the pamphlets in his hand. "I hand you evidence that your mother has been lying to you, and all you can say is *interesting*?" His grey eyes narrowed. "Is all well?"

"I … I think I'm just in shock, that's all," Gwynnie replied. "I didn't know our name — the Shadow Cutpurses — existed before us."

"I know." Tombstone sighed and took the papers back to the leather chest on his desk. "I am sorry, Gwynnie." His voice had softened. "You had a right to know."

"I told you that when you refused to show me the pamphlets before."

He winced. "I needed your help."

"You always need my help," she reminded him.

"I suppose I do." He shut the leather chest. "You're welcome to look at them again whenever you wish to."

"Thank you. That's kind of you."

"My God." He blinked. "Was that a compliment from Gwynnie Wightham?"

"Jesu! I am capable of a compliment."

"As long as it's coupled with a curse." He shook his head. "It's late, Gwynnie. We should get some sleep. King Henry will be holding many celebrations tomorrow — it's Christmas Day, you know."

She nodded. With everything that had happened recently, she had scarcely acknowledged that Yuletide was here.

"Yes, goodnight." Glad to have the chance to escape, Gwynnie hastened toward the door.

"Oh, and Gwynnie?"

She hesitated, her heart thudding as she turned back to look at him. Tombstone was hovering by the window, peering out into the darkness.

"There are many guards out tonight. After all this trouble with Devlin, they will be out in force for some time. I have persuaded Cromwell and Pascal that Devlin has headed north to the Midlands, but even so, it will be a few days before they relax the guard. Go straight to your chamber for the night."

At the mention of Devlin's name, Gwynnie felt a pain, as if a hand had squeezed her heart. She and Tombstone had arranged for the former soldier to escape back to Ireland aboard a ship, and Gwynnie now faced the very real possibility of never seeing him again. If he ever reappeared at the palace, Master Neville Pascal, Magistrate for the City of London, would see him hanged for murder.

"I will." She nodded and hastened out of the room. Taking a deep breath, she turned down the corridor and ran, heading for the tiltyard.

The night was dark with little moonlight, and it was difficult to make out Emlyn as she hovered in an archway. She blended into the wall, a well-practised shadow, just like Gwynnie.

Gwynnie reached for Emlyn's arm and grasped it tight. "Come with me," she said.

"What is going on?" Emlyn asked as they walked together through the alleys surrounding the palace. "I have never seen so many guards here. Has something happened?" They passed one of the open courtyards.

Guards were marching up and down; though they only spared a glance for the drunken revellers who were leaving the great hall, now that their Christmas Eve celebrations had come to an end. Some were heading in the direction of the chapel for Midnight Mass.

"A man was hiding here, a convict. The guards were hunting him," Gwynnie whispered, steering Emlyn past the courtyard and into another alley. The two women shivered as the wind picked up.

"What sort of convict?" Emlyn asked.

Gwynnie hesitated. Devlin may have been arrested for murder, but she now knew that he was innocent of such a crime. The Irishman had a surprisingly soft heart and had chosen not to challenge his conviction, allowing everyone to believe he was a murderer — all to save the true killer's life. *Queen Jane Seymour.*

"There are more guards this way. Keep your head down and walk beside me." Gwynnie released Emlyn's arm and walked on with haste as they passed another courtyard. She was in no mood to explain the whole story to Emlyn, to describe Devlin's good character, nor why they had deemed it necessary to protect the life of Queen Jane, a woman who had killed in self-defence.

They walked past two guards, who were too busy talking and drinking to notice them. Nevertheless, Gwynnie did not slow her pace. She glanced at Emlyn as they walked, observing that despite her limp, her mother had adopted the gait of a man, her head bowed, and her face hidden by the rim of the felt bonnet.

"You hide better than any other I know, Ma." Gwynnie found the compliment falling from her lips.

Emlyn raised her head just enough for a small smile to light up her features. "You know as well as I do that people see what they expect to. Where are we going? To your chamber?"

"No." Gwynnie shook her head. "I do not need the other maids whispering that a clerk was seen entering my chamber at night." She grinned at Emlyn. "Think of the gossip!"

"I'm sure there's many a maid in this palace who has enjoyed a night or two of —"

"You can hide in the laundry room tonight," Gwynnie cut her off as they headed toward the timber and wattle building on the far side of the compound. "I shall come and find you in the morning, and we'll talk more then." Reaching for the door, she swung it open and gestured for Emlyn to enter.

"We need to talk tonight, Gwynnie."

"No," Gwynnie hissed as footsteps sounded behind them. They both looked away as a guard passed by. He glanced at them briefly. "It's too dangerous tonight. There are too many guards. I'll find you in the morning."

"The Gwynnie I knew liked taking risks," Emlyn muttered as she stepped into the building and shut the door behind her.

For a moment, Gwynnie stared at the closed door. She was tempted to rattle it open and shout that the only reason she had taken risks in the past was to satisfy her mother, to get her the money and jewels she so craved.

Yet footsteps sounded nearby.

The guard was back, peering at her, his arms folded in suspicion.

Gwynnie gave a small wave and staggered on, pretending she had drunk too much wine. "Good feast, wasn't it?" she said with a laugh. "Goodnight."

"Goodnight." The guard glanced back at the laundry room but walked on, leaving Gwynnie to make her way to her chamber.

She followed the lane all the way to the riverbank, and was about to curve back under Donsen Tower and enter the main courtyard when she glimpsed something moving on the water.

A wherry was gliding forward. She could not make out the people within the boat, but a whisper travelled across the water, a male voice, hastily followed by a demanding, "*Hush!*"

Gwynnie melted back into the shadows on the riverbank as she watched the boat. Normally, this part of the bank would be teeming with people during the day, but as the clocks struck midnight in London town, on the other side of the river, there was no one here to observe the wherry but Gwynnie.

Slowly, the boat pulled up on the small docks. A rope was latched around a post to anchor it in position, then two men stepped up onto the dock, each holding out an arm to another in the boat. The third figure grasped their hands and allowed himself to be pulled up onto the boards. He was tall, his cloaked head towering above their own. He moved from the docks to the riverbank and stared up at the palace, his face hidden by the edge of his cloak. The two men who had helped him ashore were busy unlatching the boat, waving off the wherryman and urging him as quietly as possible to be on his way.

In the moonlight, Gwynnie could discern the glint of gold thread hemming the tall man's cloak. Behind him, his two manservants or guards — Gwynnie wasn't sure which — approached. One of the men rested a palm on his hip. He turned and she saw a scabbard at his belt, a dagger tucked into it.

Whoever these men were, it was clear they did not wish to be seen. Perhaps they hoped to sneak into the palace to rob it, as she and Emlyn had once done.

"Clothes too fine to be thieves," Gwynnie muttered to herself, dismissing the thought as soon as it had arisen.

As if her words had been caught on the wind, the cloaked figure suddenly turned his head in her direction. Gwynnie held her breath. She knew it was impossible for the stranger to see her in the darkness, just as it was impossible for her to make out his features behind his hood.

He turned back and walked up to the archway beneath Donsen Tower with his men at his heel. Gwynnie hesitated. Should she go and tell Tombstone there were strangers creeping into the palace now? Would she make it past all the guards without raising suspicion as to why she was taking messages to Tombstone in the middle of the night?

Before she could make a decision, a fourth figure appeared on the riverbank, this time not coming from the water, but from the tower itself.

Even at this distance and in the darkness, Gwynnie could not mistake the hunched stature and oversized bonnet. It was Lord Cromwell, Lord Privy Seal to King Henry. As it was Yuletide, he'd thrust a colourful feather into the rim of his hat, which stuck up at a jaunty angle, and he was carrying an ornamental staff which he used as a cane to aid his quick march.

Cromwell inclined his head toward the cloaked stranger in greeting. It wasn't a full bow, but enough of a mark of respect for Gwynnie's eyes to widen.

"Who would you greet in the middle of the night, Cromwell?" she whispered.

He stepped aside and held out an arm, gesturing for the cloaked figure to precede him into the palace. The stranger didn't hesitate, marching forward with purpose, his two men following closely behind.

As they vanished into the main courtyard, Gwynnie slipped out of her hiding place. Creeping along the wall with her back to the stone, she neared the archway under Donsen Tower and peered around the edge into the courtyard.

The four men were the only occupants of the yard, for everyone else was either at Midnight Mass or had retired for the night. The guards in the yard all looked away. Gwynnie presumed that was down to Cromwell's insistence.

The cloaked figure moved toward the main door to Donsen Tower, where the king and queen had chambers on the upper floor, but he had scarcely taken two steps when Cromwell took his elbow. The cloaked man shook Cromwell off his arm, as if he were dismissing a bothersome wasp.

Cromwell said something sharply to him, the harshness of his voice travelling, though his words did not, and pointed in another direction. The cloaked figure's head turned upward, in the direction of the royal chambers, before he relented and followed Cromwell across the yard.

Gwynnie watched with interest. Whoever he was, the cloaked man had expected to see either King Henry or Queen Jane tonight.

CHAPTER 3

"Ma?" Gwynnie whispered as she opened the laundry room door. The pale light of dawn shone through the latticed windows, casting diamond-shaped patterns upon the red-brick floor. There was no answering call, no snore, nor any sign of Emlyn.

"Ma?" Gwynnie called again as she opened the door wide and stepped inside.

The laundry bags had been stacked to one side the day before, ready for Gwynnie and the other maids to see to that afternoon. Amongst the bundles, there was a sign that someone had rearranged them, perhaps slept amongst them.

Gwynnie sighed. "Jesu, where the hell are you, Ma?"

She let the door swing shut behind her and marched across the yard, heading toward the kitchens. She glanced over her shoulder, looking for Emlyn, but there was no lurking shadow in the corners of the yard, watching her from a distance.

If her mother had crept into the palace just to risk talking to her about some treasure, then surely she would not have left again so swiftly?

Entering the kitchens, Gwynnie took in the sights and sounds. Despite the early hour, the cooks had already risen and were busy preparing the Yuletide feast.

In a vast fireplace to her right, twice her height and eight times her girth, suckling pigs were being roasted on a spit, turned laboriously by two small boys with sweat dripping from their foreheads as they stood by the fire. Across the room on one long table, peacocks and swans were being expertly cut from their skins, the cooks keeping all the feathers intact as their bodies were smothered in butter for cooking.

A young woman walked past carrying bowls of spices, the tang of nutmeg and cloves causing Gwynnie to cough.

"Gwynnie!" a familiar voice called as a large man carrying a bowl knocked into her, causing a cloud of flour to fly up into the air. It was Samuel, one of the palace cooks. "You all right, lass? Look at you. Flour all over your face and everything."

Gwynnie coughed and blinked hard. "Good morning, Samuel," she said. "Next time, just say good morning. I don't need flour thrown in my face in greeting."

"Come here. There's a cloth somewhere."

She was steered toward a table and a wet cloth was thrust into her hands. She wiped her face and looked up at Samuel. He was a big, burly man with a jolly face, though she could see he was tired.

"You and Brynne getting any sleep?" she asked. She knew it had been hard for Samuel's wife Brynne to say goodbye to Devlin, her son from her first marriage. When Devlin had been accused of murder, it had broken Brynne's heart. Though they had helped Devlin to escape with his life, Brynne had made it plain that she never wished to return to Ireland, where she had been born. Her abusive first husband would surely take revenge if he discovered she still lived and had escaped him.

Samuel lowered his voice. "Brynne isn't, no. She creeps about the chamber at night."

"Did she speak of…?" Gwynnie trailed off as old Rudyard walked past. The cook had stooping shoulders but could still beat dough into submission as well as Samuel.

"Often," Samuel whispered as he placed the bowl of flour down on the table and poured in milk from a flagon. He tossed in orange and lemon zest next, their fragrant scents tickling

Gwynnie's nose. "She didn't want me to leave her this morning, but I insisted she rest while I work." He lowered his voice further. "If anyone asks, she is unwell again."

Gwynnie nodded hurriedly. Brynne had struggled with her health this last year. "I wonder when she'll hear from him."

Samuel rubbed some of the zest between his fingers. "She'll tell you when she hears. If you ask me, lass, you'd be better off forgetting Devlin."

"I thought you liked him?"

"Liking him has nothing to do with it." Samuel returned to his task with gusto. Gwynnie had witnessed Samuel's shock at discovering his wife was a bigamist and that she had a fully grown son, but he had accepted it. Nothing would change the fact that he loved Brynne dearly. Along with Gwynnie and Tombstone, Samuel had aided them in helping Devlin escape the palace. "I don't like to see a lass's heart hurting." He glanced at her.

"My heart is perfectly fine, thank you very much."

"You're a poor liar."

"I'm an excellent liar."

Samuel smiled in amusement.

"Is there anything I can do for Brynne?" Gwynnie asked.

"No. She'll be well again soon enough, when that boy of hers is able to send a message from Ireland."

Gwynnie chewed her lip uncertainly. She knew that Brynne's ill health had started long before the trouble with Devlin. It was true that Brynne's fears for her son had only made her worse, but there was something more. Gwynnie wondered if it was fear of her first husband that made Brynne leave her bed at night and gave her nightmares.

"Very well. Enjoy your preparations for the feast." Gwynnie moved away from the table.

"Where are you going, lass?"

"I'm searching for someone," Gwynnie replied honestly, in case Samuel really could tell when she was lying.

"I hope it's not that Tombstone again." Samuel frowned. "I don't like the nature of the work you do for him."

"You don't like a lot of things this morning," she teased and waved goodbye.

Creeping through the kitchens, Gwynnie was careful to check the face of every tall man she walked past, just in case one of them was actually Emlyn disguised beneath a white cap. However, there was no sign of her mother, and Gwynnie slipped out of the kitchens, making her way through the narrow lanes toward the main palace courtyard.

The yard was just as busy as the kitchens. Maids bustled back and forth, carrying newly laundered gowns for their mistresses to wear on Christmas Day. An entire entourage of footmen entered the palace through one doorway, carrying so many pairs of duckbill shoes, chopines and heeled boots that Gwynnie gaped in wonder. As a cart was driven past, bearing more flagons and barrels of wine ready for the celebrations, Gwynnie searched the faces of those wandering the courtyard. She even examined the faces of every guard that was standing in the yard, wondering if Emlyn had changed her disguise.

"Where are you, Ma?" she murmured, glancing around.

She had been so overwhelmed to see her mother again, she had not thought to ask how Emlyn had made it into Tombstone's office the previous evening, or even how long she had been there. Could she have gone back there?

Gwynnie exited the main courtyard and looped back around the palace estate, up through the orchard, which was still quiet this early in the morning, and entered the tiltyard. At the far end, she glanced up at the windows of the clerks, lawyers and men of state who, like Tombstone, had been given a study chamber for their work in the palace. Gwynnie entered the palace and crept along the corridor toward Tombstone's office. She was about to enter his room when she hesitated and instead raised her hand, knocking.

There was no answer. She waited a moment before trying the handle. The door was locked. Cursing under her breath, Gwynnie reached deep into the sleeve of her gown. Tucked into the lining was a thin metal rod that she always kept with her. Pressing the tip into the lock, she wiggled it back and forth until the lock clicked open and she stepped inside the chamber.

All was silent. The candles that had kept her company the night before had long ago burnt themselves out and the fireplace was cold, full of ash. Gwynnie moved toward the desk, but Tombstone had cleared away the papers she had previously been reading. Turning her back on the desk, she moved to the corner of the room where Emlyn had appeared. Running her hands along the panelled walls, she searched for some sort of opening, perhaps a secret door she had not known about, yet the walls were thick and solid. She knocked lightly on the wood, listening for a hollow space, but there was none. She moved to the fireplace, though she knew from experience that hiding in this chimney was no easy task, least of all with a fire raging below.

Turning on the spot, Gwynnie's eyes darted from the door to the window. Had Emlyn entered by either the night before, Gwynnie would have seen her at once.

"You were already here," she whispered to herself, folding her arms and wondering why Emlyn had not announced herself the moment Tombstone had left her alone in the chamber. Was it possible Emlyn had been watching her?

There was a sudden rattle at the door. Someone pressed a key into the lock but upon finding it already open, thrust the door wide.

"Greetings!" Gwynnie declared with more jollity than she felt. "For it is the season to be jolly, no?" She sat down in one of the chairs by the fire and smiled up at Tombstone, pulling her woollen shawl around her shoulders.

Tombstone stood staring at her, his eyebrows arched, unamused. "Why do I even bother locking this door?" he asked drily.

"It's a good question. Why do you?"

Tombstone closed the door behind him and moved toward his desk. As he sat down behind it, the Savonarola chair creaked loudly.

"Oh, you are not happy today," Gwynnie observed. "Shouldn't you be spending Yuletide with family? What of Pascal?"

"What do you mean by that?" Tombstone's grey eyes narrowed.

"Come," Gwynnie murmured, her voice softening. "Have you forgotten I was there when you were injured in a fight, and he came to see you? Or when he was pushed out of a window and you went to his aid? There is some bond between you. Some sort of … kinship."

Tombstone looked away abruptly, sifting through the papers on his desk.

"Should you not spend Yuletide with kin?"

"Pascal and his family would not spend Christmas with me, even if I offered to be their cook and servant for the day." Tombstone spoke wryly, not lifting his eyes from the papers.

"How is he?" Gwynnie asked. Pascal had been severely injured when he had tumbled from the window — his life saved only by Gwynnie, who had kicked a haybale beneath him to break his fall. Though the lawyer was Tombstone's employer, to Gwynnie's mind there was much more to the two men's relationship. There was, at times, something distinctly paternal in Pascal's attitude toward Tombstone.

"A little better." Tombstone's shoulders relaxed. "I received a message from him. He's walking again." He smiled sadly. "He's spending Christmas in his family home to recuperate."

Gwynnie longed to ask again if he could join them, for Pascal offered Tombstone some sort of peace that no other man did, but the words faded on her tongue.

"And how are you?" Tombstone asked.

"Me? Why do you ask?"

"You know why I ask," he said, sitting back in his chair. "You said goodbye yesterday to a man whom you —"

"Whom I knew," Gwynnie cut in sharply. "Just a man I knew. And I didn't know him particularly well, did I?" Yet even as she said the words, her stomach knotted tight. After all, when she had waved Devlin off on the wherry boat, she had stood on the bank crying. Tombstone had found her. It was he who had sat with her, holding her hand in silent comfort.

"Are you well?" he asked softly.

"Yes," Gwynnie answered, far too quickly. "Yes, I am," she repeated, this time a little more slowly. Her answer appeared to satisfy Tombstone, and he went back to reading his papers. She certainly didn't need him asking how she was, or he might begin to suspect that there was more on her mind than just Devlin.

"There's something you should know," she said, sitting forward. Tombstone looked up from his papers. "I saw something last night."

"You always see things, Shadow." His name for her had at one time been strange, an odd reminder of the Shadow Cutpurse she had been. These days, she didn't mind it so much. "What did you see?"

"A man coming ashore. Fully cloaked, his face hidden. He arrived at midnight." She described how the three men had come ashore and been met by Cromwell. "I'm certain he was looking toward the royal chambers. I think he expected to see the king or queen that night."

"An uncommon thing, for the royal couple would undoubtedly have been at Midnight Mass." Tombstone chewed his lip. "Despite what King Henry says about religion, he has never not attended Mass at Yuletide." He stood and turned toward the window. "Someone has come to see the king at Cromwell's behest, perhaps? After all, Cromwell's control is slipping slightly."

Gwynnie frowned. "His control over the court? Or the king?"

"Both." Tombstone stared out onto the grassy banks surrounding the palace estate. Beyond the window was Blackheath, a large heathland known for its dark pockets and dangerous pathways. Gwynnie had heard more than one tale of courtiers being robbed by highwaymen on their way to the palace and the Thames. "I wonder how far Cromwell will go to keep the king's favour." He turned to look at her. "See if you can track down this stranger, Gwynnie. Find out who he is."

Gwynnie didn't answer. Instead, she stared over Tombstone's shoulder at Emlyn's face at the window.

CHAPTER 4

Gwynnie leapt to her feet. "I'll … I'll see if I can find him. The cloaked man may have kept his face hidden, but the two men with him should be easy to find. One of them had a scabbard at his hip, attached to a belt."

Tombstone nodded. "This cloaked man came ashore with guards? Or soldiers?"

"I do not know. They were not dressed like either, more like footmen."

Gwynnie's eyes reluctantly slid back to Emlyn, who was still staring through the window, making no effort to hide. The chamber was on the ground floor, yet there was still a drop to the ground. Seeing Emlyn's arm was still in a sling, she could only presume her mother was standing on something to be able to see through the window. Her good hand was holding the window frame tightly. "I … I wanted to say thank you for last night. For letting me read those pamphlets." If she distracted Tombstone for long enough, then perhaps Emlyn would leave.

"You're welcome." Tombstone looked up from his desk. "And Gwynnie?"

"Yes?" Gwynnie looked at him, breathing out at last as she saw Emlyn's head disappear out of sight.

"Was anyone else there to greet this cloaked man last night? Or just Cromwell?"

"Only Cromwell. The guards in the main courtyard were not interested in the stranger. I rather think Cromwell had given them an order to turn away."

"That is quite possible." Tombstone shuffled his papers. "That will be all, Gwynnie."

She moved toward the door, then hesitated. She glanced back to see Tombstone had pulled out fresh ink to write some letters.

"You don't intend to spend your twelve days of Christmas here in this chamber, do you?" she asked.

"I do." He didn't meet her eye. "We still have jobs to do. You mind your business, Gwynnie, and I'll mind mine." It was a warning, his tone heavy.

"I'll remind you of that the next time you ask me about Devlin."

Gwynnie checked the corridor was empty before darting down it and out into the tiltyard. The palace gate was guarded by two men holding pikes. One looked a little worse for wear, his head resting against the stone wall beside him. The other grinned at his friend.

"Ricard?" Gwynnie called in relief. He was one of the few yeoman guards in the palace she knew by name. They had made each other's acquaintance at the Tower of London, when a Spanish spy had attacked them in a bid to escape his prison.

"Ah, season's greetings to you, Gwynnie." Ricard performed a flamboyant bow and flicked off his hat, the red silk shining and the white feather that stuck out from the rim dancing about.

"Have you been drinking already this morning, Ricard?"

"Not yet." He chuckled and gestured to his colleague. "My friend here had so much last night, it's enough to scare any man off claret for life." He opened the gate for her.

Gwynnie laughed and waved goodbye as she slipped out, rather glad that Ricard had not asked her why she wished to step out beyond the palace walls.

Before her stretched the Woolwich road, an old track deeply rutted by cart wheels and tunnelling moles. She had seen the track fully flooded once, making it impossible for anyone to get in or out of the palace by road. Today it was coated in frost, with the dark heather of Blackheath rising up in the distance.

Careful to walk with apparent purpose down the quiet road, Gwynnie hunted for Emlyn. She at last found her mother sitting on a rock, not far from Tombstone's window. Beneath it was a discarded cart, which Emlyn must have stood on in order to peer through the window. She was cutting an apple into segments with a small knife. She didn't look up as Gwynnie sat down beside her.

"Odd man, Tombstone," Emlyn mused, handing Gwynnie a slice of apple. "What exactly do you do for him?" Her concern made her voice tight.

"I'm his shadow. His eyes and ears in the palace. That is all."

"He never asks you to do anything more? You've never risked your life for him, I hope?"

An unpleasant memory surfaced, of wrestling a Spanish spy in the shallows of the Thames, where she had pulled Tombstone to safety.

"No," Gwynnie lied around a mouthful of apple. She changed the subject. "Why are you risking walking around the palace? If Tombstone sees you —"

"I know, I know." Emlyn held up her good hand to stem the reprimand. "In case you have not noticed, Daughter, I am rather good at hiding in plain sight." She winked. "I'll be on my way again soon enough — you need not worry."

Gwynnie's stomach tightened at the thought of losing her mother's company again.

"First, I need your help." Emlyn nodded down at her arm in its sling. "I cannot find this loot on my own."

"This damn loot." Gwynnie huffed loudly. "Let me guess: this time it will be different. It's a treasure unlike any other we have stolen before!"

"It *is* different," Emlyn hissed, turning sharply to Gwynnie. "I have been searching for this for years. To have a hint of it at last, to have a clue…" She was almost breathless with excitement. "You cannot know what that means to me."

"What is this treasure?" Gwynnie muttered as a cart rolled past them. "What makes it so important?"

Emlyn waited until the cart had gone before reaching into her doublet and pulling out a scrap of yellow parchment. Wordlessly, she laid it on Gwynnie's lap.

Gwynnie blinked. It was one of the papers she had been reading the night before in Tombstone's office. It was handwritten, recording a theft from a ship belonging to King Henry in Southampton. Jewellery had been stolen in the dead of night. Two men — presumed to be the Shadow Cutpurses — had been seen sneaking away across the rooftops shortly before the theft had been discovered. They had carried two small crates with them. At the bottom of the page, added in a different hand, were the words, *The money and jewels taken that night have never been found.*

"You stole this?" Gwynnie hissed angrily. "Tombstone will notice!"

"Will he?" Emlyn didn't seem convinced. "I was surprised last night to find that paper amongst the rest. For so long that theft has been on my mind. To know the loot was out there, somewhere…"

Gwynnie stood, stuffing the parchment beneath the bodice of her kirtle.

Emlyn stood too, tucking the knife into the man's belt at her waist. "It's just one theft, Gwynnie."

"One theft? You talk of stealing jewels belonging to the king!"

"Hush, Gwynnie!" Emlyn reached for her arm, glancing warily at the cart drivers and walkers passing by.

Gwynnie pulled away, heading along the curtain wall of the palace. She heard Emlyn falling into step behind her.

"It is one last theft, Gwynnie," Emlyn insisted. "A treasure that will set us up for life. Think about it. We could escape to France as we said we would before. We could turn our backs on thieving for good."

Gwynnie tutted loudly as she entered the village of Woolwich, flush against the outer palace walls. It was busier here, with people wandering to and fro, carrying geese and plucked chickens for their Christmas dinner, some holding boughs of holly and mistletoe above their heads. Gwynnie kept her eyes averted, her sour mood at odds with their show of happiness.

"Why this loot in particular?" she asked as Emlyn walked at her side.

"I've known of it for a long time." There was something in Emlyn's voice, a tightness, that made Gwynnie suspicious.

"You're hiding something."

"Let us just say that I knew long ago Marie Duffield might have an idea of where this loot was hidden. When I found her in Bristol, my luck seemed to have come all at once. She remembered me, of course, but she didn't understand what she was telling me — the magnitude of what she was involved in. I do not believe she even realises that she may have worked out where the loot was, all on her own."

"Who is this Marie Duffield?" Gwynnie turned to face Emlyn. "Why would this woman know where such a loot is?"

"Because…" Emlyn glanced around and lowered her voice. "Because she was married to one of the original Shadow Cutpurses, Gwynnie. She heard things that no other did."

Gwynnie's mouth opened and closed. It was confirmation that the original cutpurses were indeed men. Questions raced through her mind. Who were these men? Why had they taken on the name? How did Emlyn know about them?

"Come, let us get back to the palace," Emlyn urged as they were abruptly jostled by revellers. She went to take Gwynnie's arm, but Gwynnie pulled away. She did not want people whispering about a palace maid on a man's arm.

"You need to tell me all," Gwynnie hissed as they neared another gate in the palace wall. "Everything about the original Shadow Cutpurses."

"And I will. You have my word." Emlyn's voice was solemn. "In exchange, I need your help."

Gwynnie stared at Emlyn. "You wish to barter with me?"

"That's not what I meant." Emlyn shook her head. "But you wish me to end my way of life, do you not? No doubt you have a sweet image of me baking bread, tucked up in a little French cottage?"

"Such an evil image, isn't it, Ma?"

"No sarcasm today, miting. This is our chance to escape a life of hardship and poverty for good." Emlyn's voice was low. "I must find the treasure not just for that, but for a very particular reason." She hesitated. "This loot holds a secret, a reason why our lives took the path they did. *That* is why I am so determined to find it."

Something in her mother's face made Gwynnie soften, just a little. "Where is this loot? What clue do you have from Marie Duffield?"

"I believe it to be here in London. There are two places it could be."

"You wish me to leave the palace to come and help you?"

"What is so awful about that, my child?" Emlyn asked with a laugh. "Are you actually fond of your life here? You're that man's pet, to call to heel whenever —"

"I am not!"

"Samuel and his wife are hardly a replacement for your own blood, are they?"

Gwynnie frowned. How could Emlyn have known they had become so close? "Have you been spying on me?"

"You're not the only shadow in the palace," Emlyn said with a mischievous smile. "Come with me, Gwynnie. Help me find the treasure and we can have that peaceful life in France — the one you used to talk of so much. I am offering you that dream. Would you turn your back on it so readily?"

Gwynnie's eyes danced over the gated entrance to the palace. Beyond, she caught a glimpse of the orchard where two ladies in fine dresses and French hoods walked together. Queen Jane and Lady Mary were talking intently, their heads close.

Gwynnie frowned. It was Yuletide morning. Gwynnie had thought Queen Jane would be much occupied with the king. For her to be out walking with Lady Mary, King Henry's daughter, whom he still had not spoken to since her arrival at the palace, was an odd thing indeed.

"I … I have made a difference here." The words fell from Gwynnie's lips, surprising even herself. She thought of Queen Jane crying in Friar's Church just a few nights before, fearing for her life. She had been so certain she would share the fate of

Queen Anne, ousted and then executed by the very man she called her husband — a man who claimed to love her. "I have helped to save a life."

"Then I am proud of you for it, miting," said Emlyn sincerely. "But do you truly think your life here is one you can lead? You are on borrowed time, working for that clerk, and for what? To make sure he never hunts me down for my crimes." She shook her head. "How long can it last?"

Gwynnie had no answer. Tombstone had never made any promises. He may very well send her on her way and then turn his attention to finding Emlyn.

Gwynnie approached the gate in the wall. She caught another glimpse of Queen Jane and Lady Mary walking together, then they turned and disappeared into the distance. Whatever conversation had passed between them, there had been purpose to their meeting. Gwynnie doubted they had simply met by chance in the orchard.

"Find the treasure with me and we can start a new life away from here," pleaded Emlyn.

"We could," Gwynnie found herself replying. "Let me think on it, Ma."

Once again, she was being asked to risk her life for some jewels.

CHAPTER 5

"Quick, lass!" Samuel urged, handing over a trencher of hot buns. "I wouldn't want to be there to face the king if these are late. He pelted the last maid with sugared plums!"

"A great shame — I think I'd prefer the plums." Gwynnie took the trencher and hurried out of the kitchens. She heard Samuel's laughter as she caught sight of Brynne. She was icing some cakes distractedly, making a mess. Berating herself, she cleaned up the icing and started again.

Knowing they didn't have time to talk now, Gwynnie left the kitchens and headed across the courtyard toward the great hall. The thought of leaving the palace and never seeing Samuel or Brynne again made her stomach knot.

The noise in the great hall was deafening. Voices and laughter echoed from the rafters. The long tables had been decked grandly with boughs of evergreens and mistletoe, topped with segments of Seville oranges and sprinklings of icing sugar. Between the boughs and looking resplendent were the peacocks and swans, their bodies stuffed back into their skins, their necks supported on sticks of wax. Pastry coffins were cut open, prompting live toads to jump forth. A squeak from one young man was followed by laughter and teasing, as the toads were chased across the tiled floor and around the log fire which had been erected in the middle of the hall.

Maids wandered back and forth, laying down more trenchers of cooked food. Saffron-infused meat glistened orange and copper, as the scent of cinnamon and cloves permeated the hall. The gentlemen and ladies of the court must have been drinking since sunrise, for some were already fast asleep on their benches as the sun waned outside. Others could no longer form words as they leaned against their companions, sloshing claret and hippocras across the tables.

At the top table, erected on a platform so it stood a good foot or two above all the others, sat King Henry and his favourites. Queen Jane was at his side, a little pink-cheeked as she sipped her wine with her ladies. On Henry's other side were the gentlemen of the court, though to Gwynnie's mind there were two people in particular who were missing from that table.

She scanned the hall, searching for them, and found Cromwell sitting with the other lawyers, clerks and councillors. His head was bowed and he made little effort to join in with the conversation. He stared at the trencher before him, gripping his spoon so tightly that his knuckles were white.

Across the room at another table sat Lady Mary, who looked most perturbed to be amongst the other ladies. She too made no effort to join in with the conversation, though she kept her chin raised, her demeanour as stiff as the high-necked collar of her maroon gown. Her gaze rested upon the king and queen.

Gwynnie hurriedly placed the trencher of buns on the King Henry's top table. Contrary to Samuel's warning, she went unnoticed by the king, who was busy guzzling the claret in his goblet, the red liquid running down his chin.

She made her way to the clerks' table. Most were too drunk to notice her presence, so she sat down beside Tombstone.

"Not hungry?" Gwynnie asked, eyeing some of the mouthwatering platters before Tombstone. He smiled and passed her a spoon before sliding some of the trenchers surreptitiously toward her.

"Do they not feed you in the kitchens?"

"Do you think we have time to stop and eat on a day like today?" she muttered, hastily spooning some saffron-infused chicken onto her plate. When Tombstone looked away, she took a quick gulp of his claret too. By the time he had turned back and caught the goblet in her hand, she had drunk half of it.

"Thief," he murmured, smiling.

"Only a little one," she teased, drinking more of the wine. "Have you heard any more from Pascal?"

"No. I doubt I'll hear from him for a while. He's with his family now while he rests."

"He might send a message," Gwynnie said with a forcefully cheery tone. "I'd want to hear from my father at Yuletide —"

"He is not my father!" Tombstone spoke sharply as he glanced around the table. "God's wounds, I hope you haven't been whispering such nonsense to people. You'll bring Pascal and I under all sorts of suspicion."

"I just thought…" She sighed and gestured to his face. "There is a likeness between you. You cannot pretend there isn't. It's in the arching of your brows and the angle of your chin."

"Do me a favour, Gwynnie, and don't think of the likeness. If anyone hears you…" He trailed off and shook his head.

"No one would listen to me, remember? I'm nothing more than a shadow." She elbowed him, trying to rekindle some joviality between them, but he was as stiff as a board and refused to look at her.

Silence fell between them, punctured by the laughter of others in the hall and the joyous air that seemed so incongruous with their own. Gwynnie watched Tombstone. There was a tightness in his jaw, and his shoulders were set firmly.

"You could tell me to go," she said. "I could desist eating your food and run to hide in the shadows. It's hardly an unusual order from you, is it?" she teased. Still, he did not turn to look at her. "Clearly, my conversation is sparkling! It has you captivated."

The slimmest of smiles appeared on his lips, causing his copper moustache to twitch.

"Just eat your food." Tombstone shook his head, a new lightness to his tone. "Your conversation is something I tolerate, Gwynnie."

"High praise indeed! We both know you wouldn't be without it." She winked at him and then gestured for him to push forward a basin of stewed plums. He obliged, then went back to observing the room.

"What do you make of this?" Gwynnie pointed in Cromwell and Lady Mary's direction, then at another in the room. Robert Aske, the leader of the Pilgrimage of Grace, had been given the seat of honour beside King Henry at the top table. The young man looked uncomfortable, his eyes wide at all the food before him. Like Tombstone, he had eaten very little.

"Much," Tombstone muttered. He leaned close, ensuring only she could hear his words. "This show of peace with Aske is only temporary. We all know the king's moods can change as easily as the wind. Aske is no more guaranteed safety than his pilgrimage or rebellion, or whatever you wish to call it, is guaranteed to have a lasting effect on this world."

"Wait…" Gwynnie sat forward. "You think Aske will be killed on the king's orders?"

Tombstone said nothing. His sigh was enough, though it was nearly drowned out by the minstrels who had taken up their lutes and pipes to add to the raucous air.

Gwynnie's eyes tarried on the young Aske. He had to be younger than her, a man who had scarcely started his adult life. King Henry clapped Aske on the shoulder good-naturedly, laughing with such warmth that even Aske managed to crack a smile. As the king cut into the peacock before him, brandishing his knife, a shiver ran through her.

"To think he could feed a man, laugh with him, then order him dead in the next breath."

"Have you forgotten Queen Anne?" Tombstone whispered.

"How could I forget?" Gwynnie turned her gaze away from Aske, looking at Cromwell and Lady Mary instead. "And what do you make of them?"

"Lord Cromwell's position may be more precarious. It's the first time I've ever known him be unwelcome at the king's table at Christmas. But he has his ways," Tombstone said. "The dissolution."

"The what?"

"The dissolution of the monasteries. I hear he has been tasked with ensuring all the monasteries and nunneries are closed. Where do you think that money will go? Our churches and monasteries are wealthy places, and they have land as well as riches…" He trailed off, no further explanation needed of the Church's wealth. "If Cromwell ensures that money is sent to the king's coffers, then I can't see him losing his place at court any time soon."

"You observe much," Gwynnie mused.

"Not enough." Tombstone poured himself another cup of claret, his eyes settling on Lady Mary. "I do not know why she is here."

"I thought you said she had been invited to make a show to Aske and the other rebels that the king was reconciling a little with his Catholic ways. Lady Mary is Catholic, is she not? The daughter of Queen Catherine —"

"That she may be, but the king has not spoken once to her since her arrival." Tombstone peered at Mary over the rim of his cup. "He may be putting on a show, Gwynnie, but what does Lady Mary hope for? A reconciliation with her father? Or something more?"

Gwynnie glanced across the hall at Queen Jane. She had witnessed first-hand how the queen had miscarried the child she had been carrying. It was a great secret, known only to few in the palace.

"Does she wish to be returned to the line of succession?" Gwynnie asked.

"Perhaps." Tombstone nodded slowly. "There are only her and the Lady Elizabeth, the baby the king has ousted to Hatfield House in Hertfordshire. That child can hardly do much to restore her succession, can she? Yet Lady Mary…" He paused, watching the lady in question. "She may want more than to just sit here at a table like some Bartholomew doll at her father's beck and call."

Gwynnie ate the last of the chicken on her plate then stilled as King Henry suddenly stood from his seat.

"Is he to dance?"

"Unlikely," Tombstone murmured. "He may be fond of dancing, but I've heard he complains too much about his ulcered leg as of late."

The king bent down and kissed Queen Jane on the cheek. Gwynnie saw the slightest tremble in the hand that clutched her goblet. Was it fear? Henry whispered something to his queen then stepped away from the table. He spoke to his gentlemen too, then, amazingly, waved at them.

"It cannot be…" Tombstone muttered, sitting up straight as all eyes watched the king. "Where is he going?"

"Are you to leave our feast so soon, Your Majesty?" one gentleman called. "Pray, stay, we need your company!"

"You have plenty of good company. I have an appointment that cannot be avoided. If you will excuse me, all, the responsibilities of a king are heavy upon my shoulders, but I shall bear them and the loss of your good company as best I can." He inclined his head and wished them all a happy day in a magnanimous tone.

As the king turned to leave, another greeted him at the door to the great hall. It was Cromwell, who had inconspicuously left his seat.

"Where are they going?" Tombstone whispered. "Shadow?" He turned to Gwynnie.

"I'm already departing." Gwynnie was on her feet. She snatched up an empty platter from the table and raised it high, giving her an excuse to leave the hall and follow them out into the courtyard. The door was closed heavily behind her by a guard, muffling the great laughter and music from within.

Gwynnie walked toward the kitchens carrying her empty platter, though she kept an eye on the path that King Henry and Cromwell took across the yard. No footman accompanied them, no guard, and the two walked together with their heads bent close. The king limped a little, betraying the fact that his leg was indeed bothering him. The two men disappeared under the archway into the inner courtyard, lit by the moon one moment then vanishing into the darkness the next.

In the entrance to the kitchens, Gwynnie discarded the trencher and hastened back outside, slipping from one courtyard to another. She hesitated under an archway, peering through the moonlight.

On the far side of the yard, the king and Cromwell were entering through a discreet door in the guest chambers. She waited until they had gone inside, the door closing behind them with a quiet click of the latch, then she followed, keeping to the shadows around the edge of the yard. She was careful to peer through a window before entering. Seeing nothing but a dark corridor, she lifted the latch and followed, slipping inside the building.

All was silent inside. She waited until her eyes adjusted to the darkness, then looked around. To her left was a narrow staircase, spiralling up into the rafters of the building. To her right was a closed door. Uncertain which way to go, she waited, listening. When a floorboard creaked overhead, she headed toward the stairs and crept upwards, stepping carefully to avoid creaking the boards. She passed two closed doors then reached a third, a thin strip of light at the bottom revealing that someone had lit candles and maybe even a fire beyond.

Just as Gwynnie had taken hold of the door handle, she heard a voice from within.

"That will be all." It was Cromwell's voice. "Leave us. Now."

Gwynnie snatched back her hand and moved away, but she was not quick enough. The latch lifted, and the oak door swung open. A wide man stepped out, his head bowed. He blocked Gwynnie's view into the room, but it was him she was now staring at.

The man looked up and it was plain that he recognised her too. Hastily, he shut the door behind him, then turned to face her fully.

"Gwynnie! God's blood, what are you doing here?"

"You first, Samuel."

CHAPTER 6

Samuel beckoned Gwynnie down the narrow staircase, urging her to stay quiet. She scuttled down the steps after him, glancing back at the closed door in wonder.

"You do not want to be seen here, Gwynnie. Trust me." He tugged on her arm, trying to pull her away, but she drove her heels into the step, refusing to move.

"What is happening in there? Why are you here, Samuel?"

"Please, lass —"

"Samuel, I'm not going anywhere until you tell me what is happening beyond that door."

They both fell silent as a laugh rumbled from the room. It was the king's laugh. It had always startled Gwynnie just how high-pitched King Henry's voice was, despite his broad shoulders and ever-increasing girth.

Samuel placed a finger to his lips and beckoned Gwynnie a few steps down. She followed but did not leave the staircase. Halting, she folded her arms and waited. Samuel was just visible in the darkness. The lines on his face looked deeper in the poor light.

"I received an order. One of Cromwell's men appeared in the kitchens. He asked if I was a man of quiet words. A man who could be trusted not to tell tales." Samuel sighed heavily. "With you and Brynne, there is so much I cannot tell others, so I agreed at once. He told me to bring a feast to this chamber, enough for two.

"We always store spare food, in case the king elects to throw it on the floor, as he did when he had been newly coronated." Samuel huffed. "That irascible temper of his has made it necessary to always make extra dishes. So, I brought what spares we had here. I was escorted by Cromwell's man. He is now inside with…" He hesitated, his lips pressed together.

"With the king and Cromwell," Gwynnie murmured. Samuel gave a reluctant nod.

There were footsteps from above, then a barked order.

"Leave me now." It was King Henry.

Gwynnie grabbed Samuel's arm and quickly pulled him back up the steps, this time going higher so that they could peer around the pillar in the centre of the spiral staircase to watch who left the room.

The door opened and Gwynnie and Samuel froze, their backs against the plaster wall. Gwynnie held her breath and put a finger to her lips.

"Enjoy your feast, Your Majesty." Cromwell's voice was followed by the creak of the closing door. As footsteps receded down the stairs, Gwynnie tiptoed down a couple of steps, peering around the pillar. She glimpsed Cromwell's back and the man who must have brought Samuel to this room. They were talking intently as they descended the staircase. She listened, waiting for them to leave the building and close the door at the bottom of the stairs. Once it banged shut, she looked up at Samuel.

"You said you brought a feast for two?"

"That I did. Fresh chicken and peacock, stewed vegetables, plated sugar, and sugar towers too, with one shaped like the king's crown," Samuel said proudly. "Now let us leave, before anyone realises we are here." He crept past her, but Gwynnie hesitated outside the closed door. "Gwynnie?" he whispered sharply. "Do you want to be caught spying on the king? He'd send you straight to gaol!"

But she had already stepped up to the door. She crouched down and pressed her eye to the lock, peering through. It was a poor peephole, with little light and a view that mostly consisted of the feast on the table. Samuel's hand closed on her shoulder, silently begging her to come away, but she stayed, watching.

There was movement at the table. It had to be King Henry, for she saw his large belly as he sat down in a chair. There was a glimmer of a hand too, adorned with rings. It clutched a flagon, pouring out fresh wine.

"Samuel," she whispered, leaning back from the door, "was there anyone else in that chamber? A woman, perhaps?"

"A woman?" Samuel stiffened beside her. "No. No woman. There was only the king, Cromwell, Cromwell's aide and myself."

"The king is feasting with someone. Who would he feast with but a woman? Another mistress?"

"If the king has taken another lady to his bed, we want nothing to do with it. We should leave at once, head back to the kitchens and pretend this never happened."

"A king can bed who he likes with no comeuppance," she murmured. "Only his wives would suffer for the same crime."

"But do you think the king wants his betrayal of his wedding vows to be witnessed?"

Gwynnie pressed her eye back to the lock. She had to know if the king was indeed having another affair. It could mean that Queen Jane's position at court was as precarious as Queen Anne's had been, when Henry had started noticing Jane Seymour at court.

There was a murmur of voices inside the room, then the distinct sound of another door opening. It didn't matter how much Gwynnie squinted against the lock, it afforded her no better view. She saw the great stomach of the king rise as he stood from his chair. His cup of wine was dangerously close to being knocked over as he flung his arms around someone.

A second voice joined the king's, and though the closed door meant their words could not be heard, the deep tone was unmistakable.

"That is no woman's voice," Samuel mused beside Gwynnie. "I don't think the king is breaking his wedding vows here tonight."

"No, but he's keeping something secret. *Someone* is a great secret indeed," Gwynnie replied as she pulled back from the door. "Why else not invite this person to the Christmas feast with the rest of the court?"

She looked once more into the room. The king had taken his seat and beside him, his visitor did the same. Gwynnie caught a glimpse of a lacy cuff around a wrist, and a fine sapphire and silver doublet. Whoever this stranger was, he was wealthy.

Once more, Samuel grasped Gwynnie's shoulder.

"One minute more," she pleaded.

"We are out of time." Samuel was already steering her away, and she suddenly realised why. The door far beneath them had opened again and she could hear the sound of boots on the steps. "There's another way out of this building. This way."

He led her up the stairs, the two of them careful to make as little noise as possible.

At the top of the staircase, Samuel opened a door before looking back at Gwynnie.

"We'll have to walk quietly. We're directly above the chamber where the king is feasting."

Together they crept through a long passage. Doors on either side led to smaller chambers, perhaps bedchambers for the manservants that accompanied the gentry when they visited the king. Gwynnie walked on her toes, not daring to lower her heels in case they made a noise. There was nothing that could be done about Samuel's greater weight, though. When he reached the middle of the passage, the boards creaked so loudly beneath him that the two of them froze, straining to hear if someone would come running to investigate the sound.

Nothing happened. There was even the rumble of laughter from the chamber beneath.

"The king is too busy enjoying himself to notice us," Gwynnie assured Samuel, waving him on.

They continued to a staircase at the far end of the passage and hastened down the steps, moving as carefully and as quietly as they had done before. Passing a myriad of doors, Gwynnie hesitated, wondering if the man with the fine doublet had used one of them in order to meet the king for their private feast. She hesitated by a door, a chink of candlelight at the bottom, but before she could investigate, Samuel steered her forward again.

"We've seen enough," he muttered.

"That man could have come in this way," Gwynnie said as they reached the bottom of the steps.

"He could. All the more reason not to get caught sneaking around." He opened a door and stepped out into the inner courtyard. He came to such an abrupt halt that Gwynnie walked straight into his back. She stumbled, nearly falling over.

"Ho, what are you two doing?" a sharp voice demanded.

Gwynnie halted beside Samuel, staring into the faces of two men who appeared to have been standing guard in the yard. One was tall and gangly, the other just as tall but carrying more weight. The former was dressed head to toe in green, the latter as brightly as some of the ladies in the great hall, with holly thrust into his belt and a gold medallion swinging from his neck. The man in green laid a hand across his belt, his thumb resting above a scabbarded dagger.

Gwynnie's mouth went dry as she stared at the scabbard. This had to be the same man who had helped the cloaked stranger ashore from the wherry the night before.

"Forgotten how to use your tongues?" he barked, shifting his hand to the hilt of his dagger. "I could cut them out, if you have no need of them —"

"Woah, stranger." Samuel affected a laugh and raised his hands. "Don't mind us. We were just given orders to deliver food to a private dinner in these chambers. We'll be on our way back to the kitchens. Is this courtyard off limits? Have we missed an order?"

"No," the other man said. He was dressed in an overly fussy doublet with so much lace around his throat that it resembled loose skin dangling from his chin. "Let them pass, Amaro. We don't need to start a fight wherever we go, do we?" He laid a bejewelled hand on Amaro's shoulder. "Be on your way, friends."

"Thank you, sir." Samuel bowed, and Gwynnie hastened to curtsy. The two of them walked around the pair and headed toward a distant archway in the yard.

"Wait," the fussily dressed man called after them. Gwynnie and Samuel both halted under the archway. They exchanged a nervous look before turning round. Amaro had pulled out the dagger and held it surreptitiously at his side. The blade flashed in the moonlight. "Who were you delivering your feast to?"

Samuel held the man's gaze. "I don't know, sir. I receive my orders, and I follow them. That's all."

"Very well. On your way."

Samuel turned, and Gwynnie fell into step behind him, hurrying through the archway as they headed back toward the kitchens.

"They never speak to a woman, to a maid, do they?" Gwynnie scoffed as she caught up with Samuel. "You'd think I was nothing but horse shi—"

"Gwynnie." Samuel turned to look at her, bringing the pair of them to a stop. "What we saw tonight, we never saw, all right?"

"What?"

"We never saw it." Samuel shook his head. "Whatever was happening in that room, it's none of our business."

"Are you telling me to keep my head down and not cause trouble?"

"I know, it's like telling a bat not to fly at night." Samuel sighed. "But I'm begging you all the same. Tell no one what we saw here tonight, Gwynnie."

"As you wish." Gwynnie chewed her lip. There was one person she would have to tell, someone who could perhaps make sense of what they had just seen. She would have to tell Tombstone.

"Have you finished all your tasks for the night?" Samuel asked as they hovered by the entrance to the kitchens. The moon had come out from behind the clouds, casting a silvery light upon their surroundings.

"Yes."

"Then why don't you run along to bed?" Samuel urged, glancing back toward the distant archway in the yard.

"You're concerned for me," Gwynnie realised abruptly. "You do not need to worry for me."

"Don't I?" Samuel raised an incredulous brow. "This from the lass who frequently gets herself into scrapes."

"They didn't even notice me," Gwynnie said simply. "That's the thing about being a maid. You can go to a lot of places unseen."

"You're not unseen by everyone, Gwynnie." His voice softened. "Now, go and get some rest, lass. I'll see you in the morning."

Gwynnie smiled at him. It was strange to have someone watching out for her safety, yet Samuel had done that since she had first arrived at the palace, picked up an apron and started work as a maid.

"Goodnight."

He nodded goodbye, and Gwynnie hastened across the courtyard. Like Samuel, she shot a glance toward the distant archway. She could see nothing, though she felt the hairs rising on the back of her neck, as if someone was indeed watching her.

She walked around the kitchen building and headed for the maids' chambers, thinking about Amaro and his friend, the man in the flamboyant lace collar. They could indeed be the two men who had helped the cloaked stranger out of the wherry the night before, then followed him and Cromwell into the palace.

The cloaked stranger… Gwynnie paused as a thought occurred to her. *Was that who the king was meeting?*

It was just possible that the cloaked stranger and the man wearing the sapphire and silver doublet, who sat feasting with the king right now, were one and the same.

Gwynnie hurried on. Despite what Samuel had said, she knew that come morning she would have to tell Tombstone. She was so lost in thought that she didn't notice the tall shadow leaning against the wall, watching her.

"Tut-tut." The shadow stepped forward off the wall, arms folded. "You're getting careless, miting."

CHAPTER 7

"I thought I told you to hide in the laundry," Gwynnie hissed. "Anyone could see you."

"No one looks into the shadows, you know that. And the laundry room was rather dull." Emlyn shrugged. "I much preferred to go to the feast."

"You went to the feast?" Gwynnie spluttered.

"Quite something at Yuletide, isn't it?" Emlyn sighed. "All that sugar." She picked at her teeth. "To think the king can have such delicacies every day! It's a different life, isn't it?"

"Inside!" Gwynnie pointed toward the maids' chambers. "We can't risk you being seen. If anyone sees you here dressed as…" She trailed off, for Emlyn had shed the clothes of the clerk she had worn before and now wore a rather fine copper and scarlet doublet, a neat collar at her throat. She still wore her sling, but it was loose, as if she no longer needed it so much, and she had the same long boots on her feet. Gwynnie eyed the injury, presuming it was not as bad as Emlyn had first feared. Her mother had taken extra care to pin her hair beneath her felt hat. Gwynnie could well believe that Emlyn had been mistaken for a courtier in the great hall. Her hands were hidden in long silk gloves and across her chin she had peppered something dark, to resemble stubble.

"No one saw me," Emlyn assured her, as they entered the building and Gwynnie hastily lit a candle from a tinderbox on a shelf in the wall.

Gwynnie marched up the steps, beckoning Emlyn to follow her. "Let's just get you inside my room before anyone sees you."

"I saw you at the feast," Emlyn went on. "I saw you stealing some of that clerk's food. Well, I say steal. It looked as if he *gave* you most of it. Why would he do that?"

"Tombstone has a rare quality." Gwynnie looked back over her shoulder as they reached the top of the flight of stairs. "Kindness." Emlyn's brows rose in disbelief. "I see you have forgotten all the dealings you had with him in January."

"He vowed to arrest me for murder, Gwynnie."

"And he chose not to arrest us for being thieves." Gwynnie bundled Emlyn into her chamber. There had once been two beds in the tiny room which she and Emlyn had shared. One had since been removed to another chamber. It had freed up a little space, but it was still more like a cupboard than a bedchamber. The bed was pushed firmly under the window, where she now urged her mother to sit as she locked the door. Gwynnie washed her face in a basin resting on a small table as Emlyn continued to praise the feast.

"Such ladies!" Emlyn gasped. "Did you see the way they danced? Fashions are changing, are they not? Mind you, Queen Anne changed much. Everything was a little more relaxed with Queen Anne. I've noticed high necklines have returned this year. Is this the influence of Queen Jane, do you think?"

"Ma? Did you have wine tonight?"

"Unlike you, I have not forgotten how to steal," Emlyn teased with sparkling eyes. "I may have had a drink or two."

"I have not forgotten how to steal," Gwynnie muttered peevishly, unpinning her hair and combing out the light brown strands.

"So you say." Emlyn's tone made Gwynnie pause. "What a curious conversation I overheard this evening between Queen Jane and the king's daughter. What's her name? You know, the one he had ousted?"

"Lady Mary?"

"That's her!" Emlyn flicked her fingers in the air. "Well, the two were pressed together in conference in the corner of the room. They seemed completely unaware of all the dancing and games. Mind you, I don't think they particularly wanted to be overheard."

Gwynnie dropped her comb and turned to Emlyn, who was swaying a little from the wine. "And what did they say?" she asked.

"It seems the dear young queen is determined to reconcile her stepdaughter with her husband. But who is older — the queen or Lady Mary? They look much the same age to me."

"There are not many years between them." Gwynnie waved a dismissive hand. "So Queen Jane wishes to reconcile them? Was it her idea or Lady Mary's?"

"That I do not know." Emlyn shook her head and leaned back, resting her against the wall. "It would take something, would it not, to change the mind of such a man? Well, I say man. He's more like a giant sow dressed up in a doublet and hose, with pointed shoes they've thrust onto his trotters."

"Shh!" Gwynnie hissed, for Emlyn's voice had risen with the insult. She looked at the door in panic, but could not hear anyone in the corridor. "I think you have drunk too much."

"Nonsense."

Gwynnie poured a glass of water from a flagon that had been left in her room. She passed it to Emlyn, who took a sip.

"Now you know where I was, where were you?" Emlyn asked, lifting her chin and looking at Gwynnie.

"I followed someone." Gwynnie used the candle to light a rushlight, placing them both on the table beside the water basin.

"The king?" Emlyn leaned forward. "He was the only one to leave the great hall early tonight, after all. Do you know, many whispered that he has a mistress. Why else would he leave the Christmas Day feast so early but to entertain another woman?"

"It was no woman he met, but a man." Gwynnie sat down in a rickety chair that had been discarded from the main palace, as one leg was shorter than the other. Retrieving her comb, she resumed tidying her hair, thinking once again about the richly patterned doublet that she glimpsed through the keyhole, the laughter that emanated from the room, and the cloaked figure that had crept into the palace grounds the night before. "A man who does not want to be seen by anyone else, it seems."

"Who? A spy? Perhaps a political envoy from France or Spain?" Emlyn asked excitedly.

"I do not know."

"It was a risk to follow the king." Emlyn downed the last of the water, not noticing that she had sloshed a little onto Gwynnie's straw pillow, even when Gwynnie frowned at her. "What if you are caught watching him? What then?"

"I shan't be caught."

"That's what you say, but you do not see everything." Emlyn smiled, looking pleased with herself.

"What?" Gwynnie asked. "What have I missed?"

"Tonight was not the only time you did not see me watching you. I was watching you yesterday too."

Gwynnie's mind raced. Much had happened on Christmas Eve. She recalled how she had searched Tombstone's office, looking for another way into the chamber. She'd found no passage, no hidden door in the panelling through which Emlyn could have crept. "You were already in Tombstone's room, hiding, weren't you? You watched me as I was reading those papers."

"I was," Emlyn replied unashamedly.

"You're impossible," Gwynnie muttered, throwing down her comb. "Why were you watching me? Why could you not just speak to me?"

"I had to make sure Tombstone wasn't coming back, that we were truly alone. Besides, that was not the time I was thinking of. I was watching you much earlier in the day too."

"When?" Gwynnie stiffened.

"You were sitting on the docks. You were with Tombstone, holding his hand, like children together." She giggled drunkenly. "You had just waved goodbye to a man. It looked very much as if you had just sneaked him out of the palace. He kissed you goodbye."

"Ma!" Gwynnie barked, then lowered her voice. "What happened that day has nothing to do with you. What you saw … you never need to mention it again."

Gwynnie could still feel Devlin's lips upon hers. It had been a fleeting thing, sweet, meaningful, then gone like a puff of smoke. What affection she felt for Devlin could not be dwelled upon.

"You and I spoke of love, long ago. It causes nothing but pain. I warned you of that, miting." All humour had left Emlyn's face, her dark eyes serious. "I do not say any of this to hurt you, dearest, but to warn you." She leaned forward. "Who was that man? Can he be trusted?"

"It doesn't matter anymore." Gwynnie sat down heavily in the chair. "That man is gone. He'll be in Ireland in just a few weeks. I am unlikely to ever see him again." Her throat tightened. She prayed Emlyn would ask her nothing more, for she didn't think she could manage to speak at that moment. Emlyn reached out and laid her hand over Gwynnie's. That simple kindness, the soft touch, made the tears well in Gwynnie's eyes.

"He's gone," she whispered again. She knew she would never speak to Devlin again, never lean her head upon his shoulder, nor take his hand as she had done at their parting. She heard his voice in her head.

Well, flower, I wish I didn't have to say goodbye to you. I would have liked to know you better.

"I am sorry." Emlyn's voice was soft. "I hate to see you in pain, my child. Truly. Your pain causes me pain."

Gwynnie nodded. Only when she was certain that no more tears would fall did she lift her chin and stare back into Emlyn's open face.

"But you do need to be more careful," Emlyn pleaded. "I have watched you these last couple of days. You may be the shadow that follows others, Gwynnie, but don't let yourself become prey to someone else someday."

"I'll be careful," Gwynnie vowed. "I will not let that happen." She leaned back, increasing the space between them. Emlyn sensed the change and sat back on the bed.

"You know what I said this morning is true," Emlyn told her. "There is no future for you here at the palace. We have but one life, Gwynnie. Surely you do not wish to spend it unseen in the corridors of this palace?"

Gwynnie began to plait her hair, ready for bed, aware that Emlyn waited patiently for her to answer. It was true — she had never thought her future as a maid and informant. Would she still be here when she was an old woman? Still at Tombstone's beck and call and hiding in the shadows?

"It's a way of life," Gwynnie muttered as she stood to remove her shoes, stockings and kirtle. "At least I'd have good meals."

"That you would. But with what I'm offering, we'd have more food than you could possibly imagine." Emlyn reached into her doublet and pulled out the handwritten account of the theft she had taken from Tombstone's chamber. Gwynnie stared, open-mouthed.

"I had that last. I stuffed it here." She gestured to her kirtle, but Emlyn smiled with a glint in her eye.

"Don't forget where you learned to steal from. You never even noticed when I took it."

"Ma!"

Emlyn flattened out the parchment on the table beside the bed. Gwynnie stepped forward, peering down at the writing. The more she looked, the more convinced she was that the additional spiky handwriting at the bottom was Tombstone's. He was the one who had detailed the fact that the money and jewels had never been found.

"It must have been some scandal, when the king's jewels went missing," she mused.

"Oh, it was. I remember it well." Emlyn sat forward to pour another cup of water. "We were in Southampton at the time, staying in a small lodging house behind an inn, not far from the docks. The soldiers searched every lodging house, every inn, every rickety thatched house they could find. I even caught sight of King Henry that day, from a distance. He shoved over a poor footman who was probably just trying to help him. I came back to find you, told you that we had to leave at once, that we could not stay there, so we moved. We took a cart out of town and came back to London. Your father … well, he was already on the road."

Gwynnie froze as a childhood memory stirred. Bundled in a second-hand gown that was too long for her, she had sat on a windowsill, watching the waves crash against the ships in the dock as soldiers marched up and down and someone barked orders.

"Some of the soldiers were brutal," Gwynnie murmured.

"You remember?"

"I watched from a window. They demanded to search people, their carts." She shuddered as she recalled a young man being struck by a soldier. Bleeding, he had fallen to the ground. She had still been watching that man when Emlyn had burst through their door, telling her they must leave.

"We came to London, though here it was little different. Within days the pamphlets were full of the news and soon enough, a ballad was written about the theft. Some carelessly written jig that painted the thieves as demons with springs in their shoes."

"And you have wanted to find the stolen loot ever since? Why?"

"No, not immediately." Emlyn shifted on the bed, pulled at the fine collar of her doublet and peered out of the window. "I thought the jewels were safe. I thought we would see some of them. That is what Marie Duffield's husband had promised, after all. Titus Duffield was his name. Do you recall him?"

Gwynnie's brow creased in thought. A tall, loping man with a stoop came to mind. His dark red hair had been loose around his ears, and his face had been pockmarked.

"He had smallpox once."

"He did!" Emlyn gasped. "Do you recall anything else?"

The figure in her mind vanished, as if walking into a mist, and she shook her head. "I don't understand. Why would he promise to give you some of the loot?"

"It was the agreement the two of them had," Emlyn said, looking out of the window again. "To split what they managed to take between the two families. Titus paid for him and Marie, and your father, well, he took care of us."

Gwynnie stared at Emlyn, her heart suddenly pounding. "Ma," she whispered, "are you telling me that the Shadow Cutpurses, the first thieves to bear that name, were Titus Duffield … and my father?"

CHAPTER 8

"They were the Shadow Cutpurses." Emlyn's words came to Gwynnie as if from a distance.

Wordlessly, Gwynnie reached out. She found her chair and sat down, staring at the candles. Her father had died so long ago, she struggled to picture him.

Physically, Gwynnie was more like him than Emlyn. He had been short, as was she, with the same hazel eyes. She recalled a joyous smile and a quick wit that often had Emlyn laughing. Some of Gwynnie's fondest memories were of seeing her parents dancing together in their tiny lodgings, tucked into the eaves of an old timber building.

"Dear John-Louis," Emlyn said with a sigh. "There is not a day that has gone by since his passing that I have not missed him with an aching heart."

Gwynnie covered her face with her hands. She had always presumed that her father had had some form of honest occupation. Now that she considered the matter, was it not strange Emlyn had never volunteered information on what he had done for a living?

"I thought we started thieving in order to eat after Father's passing," Gwynnie murmured behind her hands.

"Oh, it was time you learned the family trade, after he passed—"

"Family trade?" Gwynnie spluttered, lowering her hands.

"It was how your father and I were raised, Gwynnie. The slums of London town are kind to few. You quickly learn there is only one way to survive and that is to *take* what you need." Emlyn's voice was firm. She reached up and took off her bonnet, unpinning her dark brown hair so that it fell in soft locks around her ears. She'd cut it since Gwynnie had seen her last, so it didn't even reach her shoulders. "Your father and I were raised to pickpockets and cutpurses. When John-Louis met Titus, the two realised there was a better way to live than just hand to mouth, that they could pull off thefts of such daring that we wouldn't need to worry about hunger."

Gwynnie shook her head. "Why did I not know this?"

"You can blame me for that," Emlyn said sadly. "I wanted to protect your innocence. I wished you to grow up believing that life was possible without testing the bounds of the law. Such foolish naivety left me the night your father died."

"The night he died," Gwynnie repeated. "Was it the same year that he and Titus took the king's loot?"

Emlyn's eyes held hers. "It was the same week, Gwynnie."

"Oh!" A pained gasp escaped her. "Are you telling me that he died because of what he took? That he and Titus were killed by the king's soldiers?"

"No, no, that is not what I am saying." Emlyn moved to sit on the edge of the bed. "Now, listen carefully to me, dearest. When you and I reached London, I could not find your father. He was supposed to meet us at our lodgings that night, but he was nowhere to be seen. I left you home alone and went in search of him. I found him in the middle of the night." Her eyes glazed over. "He was at Titus's lodgings. Poor Marie was sitting outside, saying they had ousted her, refusing to let her in on their discussions. Well, she never had the strongest of resolves. I marched in there and demanded to know what they were speaking of.

"What I saw…" She trailed off, rubbing her face. "Two small crates, small enough to be carried in your lap, were open on the floor. One contained jewels, such rich jewels — rubies, sapphires, emeralds, you name it. The value was unfathomable. The other crate was full to the brim with gold coins. John-Louis and Titus stood over the crates, arguing about what they were going to do with them.

"Titus was all for splitting the loot evenly between the pair of them that night. He was certainly right that they would never need to steal anything again. With such jewels, we could live our lives in luxury.

"Your father thought it was too much for two men, even with families to keep. His argument was that we knew many in the slums who needed help. If he could distribute the jewels and money amongst those who needed it, was that not a better plan? He didn't want to own a king's fortune. He wanted to share it."

"Let me guess — they argued," Gwynnie surmised. "And the argument got out of hand."

"I had to step between them." Emlyn's face had paled. "I had never seen Titus so furious. He was a tall man, taller than me, and he could certainly be violent. He'd had his fair share of pub brawls. Even Marie was scared of him." She paused, her hands fidgeting. "I stood between them and Titus backed down. I urged the two of them to cool off, to take some time to think about what to do with the loot and in the meantime, to hide what they had taken."

"And so they did? Somewhere here in London?"

"I couldn't be sure they had hidden it in London." Emlyn shook her head. "Your father and Titus went the next day to hide it, but John-Louis was home so late, I thought perhaps it was beyond the city's walls. He didn't share with me where they had hidden the jewels. He said it was for the best, that there was something in the loot that was more dangerous than he had first realised. I believe he was afraid of what he had found."

She paused and in the silence Gwynnie lit another rushlight, placing it on the table beside the others.

"The next day, John-Louis did not come home." Emlyn spoke quietly now. "He always, *always* came home. I went searching for him, stopping at Titus and Marie's lodgings. Titus insisted that he hadn't seen John-Louis that day. He even suggested that maybe John-Louis had run, turning his back on you and I. Pff!" she scoffed. "John-Louis loved us far too much to ever do that. I saw Marie hiding in the shadows of their lodgings. She was scared." Emlyn paused and took a deep breath.

"I went looking for him later that night. I dressed in a man's clothing, hoping it would make me less conspicuous. I found John-Louis in the early hours of the next morning. He was barely alive. I will not tell you what state I found him in —"

"Ma, please —"

"No." Emlyn's voice was firm. "No child should have to hear what became of her father."

"I am hardly a child anymore."

"You will always be my child, Gwynnie." Emlyn's voice softened. "And I shall always protect you from what I saw that night, from what we said to each other in his last moments."

Gwynnie saw tears in Emlyn's eyes and did not press her.

"I went to Titus, to challenge him for what he had done."

Gwynnie stiffened. "No, no … do not tell me that this Titus Duffield … that his own partner … that he was the one…"

Emlyn nodded.

A cry escaped Gwynnie's lips. "He killed my father? Because they argued over the king's jewels?"

"I challenged him," Emlyn went on. "I demanded that he tell me the truth about what happened. He practically threw me out. Poor Marie raced after me to help, but there was nothing she could do. She never admitted it, but she knew as well as I did that her husband was a killer. She disappeared the next day." Emlyn sat up straight. "At first, I thought Titus had hurt her, too, because she knew what he had done to John-Louis. But later, when Titus was out, I broke into their lodgings. Marie had taken all her clothing, all her meagre possessions, and run."

"You found him, didn't you?" said Gwynnie, her mind working quickly. She had known for a long time that her mother had been accused of murder. It was well known that one of the Shadow Cutpurses had been guilty of killing someone. "What happened?"

"I caught him sneaking across the rooftops on his own the next night," Emlyn told her. "He'd been seen, the fool. He was being followed by nightwatchmen from the ground. I had donned a man's garb again and followed to confront him. The watchmen mistook me for his fellow Shadow Cutpurse. One of them must have seen what happened when we reached the docks. They must have seen me as I grabbed hold of Titus."

She looked away. "He did not deny it. He couldn't. I told him I knew that he had hurt John-Louis. That I would have my justice. He was strong, stronger than I thought..." Emlyn blinked and turned to Gwynnie. "It all happened so fast. You do believe me, don't you, when I tell you it was self-defence? The details, oh, how can I tell you? I can't speak of it. It's too awful, but it was self-defence. Believe that."

Gwynnie said nothing. She merely stared at her mother, waiting to hear something more.

"I left him in the Thames."

A cold chill washed over Gwynnie. She stared at Emlyn. There was no remorse in her face, no sign of guilt. Only resolve.

Closing her eyes, Gwynnie recalled the night Emlyn had come stumbling back to their attic rooms in the early hours of the morning, clothed in hose and jerkin. The rushlight had nearly burnt itself out, but there had been enough light to reveal that Emlyn's hands were stained dark red. Emlyn hadn't realised Gwynnie was watching her from the corner of their attic room at first. She'd stumbled against the wall, a strained cry escaping her lips before their eyes met across the room.

Gwynnie knew now what had happened that night. That was the night Emlyn had murdered Titus Duffield.

Now, as her mother had told her the story, she had left out why her hands were stained with blood. There was still something she was keeping secret.

"He was a murderer, Gwynnie."

"So are you, Ma. I … I need some air."

"Some air? It's the middle of the night —"

Gwynnie grabbed a fresh kirtle and laced it up around her waist. She pulled on her boots and wrapped the woollen shawl around her shoulders.

"Gwynnie? Gwynnie, please do not leave like this. Can you not understand why I did it? Can you not see what it was all for?"

Gwynnie reached for the door, flung it open and marched out. She made her way along the dark passage and down the staircase, nearly tripping on the stairs in her haste.

She didn't know where she was going. All she knew was that she needed time to think and space to breathe.

She burst out into the courtyard, stumbling across the cobbles. Dimly, she was aware of some guards in the distance, lit by a burning torch fixed to the stone wall beside them. They were too busy passing a flagon of ale between them to notice her. She crept along the edge of the courtyard, moving around the buildings and keeping to the shadows. The moon was hidden behind thick clouds, the chill air making her shiver as she walked. Gwynnie trailed her fingers along the walls, using them to navigate through the palace grounds and toward the Thames. She dipped through the same archway she had taken the night before, but tonight there was no one sneaking ashore from the docks. All was quiet on the riverbank.

Gwynnie headed for a small boathouse that stood on stilts at the side of the Thames. When she reached the building, she sank down against it, her feet nearly falling into the river that lapped against the building.

Her mother's words from that fateful night came back to her, echoing like a bell that wouldn't be dampened.

Vengeance has been served tonight, miting.

Was it vengeance? Or was it self-defence? Her mother had claimed once in the past it had been, and yet the description Emlyn had given her now had sounded more brutal.

She had known her father had been killed. She had also known Emlyn was blamed for a murder. She had even understood that her mother saw her crime as an act of justice, for the loss of her father. But was this justice?

"It was murder," Gwynnie murmured in horror.

The moon peered out from beyond the clouds, the river reflecting its silvery glow.

I left him in the Thames.

That's what her mother had said. Did that mean Emlyn had killed him before dumping his body in the river? Did it mean she had drowned him? Or had she injured him in such a way that it meant he would never make it out of the water? Gwynnie remembered the blood on her mother's hands that night. If she had drowned Titus, why was there blood on her hands?

Gwynnie trembled as the questions raced through her mind. She wasn't even certain if she wanted to know the answers. She inhaled deeply, trying to calm her breathing.

Gwynnie now understood why she and Emlyn had become the Shadow Cutpurses. It made sense. If Emlyn had been seen that night by a watchman, mistaken for a jewel thief, then it was little wonder pamphlets had appeared, blaming one of the infamous cutpurses for murder. Gwynnie supposed it had been too easy for Emlyn to believe that they could make the name live on, that between the pair of them, they could survive by stealing what they needed.

Her throat tight, Gwynnie leaned her head back against the wooden boathouse, her gaze drifting across the river to London town in the distance. Even at this time of night she could hear people making merry in the taverns, celebrating Christmas, their laughter carrying across the water.

Suddenly another thought came to her. Emlyn had not said what had become of John-Louis. Where was his body now?

"What became of him?" she murmured, as if the cold breeze would answer her. She shivered and pulled the shawl tighter around her shoulders. In her mind's eye, she saw her father laughing at some jest. He had been a jovial man, always smiling, always teasing. "Where are you, Father?"

It was hardly unusual for a man of his station to be buried without a headstone. Such things cost money, money that they had never had. But in that moment, Gwynnie longed for somewhere to go, to stand by the grave of the father she had loved.

"He was murdered by a friend." The quiet words escaped her lips. "A man he trusted."

"That he was," said a voice in the darkness.

"Ma!"

CHAPTER 9

Gwynnie staggered to her feet, glaring into the darkness.

Emlyn was standing against the palace wall. "I told you," she said. "You have to be more careful. Anyone could be watching you from the shadows."

"It always seems to be you!" Gwynnie snapped, taking a step back. She was suddenly off balance and tipping toward the river.

"Gwynnie!"

She tumbled into the water, her whole body submerged in the icy depths. The sudden cold made her chest constrict, making it impossible to breathe. For a moment, she could not move. Suspended, she fought to kick her legs, then a hand thrust through the water. Gwynnie's fingers gripped the wrist, and she was pulled upwards.

She coughed as air rushed into her lungs. Her whole body shook as Emlyn pulled her from the water, and she collapsed to her knees on the grassy riverbank.

"God's blood, that water's cold!" Gwynnie cursed.

"Hush, miting. Do you want all and sundry to come running?" Emlyn flung off the doublet she had been wearing, pulling it around Gwynnie's shoulders. "Watch where you're putting your feet next time."

"Oh, yes, because that's something I did entirely on purpose."

Instead of reprimanding her for her sarcasm, Emlyn just frowned, adjusting the doublet as Gwynnie squeezed the water from her hair.

"That's what happened to Titus, wasn't it?" Gwynnie looked at her mother, her teeth chattering. "You said you left him in the Thames."

Emlyn didn't answer.

"God's wounds," Gwynnie muttered, closing her eyes as she considered the horror of it. Titus Duffield, a man her father had once called a friend, had ended his days in that icy water. No hand had reached in to pull him free.

"He was a murderer," Emlyn said sharply. "Hate me for it if you want to, Gwynnie, but I know what I did. I know all that happened. I sought justice. That was all. *Justice*."

"Justice? Or revenge?"

"What's the difference?"

"Oh, no difference at all," Gwynnie snapped. "Only that one is just and fair, the other bloodthirsty."

"Gwynnie, this is not the place for this argument."

"I quite agree!"

"Hush." Emlyn pulled Gwynnie to her feet and steered her into the boathouse. It was a small building, barely big enough to hold two wherries on the water, but other small boats rested on shelves along one wall. It left just enough floor space for the two of them to stand as Emlyn shut the door behind them.

"Titus took your father's life," Emlyn said bitterly. "Can you say you are not angry at him for what he did?"

"Of course I am," Gwynnie hissed, pulling the doublet tighter around her shoulders to fight the cold. "Yet if you ask me if I would have done the same…?"

"In my experience, we never know what we are capable of until we are forced to act."

The statement hit uncomfortably close to home. Gwynnie tried not to think about the moment she had brandished a knife at a Spanish spy in the shallows of the Thames, nor how she had tussled to save her own life, ready to hurt another in order to survive.

"It was one decision. That was all, Gwynnie. Will you judge me for one act alone?"

"One act?" Gwynnie stared at Emlyn. "Do you not remember what happened here in January? What you did then?"

"What did I do?" Emlyn's face was a picture of innocence.

"Master Florian Battersby. Do you remember him? The poor man killed by Fitzroy?" Gwynnie shuddered at the memory of what Henry Fitzroy, the king's illegitimate son, had done.

"Of course, I remember." Emlyn waved a hand in dismissal. "Fitzroy thought he could get away with anything — including murder."

"And he did," Gwynnie reminded her. "Do you remember Florian's wife — Esme Battersby? Her anger and grief?"

"I remember her." Emlyn stilled. "Do not say another word—"

Gwynnie ignored her. "Then you will remember Renard, the man who worked for Fitzroy, who protected him and hurt God knows how many people to do so. You stepped out of the way so that Goodwife Battersby could take her revenge. You let her plunge a knife into Renard's back."

"And as you said, dearest —" Emlyn stepped forward, her face appearing in a shaft of moonlight, her expression serious — "Renard had hurt many people. He tried to kill *you*."

Seeing Gwynnie's shocked expression, Emlyn sighed. "Are you afraid of me, miting? Is that it?"

"No." Gwynnie's answer came swiftly. "I'm not afraid of you. But sometimes I am afraid of what you can do…" She trailed off.

Emlyn turned and sat down on the wooden ledge of the boathouse, her feet dangling over one of the wherries tacked to its moorings. She stared out over the river.

"I'm sorry," she whispered after a moment. "Truly, Gwynnie. When you were a child, I wanted to give you the best life. To persuade you that the world is a good and safe place." Her shoulders slumped. "Yet I was a fool to think I ever could create such an illusion. The world is no friend to people from the slums, like you and I."

Gwynnie felt her eyes prickle with tears. She blinked fast, staring at Emlyn's back.

Briefly, she saw the young woman her mother had once been. A woman full of hopes and dreams of what the future could be, making a happy home for her husband and the daughter she loved. Gwynnie could remember being tickled by Emlyn until she'd cried and the warm embrace of her mother's arms when she'd woken from a bad dream.

Those happy memories had died with John-Louis.

Gwynnie wiped her eyes with the back of her hand as she sat down beside Emlyn, their elbows bumping together.

"I'm sorry you've not had the life you wanted, Ma," Gwynnie murmured.

Emlyn wrapped an arm around her shoulder and held Gwynnie tight. Resting her head on her mother's shoulder, Gwynnie closed her eyes.

"Why do you want to find these jewels, Ma? What good can it do now, all these years later?"

"You mean besides giving us a new future, a life without want, without thievery?" Emlyn shook her head.

"You said my father said it was too much. What would you do with it all? Would you give some of it away, as he wanted to? Would you honour his wishes?"

"Of course I would. I would only take what I needed. But that is not the only reason I want to find the loot. I want to lay your father's ghost to rest, Gwynnie."

"What do you mean?" asked Gwynnie. "You already avenged him. You told me so that night."

"I mean, to give him *real peace*," Emlyn said gravely. "When John-Louis and Titus argued, Titus talked of using something they had discovered to persuade someone to pay them more to keep quiet. *That* was what your father was afraid of."

Gwynnie frowned. "Titus wanted to blackmail someone?"

"That's what it sounded like." Emlyn nodded. "Now, what could possibly be amongst the king's jewels that pertained to a secret? Titus could have been trying to blackmail the king himself, or one of his councillors. Perhaps the steward whose responsibility it was to care for the jewels. There are so many possibilities —"

"Try to sound a little less excited, Ma," Gwynnie said wryly.

"All I'm saying is there's a secret here. Maybe *this* is why Titus killed John-Louis. Not to take the loot for himself, but for the chance to blackmail someone for more. He clearly thought it would be the making of him. But what secret would persuade him to kill a friend?" Emlyn shook her head sadly. "I want to find out. And when I do, I'll know once and for all why your father was killed. Then his ghost can rest peacefully."

Gwynnie stared at her mother. Emlyn may have claimed it was so that John-Louis could find peace, but Gwynnie knew the truth. It was so that Emlyn could find her own peace.

"Does the past follow you every day?"

"Every second of every day," Emlyn replied.

Gwynnie nodded. The obsession was frightening. To think her mother could not live for anything else but this secret. It was just possible that if they could find the loot, the two crates which held the jewels and gold coins, her mother could start a new life. Not just turn her back on thieving, but be able to think of something else each day.

"You said Marie Duffield had given you some hint as to where the loot is now," Gwynnie murmured. "What was it?"

Emlyn's head jerked up. "Does this mean you are agreeing to help me, miting?"

"No, no. I didn't say that," Gwynnie said quickly. "I'm only asking what the hint was. How did you find her?"

"I remembered her talking long ago of family, though I couldn't recall if it was Bath or Bristol, and an idea occurred to me. Perhaps she had gone to hide with her relations. I tried searching for her in Bath, with no luck, so I moved on to Bristol. It took a long time, a lot of standing and watching in streets, and many questions asked at markets, but eventually someone knew her. They knew her by her maiden name, Marie Knollys. It was not difficult to find her then." Emlyn sighed. "Poor Marie was shocked to see me at the door, afraid the past had come to find her."

"She thought Titus was still alive? That you were leading him to her?"

"She didn't know he had died. I broke the news to her. She couldn't grieve for him — she had hated him for too long. Instead she cried with relief to know he was gone, that she was safe. I spent a few days with her." Emlyn paused. "Marie had some papers she had taken when she had left Titus, including a map. It was plain she hadn't grasped what it meant. It's a scruffy drawing. I keep it close."

"Where?"

Emlyn ignored the question. "I believe it is a map to where Titus and John-Louis hid the loot. He was probably waiting for the right moment to go back for it. The map has no words, only a drawing. It's a small plan of a building, and that building could be anything. They knew what building it was, so they sought to document nothing further about its location. I suggested that Marie and I could try to find the jewels, but she refused. She wanted nothing to do with it. She had a quiet life; she worked as a seamstress, and she was happy. She did not wish to rake up the past. So, I asked her if she knew anything about where the loot was hidden. She was reluctant to speak at first. Then she remembered poor John-Louis. She talked of Titus coming back to their home … the blood, and the words poured out.

"The day John-Louis and Titus went to hide the jewels, they went to two places. Marie thinks either one could be the hiding place. And both are in London." From the open window in the boathouse, they could see London glimmering in the distance, the torchlights still burning. "It's out there, waiting to be found, but I can't find it alone."

Emlyn looked down at her arm. Even though it was out of its sling, it did not move as freely as it once had. She stretched her leg out in front of her. Gwynnie had noticed that her mother was still limping.

"I need help. I need *your* help, miting."

Gwynnie cursed and looked away.

"I know you hate the name —"

"I do."

"It's my name for you. You always were my little miting." Emlyn reached out and brushed some wet hair back from Gwynnie's forehead. Gwynnie tried not to be swayed by her mother's gentle touch. Yet the temptation was there, the temptation of another life, far away from this one, and the chance to know the truth behind her father's death.

"If I help you, Ma — and that is a big *if*," she emphasised, for Emlyn had leaned forward in excitement, "you have to promise me that this will truly be the end of it. No more thefts. You will go and start a new life."

"Baking in a cottage in France?" Emlyn teased.

"Yes, why not? Promise me that you will no longer steal, risk arrest, or brawl at night." She gestured to Emlyn's wounds. "You can rest your sore bones and live a life of peace. If you want my help, then you have to promise me that."

Emlyn held out her good hand without hesitation. "I promise you, dearest. You have my word."

"Thank you." Gwynnie took Emlyn's hand and gripped it tight.

"Does that mean you will help me?" Emlyn asked eagerly, not yet releasing her hand.

"I…" The words were on the tip of Gwynnie's tongue. She was ready to say yes, when there was a sound behind them. Emlyn held a finger to her lips. They both stood as quietly as they could, then tiptoed toward the door of the boathouse. Emlyn peered easily through the window set in the door, but Gwynnie had to raise herself up on her tiptoes.

A shadow was moving along the riverbank, a guard marching up and down, keeping watch.

"Well, we'll need a way to get us back into the palace now, then," Emlyn said, pulling her bonnet from a pocket in her hose and fastening it to her head, then tucking her hair beneath. "Wait here, miting."

"What are you going to do?" demanded Gwynnie, but there was no response.

Emlyn had already slipped through the door.

CHAPTER 10

Gwynnie peered through the window of the boathouse. Emlyn had walked quite openly along the riverbank, apparently without a care in the world. She was doing her best to hide the limp, though she made a poor job of it. When she reached the guard, he had turned toward her in alarm.

The two talked for a moment, then they walked on, heading toward the docks and Donsen Tower. Gwynnie saw the opportunity Emlyn had created by drawing the guard away.

Pushing the door open, Gwynnie slipped through the crack. She kept her back flat to the wall of the boathouse, checking that Emlyn and the guard — their figures silhouetted in the moonlight — were facing the other way, before she crept toward the archway and hid in the shadows. She waited, her ears straining to hear their conversation.

The guard laughed at something. Emlyn, affecting a deep voice, bid him goodnight, and the two parted ways. Gwynnie heard her mother's footsteps making their way back toward her end of the riverbank. Soon enough, Emlyn appeared beside her.

"You melt into the shadows better than anyone I know," said Emlyn and took hold of Gwynnie's arm, pulling her through the archway. "Come. I may have made him believe I was a man out for a short walk to clear my head after all the ale I drank at the feast, but I do not think it will be long before he follows us."

"Why?" Gwynnie glanced over her shoulder, warily watching for the guard's approach. "Why would he follow you if he believed you?"

Emlyn raised her good arm. Dangling from her fingers was a man's leather purse, the drawstrings cut.

"You cut it from his belt!" Gwynnie hissed. "What a grand idea when we're trying to go unnoticed."

"Hush now, dearest. He may not notice. Besides, he must be paid well as a palace guard, and these coins could buy us food for two days."

"I have food enough in these walls!"

"Well, I do not."

"Ma!"

"Hey! You!" The guard appeared on the riverbank, running toward them.

"Like old times, Ma." Gwynnie tugged Emlyn's good arm and the two of them sprinted into the adjoining courtyard, heading toward the kitchen and staff quarters. Gwynnie quickly became aware that Emlyn was not able to keep up with her.

She glanced back across the cobbled yard. With her limp, Emlyn was falling behind. The guard behind her was swiftly catching up.

Gwynnie looked around desperately for a way to help Emlyn escape. The door to the kitchens opened and some of the cooks stepped out. They were mopping their brows after the day's hard work, some of the men drinking languidly from cups of ale as others followed tiredly behind.

Without hesitation, Gwynnie walked toward them, her head bowed. None of them glanced her way in the darkness. Gwynnie slipped behind one man. It was old Rudyard, the baker with the stoop who often helped Samuel out in the kitchens. He was known for flying off the handle at the smallest provocation. Gwynnie elbowed him sharply in the back.

"Who did that?" By the time Rudyard spun around, Gwynnie had jumped behind another in the group, reaching up and pulling on his ear.

"Argh! 'Ere, who did that?"

She slipped away into the shadows, just as Rudyard pushed the man.

"You looking for a fight?"

"Look what you're doing, old man!"

"I'll give you old man, you knave —"

A punch was thrown, quickly followed by another, until all were striking and lashing out at one another.

"What's going on here?" The guard who had been chasing Emlyn came to a halt beside them. "Hey! Stop this." He ran forward and ended up joining the fray rather than separating them.

In the commotion, Gwynnie grabbed Emlyn's wrist and ran. If any of the cooks noticed her, they did not call out. She suspected they were all too tipsy to see anything beyond their immediate circle. Gwynnie dragged Emlyn around the laundry building, her mother wincing with every step.

When they reached the door to the laundry, Emlyn fell against the wall, breathing hard.

"You need a physician," Gwynnie urged.

"I cannot afford one. And don't you think it would be suspicious, with all my injuries?"

"You need a physician who would ask no questions." Gwynnie flung the laundry door open. "Hide in there. No one will come in until morning. You can at least have a decent night's sleep. Go!" Gwynnie urged, pushing Emlyn inside.

"You have not yet given me an answer," Emlyn responded as she stumbled inside. "Gwynnie, are you going to help me?"

"Help you? It's all I seem to do!" Gwynnie hissed as she followed her inside, closing the door behind them. "Have you not noticed that the reason I stay in this palace is to stop Tombstone from following your trail? To prevent anyone from arresting you for murder? You think I could see you hanged from a noose?"

"I know, child. I know." Emlyn held out a hand placatingly.

Gwynnie sighed. She'd seen her twenty-eighth summer and yet Emlyn still spoke to her as if she had much growing up to do.

"I told you, no more thieving," she said. "And what did you do? You went and stole the purse of the first man you saw."

"We agreed no more thieving *after* we have found the treasure. How else am I supposed to live in the meantime? Or have you forgotten how hard it can be to find food?"

"Ma, you risked so much, and for what? A few coins." Gwynnie shook her head. She was starting to feel a little nauseous. She felt tired after their run, and she still shivered from her dunk in the Thames. She slid the damp doublet from her shoulders, finding it offered no warmth anymore. "How can I help you?"

Emlyn's lips parted. "You're refusing me? You will not help me, Gwynnie?"

"How can I, when you will not keep your word?"

"I will keep my word," Emlyn said firmly. "But in the meantime, I have to eat somehow."

"Sometimes, I think you crave the danger — the risk," Gwynnie muttered.

"Maybe you do not know me as well as you think, child."

"Stop calling me that!" Gwynnie snapped. She marched back to the door. "Stay here for the night. I'll come and find you tomorrow and we'll talk more then."

"Will we talk? Or will you just continue to shout at me?"

Gwynnie paused, her hand on the door. "You want me to help you, Ma? To find this loot so we can start a new life together and lay the ghosts of the past to rest? Then make me believe you'll keep your word this time." Without another word, Gwynnie opened the door and left.

She hastened along the wall, making her way through the courtyard and down the narrow lanes. She glanced over her shoulder, looking for the guard who had chased Emlyn, or the drunken cooks, but there was no one around. This part of the palace was quiet, with people in their beds and the night ticking on.

Gwynnie hesitated by the door to the maids' lodgings. Her nausea was still there, and she swayed a little on her feet, as if she too had been drinking. She tried the door handle, but her fingers were surprisingly stiff and she struggled to make the small movements required to unlatch it. Soon enough, all she could think about was how cold it was. The air was closing in around her, making breathing difficult.

Stepping back from the lodgings, she crept away. She could go to Emlyn in the laundry and ask her to start a fire. Yet somehow it seemed a poor idea to return. They would simply argue again. After all that Gwynnie had discovered that night about her parents and their past, Emlyn was the last person she wanted to see.

Woodenly, she headed toward the tiltyard. If there had been guards on this particular gate, then they had long since abandoned their post, their pikes and halberds resting against the stone wall. It struck her that the guards could have been called away by the one who had been chasing Emlyn. Perhaps they were even now searching the palace grounds for her.

Gwynnie picked her way through the gate, once more struggling with the latch. Somehow, she managed to open it, though her fingers trembled as she did so.

She couldn't remember entering the clerks' corridor, nor even the building, but soon enough she was standing outside Tombstone's office. It was late, so late that he had surely gone to bed. Yet with some vain hope, she raised her hand and knocked on the door. Something creaked on the other side. She knocked again and footsteps followed.

She stepped back as the door was opened wide.

Tombstone stood on the other side. His black doublet was undone at the neck, his copper hair tousled, and his cheeks pink from the warmth of a fire, or wine, or both.

"You usually pick the lock and let yourself in." He frowned. "Gwynnie, what is it? What's wrong?"

"I … I think I need your help," Gwynnie whispered, stepping forward. Her nausea took over, and she held a hand to her lips.

"What happened to you? Dear God, why are you shaking so much?"

"I fell in the Thames."

CHAPTER 11

"Well, you've had a merry Christmas Day, haven't you?" Tombstone said as he tossed a fresh shirt and hose onto the floor. "Change into those and hurry. We have to get you out of those cold things." He steered her toward the roaring fire in his room.

Not for one moment did Gwynnie doubt Tombstone's resolve not to look as she changed. She knew that Tombstone's romantic interests lay in a different direction. He would have no interest in looking at a naked woman.

Gwynnie fumbled as she undressed, struggling to move her frozen limbs. She discarded the wet kirtle and chemise, kicking off her damp boots, then pulled on the hose, but her hands failed her when it came to the shirt.

"Elric!" She called his Christian name as she sank to her knees. Before she knew it, he was pulling the shirt over her head for her.

"Don't worry, I didn't look," he promised, though she realised she didn't care if he had. She was safe here.

He took her shoulders and turned her to sit on the hearth. "Warm yourself by the fire."

She did as he said, leaning toward the flames and breathing deeply as Tombstone picked up her damp clothes, hanging them from little iron hooks. Next, he took a flagon of water, added it to a cauldron, and placed that on a grate over the flames. He went to his buffet cabinet and pulled out the wooden box, searching for something inside.

"Dry your hair by the fire if you can," he urged, glancing her way. "It will keep you cold, otherwise." He added something to a cup, then returned to her side, throwing a blanket over her shoulders.

"What's wrong with me?"

"Cold shock, I think," he murmured, sitting beside her on the hearth as he stirred the contents of the cup. "My ma saw it, many times. She said a man's body can freeze up if it's exposed to the cold for too long."

Gwynnie's ears pricked up. It was rare to hear Tombstone talk about his mother. All she knew was that she had been a healer, and that she had died some time ago.

"How long were you in the water?" he asked.

"Not long." Gwynnie pulled the blanket tight around her shoulders. "The cold — it feels as if it has seeped into my bones."

"That Thames looks ready to freeze. You're lucky you were not in there for long." Tombstone fell quiet as he fussed with the water in the cauldron. When it was boiling, he poured a little into the cup he had prepared, then pressed it into her hands. "Drink this with care. It will help."

"What's in it?" She blew hard on the hot liquid and took the smallest of sips, coughing and spluttering. "That burns!"

"This will help." Tombstone returned to his medicine box and picked up a glass jar of golden liquid. "Honey," he assured her softly as he placed a large spoonful into the cup and stirred. "There's cinnamon and ginger in there. My mother always said it helped the blood to move. It warms you through."

"God, I hope she's right." Gwynnie took another sip. It was bearable now, with the added sweetness. As her nausea eased, she became aware of Tombstone watching her closely. "I cannot believe you're working on Yuletide night," she murmured.

"I cannot believe you fell in the Thames. Are you going to tell me how?"

"No."

"I thought not. Drink up." He didn't reprimand her but stood again and went to fetch a second blanket out of a coffer. When he returned, he wrapped it around her feet.

"Thank you," she whispered. He smiled a little and moved to sit in one of the chairs by the fire. "Can I ask you something?" she asked after a moment, noticing that she was no longer shivering so much.

"You usually ask without permission," he said wryly. "What's to stop you now?"

"What's your opinion of family?" She paused. "And … of loyalty?"

"Loyalty?" He frowned deeply. "If you're asking if Pascal and I are related again —"

"No, no, I just want your opinion," she cut in. "Should we be loyal to our family? Always?"

"An interesting question." Tombstone sat forward, ruffling his copper hair as he thought about the answer. "I suppose I do not think loyalty should be born from blood alone. Loyalty must be earned."

"And Pascal has earned yours," she said lightly.

Tombstone inclined his head and Gwynnie took another sip from the strangely spiced and honeyed drink, praying that he would not think too hard as to why she had asked that question.

"You can sleep here tonight, on the rug, if you wish. It will certainly be warmer than that chamber of yours."

"You do not mind?"

"No, Gwynnie, I do not mind. I don't particularly want to see you die of cold." He smiled teasingly. Rather glad to feel any comfort at all after the night she'd had, Gwynnie smiled back.

"God's blood! Have they swapped the wassails for shrieking cats this year?"

Gwynnie hastened to keep up with Tombstone as they entered the great hall, carrying a tray of mead. It was the second night of the Yuletide celebrations, a night typically given to charity, folk plays and wassailing. A service had been given at the chapel earlier, attended by both King Henry and Queen Jane, though Gwynnie had seen nothing of the service. She'd heard the distant chanting, even a carol being sung, but nothing more. She had spent most of the day huddled by the fire in Tombstone's office, while he kept an eye on her and brought her warm food. Only when she had pleaded that questions would be raised if she didn't help with the feast did he agree that she could leave, on the strict understanding that if she felt cold again, she would return at once to sit by his fire.

"I see they have spared no expense tonight," Tombstone murmured, stepping toward the clerks and lawyers' table, which had to be the demurest of the tables present. At all the other tables, the courtiers had dressed flamboyantly. There seemed to be an understanding that only red and gold could be worn tonight, but the clerks and lawyers were dressed in their usual black. There were more evergreen boughs hanging from the ceiling than the day before, more grand sugar structures set on each table, with one that even looked like Greenwich Palace itself.

Tombstone took his seat at the end of the table, far from the other lawyers, apparently not wishing to join in with their conversation. Gwynnie stepped away, handing out flagons of mead to the other tables. Her eyes lingered on the top table, where the king and queen sat together.

As before, Robert Aske sat on the king's right-hand side, though he looked uneasy. He had not eaten from the trenchers in front of him and his fingers fidgeted with the spoon in his grasp. The king and queen were in high spirits, and Gwynnie found a smile tugging at her own lips when she saw the queen laugh so freely.

Queen Jane was safe and happy. Such a thing was rare indeed in this palace.

Gwynnie returned to Tombstone's table, being careful to give a wide berth to the wassailers who stood in the middle of the room, singing so loudly that they seemed to make the rafters shake.

"When you fell in the Thames last night," Tombstone whispered as she poured mead into a cup for him, "were you still following the king?"

"I had just finished," Gwynnie replied, reasoning that it was not entirely a lie.

"And? Where did the king go?"

Gwynnie glanced around. Seeing that everyone was too busy either teasing the wassailers for their inability to hold a tune, or joining in with the poor show, she hastened to sit beside him. She hurriedly told Tombstone how Samuel had been ordered to deliver a feast for two, and had been escorted there by one of Cromwell's men. Then she described the arm of the finely dressed man she had spied through the keyhole.

"Who was he?" Tombstone asked, his mead long forgotten.

"I do not know, but…" Gwynnie paused, checking once again that there was no one close enough to hear them. Everyone seemed much more interested in the folk play that had now begun, in which one particular actor was kicking another around the room, making King Henry roar with laughter. "I believe that whoever dined with the king last night was the same man who came ashore under cover of night on Christmas Eve."

"Why?"

"Because when Samuel and I left, we found two men guarding the door. It was *them*. The same two men who had helped the third onto the deck from the wherry. I am certain of it. Both are tall, and one carried that scabbard at his hip I mentioned to you before. They seemed most concerned that Samuel and I had been inside the building. When Samuel explained we were following orders and delivering a feast, they relaxed a little and let us leave."

Tombstone nodded, deep in thought. "Do you see those men in this room now? Would you recognise them?"

"I would recognise them, but not their master." Gwynnie stood with her tray and walked around the room. Collecting empty flagons, she circled the hall, avoiding the actors in the folk play and diving out of the way of the wassailers, who seemed rather keen to join in with the jollity and start singing again. As she picked up flagons, she took the opportunity to look at every face she passed. She even examined the scabbards of men who had dared to bring a knife to the feast, and the fussy laces and collars to see if she could recognise the second man, but neither were present.

She eventually returned to Tombstone and laid down the tray, sitting beside him.

"They're not here."

"So, who could he be?" Tombstone murmured as he looked out over the room.

"I wondered if he could be some diplomat, some political official the king shouldn't be seen to meet in public," Gwynnie suggested. "Perhaps from France or Spain?"

"A risky position for the king to take. Since he dissolved the monasteries, peace with both countries has been at risk." Tombstone shook his head. "Any alliance would surely have to go through official routes. Yet you said Cromwell escorted him?"

"Yes, he did."

"Then the pair of them are up to something." Tombstone nodded in Cromwell's direction. "Have you not noticed where Cromwell sits tonight?"

Gwynnie sat forward with interest, for Cromwell had been welcomed back to the top table.

Before any more could be said between them, King Henry stood from his seat. Others at the top table tapped their cups with their cutlery and a manservant stepped forward, ringing a bell to silence the great hall. The folk play stopped at once and the wassailers desisted, all except one particularly drunken singer who had to be elbowed sharply in the ribs.

"Ladies and gentlemen of the court, I thank you for the generosity you have shown today, on this day of charity. The donations you have made in the church will do more good in my country than I can tell you." With a show of humility, King Henry laid a hand on his chest.

"Curious," Gwynnie muttered. "All this charity — I do not remember seeing a shilling of it on the streets of London."

"Shh!" Tombstone hissed. "Do you want to risk being heard?"

"It is on this day of charity that my good wife, that my dearest friend…" King Henry paused and held his hand out to Queen Jane. She hurriedly stood, taking his hand with a smile on her face. "My dear wife has reminded me that Christian charity, of course, must start at home. We must forgive, we must move forward with kindness and goodness in our hearts." He kissed the back of her hand. There was a soft sigh from the watching court, but Gwynnie and Tombstone exchanged an uneasy look, wondering where this speech was leading.

The king stepped away from his wife and moved along the platform.

"That is why, tonight, I shall be one with such charity. I shall forgive. I shall move with kindness and goodness in my heart." He stepped down from the platform, leaning momentarily on a footman's shoulder. Henry moved toward the far table, where Lady Mary sat. "Today I extend my hand and my forgiveness to my daughter, Lady Mary."

Gwynnie's eyes darted around the room. There was a general wave of astonishment and wonder. Some muttered, others shook their heads, but a few people applauded at once.

Lady Mary took her father's hand and allowed herself to be drawn to her feet. She did not seem shocked.

"A reconciliation," Tombstone said to Gwynnie, under the cover of the applause. "Some of the more forward-thinking councillors will not be pleased to hear that a Catholic daughter is to be returned to court so highly favoured." He nodded at some of the political councillors further down the table who had bent their heads together to speak in quiet tones.

"Tomorrow, we shall have a reconciliation ceremony," Henry announced, now holding his daughter's hand between both of his own. "Come, daughter. Take your place where you belong. Join me at my table."

"Well, well," Gwynnie said as the applause began again. King Henry and Lady Mary moved to the top table as two servants hastened to add another place, between the king and queen. "It seems that Queen Jane has more influence over the king than she has given herself credit for."

"Was it her doing, I wonder? Or was it all at Lady Mary's behest?" Tombstone asked with interest.

"Now, now." King Henry called for attention once again, standing beside his daughter and his queen. "In the spirit of friendship, I also wish to welcome another to our celebrations tonight. He is a new friend and a fiercely loyal gentleman, with a heart as pure as gold. Please, open the doors." The king gestured to the double doors of the great hall. "I'd like to introduce you all to Viscount Hereford, Walter Devereux."

The doors were swept open and two men stepped inside. One was dressed in such fancy lace that the cuffs hid his hands, while the other entered with his hand resting on his weapons' belt, from which a scabbard hung.

Gwynnie gripped Tombstone's elbow under the table.

"I know, I know. I have eyes too," he assured her hastily. "God's wounds…" It was so rare to hear Tombstone curse that Gwynnie glanced at him quickly. He was not looking at the two men, but at another who had followed behind them.

This man was dressed grandly, wearing the same sapphire and silver doublet that Gwynnie had glimpsed through the keyhole the night before. He had russet hair, which had grown long around his ears and had been excessively styled. On one side of his face, which had once been quite handsome, a long scar travelled from his forehead to his chin.

"It can't be him," Tombstone muttered. "It can't be."

Yet Gwynnie had no doubt in her mind as she stared at the man. "That's Henry Fitzroy."

CHAPTER 12

"It can't be him," Tombstone said again as Walter Devereux, Viscount Hereford, walked down the aisle between the tables, heading toward the top table and King Henry.

The great hall had erupted in whispers. Surely everyone was thinking the same thing.

The king's voice boomed out. "Here is a man pledged to my cause, a man who has vowed to help us if there are any more rebellions in the north." Henry glanced at Robert Aske. The threat was subtle but clear. Aske simply stared at the approaching man in wonder. "Please, raise your glasses in a toast. To reconciliations —" the king nodded at his daughter beside him — "and to new friends."

The men in the room stood and toasted as the women raised their glasses. With one clap from the king, the revellers began again, the wassailers singing and the actors performing their skits. Viscount Hereford had been shown to the top table, where yet another place was added so he could sit.

"Gwynnie, you can let go of my arm now," Tombstone said with a sigh.

"It's him!" she hissed.

"I know."

"Is the king actually claiming that Fitzroy is Viscount Hereford? That this man is not his son?"

Tombstone gulped from his cup of mead. "The damn daring." He shook his head. "To think that man would walk here again, after what he did…" He trailed off.

They both knew that Fitzroy had been exiled from Greenwich Palace because of murder. One of the two men he had killed had once been Tombstone's lover. Though the love between Tombstone and the murdered man had dwindled, Tombstone's lingering affection and pain had been evident when Gwynnie had helped her friend find his body.

"Cromwell hinted that Fitzroy could still be alive," said Tombstone, his voice low. "He even warned me to stop asking."

"The king lied about Fitzroy being dead. He lied to the whole court — to the country! Prayers were said for him, a service held in London," Gwynnie muttered angrily.

"He had to lie," said Tombstone, his tone bitter. "His son is a killer."

Gwynnie shuddered. She had been hiding in Fitzroy's garderobe, about to steal his jewels, when she had overheard Florian Battersby attempting to blackmail him. Fitzroy had silenced such demands by placing his hands around Battersby's throat.

Still little more than a boy in age, yet strong in build and taller than most men, Fitzroy had been an impressive presence in the palace. As Gwynnie peered at the man now at the top table, she saw that much about his appearance was as she remembered. He was the same height as before, with the same broad shoulders and the same long-fingered hands that reached for a flagon of claret. Yet there was much that was different. The scar on his face was new, the beard too, and his cheeks had become more prominent, having matured with age.

"He's put on weight — that will prevent some from recognising him," Tombstone commented. He too was staring at Fitzroy.

"That scar…" Gwynnie frowned at the scar that ran down one side of the man's face, disappearing into a full, russet beard. "That will make others doubt their convictions."

Had Gwynnie not seen the man's face so often in her nightmares, she may have been able to persuade herself that she was not looking at Fitzroy. But she could not. She knew exactly who he was.

"Henry was determined to have him back at court, even after he exiled his son to his country estate," Tombstone muttered. "Only Queen Anne saw Fitzroy for what he is, a murderer, and look what happened to her. Henry had her silenced. What a weak king."

"Or just a selfish one. It is a crime we already know he is guilty of." A memory stirred in the back of Gwynnie's mind. She had glimpsed Fitzroy at Queen Anne's execution. He had crept into the Tower of London to watch his stepmother, the woman who had insisted he pay for his crimes, be executed. Fitzroy and King Henry had met in secret that day, and Gwynnie had caught a few snatched words. "Fitzroy was determined to return to court someday."

Tombstone sighed heavily. "Today is that day, it seems."

Gwynnie delivered fresh food and cleared away empty trenchers before she returned to her seat at Tombstone's side. In that time Tombstone hadn't eaten anything. He simply stared over a very full pewter plate, watching Fitzroy intently. Gwynnie topped up his cup of mead and pushed it toward him.

"You have to eat something," she said. Tombstone took a small sip of his mead. "That's not what I meant."

"I cannot believe this," Tombstone hissed.

They both stared at the top table. Lady Mary's initial happiness at being welcomed back by her father appeared to have waned. She could not stop glancing at the man her father called Viscount Hereford. Perhaps, like Gwynnie and

Tombstone, she knew exactly who he was, though plenty of others in the room seemed to have accepted King Henry's word, that he was some distant viscount from the north.

"The question is," Tombstone went on, "if we recognise him, will he recognise *you*?"

Gwynnie flinched. She remembered all too well how Henry Fitzroy and his man, Renard, had hunted her through the palace. She had been attacked by them in the tiltyard, and had thought she would die out there on the cold earth, with no one to help her.

Her eyes darted toward the two men who had accompanied Fitzroy. They sat at the far end of the one of the tables. Amaro talked to no one, shovelling food into his mouth. The other, whose name she hadn't yet discovered, was happy to talk in a loud voice to all around him about Viscount Hereford, telling them stories of the distant borders with Wales and the land he helped to steward, which stretched on for miles.

She shivered as she looked at them. Amaro certainly carried a dangerous weapon, yet it seemed to her that the other man had seniority over him.

"Do you think Fitzroy would risk hurting me now?" Gwynnie asked. "He comes here under another name. He must think himself invincible."

"Perhaps he does." Tombstone nodded, placing down his cup. Gwynnie quickly swiped it and took a sip. "Either way, I think it best you go back to your chamber. I do not think it wise for you to risk being seen by him."

"I am in a hall full of people. He would not do anything to me now."

"It doesn't mean he's incapable of seeing you." Tombstone stood, urging her to do the same. "I must speak to Cromwell."

"What about?"

"Cromwell knows what happened in January, all that Fitzroy is responsible for, and yet he aids his return to the palace?" Tombstone muttered a curse under his breath. "I fear he is prepared to do anything, even welcome a known murderer back into our midst, if it means keeping his place at the king's side." He glanced up at the top table. "I wish to see his reaction when I challenge him about Viscount Hereford being Fitzroy. Now go."

Gwynnie moved toward the door, only hesitating long enough to pick up a few empty trenchers. The wassailers had started up again, reaching new pitches, so high and piercing that many in the room covered their ears to block out the sound. Struggling with so many trenchers, Gwynnie fumbled with the door. Another hand suddenly appeared above her own, jerking the door open. She looked up to see Tombstone. He was pink-cheeked, as if he had crossed the hall in a hurry.

"Go!" he commanded. She slipped through the doorway, expecting him to follow. Instead, he quickly pushed the door closed behind her.

"Ah, good evening to you, sirrah." The familiar voice on the other side of the door made Gwynnie freeze, her knuckles white as she clung to the trenchers, straining to hear more. "A merry Christmas to you."

"A merry Christmas to you, my Lord *Hereford*." Tombstone's voice was tight as he greeted Henry Fitzroy. Gwynnie's mouth became dry. Little good could come from revealing to Fitzroy that he had been recognised for who he really was.

"I do not believe we have met. Would you do me the honour of sharing your name?"

"Elric Tombstone, my lord," Tombstone replied, his tone cool. Gwynnie stiffened. Fitzroy may have been conducting the conversation as if it were merely a chance meeting, but she was not fooled. Fitzroy was handling this exchange with great care.

"An unusual name. One I'm sure I am unlikely to forget. Your face, of course, was familiar. I pointed you out in the crowd just now and wished to be acquainted with you. I hope you do not mind."

"Not at all." Tombstone's voice showed just how much he did mind.

"My companion knows your face. He says you are a man of this palace — a clerk and lawyer in Cromwell's employment. Is that correct?"

"Yes, my lord."

"And you know the palace well? You know all who work here?"

"I know many who do, my lord. Not all."

"I wonder if you know a young maid. Short, very short, with light brown hair. Rather … undistinctive."

Gwynnie's jaw dropped in horror. He had to be speaking of her.

"May I enquire why you ask, my lord?" said Tombstone. "Could it be that you have seen such a maid before?"

"No, no. This is the first time I have been to the palace. Was the king's introduction not clear?"

"Yes … of course. This maid, do you know her name?"

"Do you know, I have quite forgotten it. Do you know of such a maid?"

"No, I'm afraid I do not," Tombstone replied firmly.

Silently praising Tombstone, Gwynnie turned on her heel and ran to the kitchens. She shot through the doors, discarding the trenchers on a nearby table.

"Ho, lass. What's all this?" Samuel's voice brought her up short. He stood before her, hands floured as he prepared dough for the following day's feast. "You look as if you have seen some phantom. What is it, lass?"

"Nothing, nothing," Gwynnie said as brightly as she could. "I'm quite well. Completely fine." Samuel's eyebrows were raised. "Just some drunkards from the feast," she said with much more forced ease. "They sometimes grab too much with their hands."

Samuel sighed and pummelled some dough in clear anger. "Go out the back way. You don't want anyone following you to your chamber."

She squeezed his arm in thanks, about to walk away when she thought of Brynne. "How is Brynne?" she asked gently. "Has she had any news —"

"No news yet." Samuel halted with the dough. "I think, once she hears, she'll be a lot better."

"I hope so." Gwynnie released his arm and scuttled off to the back of the kitchens. The other cooks sat around the fire, their tasks for the day done. They passed a flagon of ale between them, exhausted from preparing their second grand feast in two days. She crept out of the building and into a narrow lane. Pausing long enough to lean against the wall, she clutched her chest and breathed heavily. "He remembers me," she muttered to herself, thinking of Henry Fitzroy.

Had he seen her across the great hall and moved to follow her? Was that why Tombstone had caught up with her, in an attempt to mask Fitzroy's view and stop him from following?

Glancing over her shoulder, she headed toward the maids' lodging house. The courtyard was empty. There were no guards this evening to watch her, no drunkards that had left the feast early. She was careful to check every shadow for a sign of movement, knowing that Amaro or his companion could be watching her on Fitzroy's orders.

On reaching the maids' lodgings, she halted, staring into the darkness where she had seen Emlyn the night before. She did not doubt that Emlyn had taken the first opportunity to leave the laundry room that morning. She was likely to have crept around the palace all day, stealing food and watching the feast, though Gwynnie had not glimpsed her in the great hall.

Seeing that Emlyn was not watching her from the darkness tonight, Gwynnie crept up the stairs. She halted on the top step. There was someone in the shadows in front of her.

Gwynnie held her breath. Could it be one of the two men that had accompanied Fitzroy? Yet that was surely impossible. She had left them behind in the great hall.

The figure stepped forward, just visible in the darkness.

"Ma?" Gwynnie whispered.

"What's wrong?" Emlyn asked. "Miting, what has happened?"

Gwynnie reached for Emlyn, clutching her hand.

Far beneath them in the entrance hall, a door creaked open again. Both women flinched at the sound of the door closing sharply. Gwynnie peered over the banister, down at the new shadow which had appeared.

"Gwynnie? Are you there?" Tombstone called from the bottom of the steps.

CHAPTER 13

"Tombstone?" Gwynnie hissed through the darkness. "Do you want to be seen sneaking into the maids' lodgings?"

"That is hardly my worry at this moment." Tombstone started to move up the stairs, scrambling for a candle from the shelf. He hastened to light it with a tinderbox, the tiny flame casting a warm yellow glow across his face. "Fitzroy saw you."

Gwynnie hurried down the steps to meet him, preventing him from climbing higher and glimpsing Emlyn.

"I feared as much."

"I don't think he got a good look at you; that's why he was asking me questions." Tombstone spoke quickly. "I saw him walking your way and hurried to halt him. The only thing that made him return to the top table was my promise to come to him if I saw a maid that matched your description."

"That's mad."

"Of course, I'm not going to do it," Tombstone hissed. "But I need to know why he's back here."

"Isn't it obvious?" Gwynnie asked. "King Henry was clearly determined to bring his son back to court."

"That may be the case." Tombstone ran a hand through his hair. The candle in his other hand shook a little, making the yellow light dance around the stairs. "I managed to speak to Cromwell, briefly. He made it plain the subject was not up for discussion, but he's asked me to meet him in his chambers."

Gwynnie's eyes widened. "He's asked for a private audience with you?"

"Yes, and I have a strong suspicion that he is about to tell me all the things he felt he couldn't say in the great hall, where there were listening ears." He glanced above her head at the passage. Gwynnie bit her lip, hoping that Emlyn had had the good sense to hide. "Go to my office, Gwynnie, and hide there."

"Why?"

"Because Fitzroy is hunting for a maid. A maid who can point the finger at him for what he did earlier this year. Where do you think he'll look first?" He gestured around them. "Go quickly. I shall meet you there later, after my meeting with Cromwell."

Tombstone hastened back down the stairs, blowing out the candle when he reached the entrance and slipping out into the courtyard beyond. Gwynnie stared at the door as it shut behind him, and did not hear Emlyn approach until she rested her hand on Gwynnie's shoulder.

"Jesu!"

"Hush, miting."

"Are you trying to scare me to death?"

"What was all that about?" Emlyn asked. "He mentioned Fitzroy."

"He's back, Ma. Henry Fitzroy is back in the palace. He's been given a new name, and practically looks like a new man, but it is him." Gwynnie looked up at Emlyn. "We are both in danger. Ma, we need to get you out of the palace."

"I have only been here a couple of days," Emlyn said. "You know why I came, Gwynnie. I came for your help, and I shall not be leaving without it."

"You're a stubborn mule, sometimes."

"Runs in the family, dearest."

Gwynnie took Emlyn's hand and drew her toward the door. "You must leave the palace. I shall come and find you in a few days' time. Just tell me where you are going and then leave."

"Quite the send-off," Emlyn scoffed as she reached for the door, opening it a crack and peering out. A glimmer of torchlight fell upon her face. "And perhaps a little more difficult than you anticipated."

Gwynnie took Emlyn's place and peered out into the courtyard. She could see Tombstone's retreating back. He was heading through an archway, in the direction of the guest chambers, probably for his meeting with Cromwell. Coming the other way were three guards. They inclined their heads respectfully as they passed Tombstone, then took up their posts around the yard, keeping watch.

Hastily, Gwynnie shut the door, plunging the two of them back into darkness.

"Any other bright ideas?" Emlyn whispered.

"I'm thinking!" Gwynnie's mind raced. "We cannot risk Fitzroy seeing either of us, neither can we risk Tombstone seeing you." She glanced at Emlyn. "You may be willing to risk your neck at the gallows, but I am tired of it, Ma."

"All right, miting." Emlyn's tone softened. "I crept into the palace grounds easily enough. The guards were too busy looking for that soldier friend of yours. Apart from one lad who was dissuaded from following me after a short tussle, they did not pay attention to a woman who followed a cart delivery of fresh mead. There must be an equally simple way to get out tomorrow."

"Tomorrow? No, Ma — it has to be tonight."

"Tonight? Would you be rid of your mother so soon?"

"I'd be rid of you this very moment."

"How charming."

Gwynnie gripped Emlyn's arm tight. "I'm doing this to keep you alive, Ma. We will find a way to get you out of the palace — tonight!"

This time, Emlyn did not argue.

Gwynnie stood by the door of the maids' lodgings, carrying a bundle of laundry she had taken from the chambers upstairs. She peered out across the courtyard, watching the three guards who stood beneath the burning torches. Two were talking jovially together, but the third took his responsibilities more seriously, watching the courtyard avidly.

"Are you ready?" Gwynnie asked Emlyn behind her.

"I'm ready." Emlyn adjusted the bonnet on her head. Over her shoulder was a long stretch of rope they had found in a store cupboard upstairs.

"Then keep watch." Gwynnie stepped out of the door and into the courtyard.

The diligent guard turned his head toward her, though the other two didn't take any notice. Carrying the bundle of laundry in front of her, Gwynnie yawned widely and then pretended to slip on the ice beneath her boots. Regaining her balance, she walked on, heading toward the archway where the men stood guard.

When she was close enough, she made a show of slipping completely. "Oh!" she cried as she fell on her back, tipping the linen sheets onto the ground.

"Woah! You well there?"

Two faces appeared above her, as the third guard picked up her laundry.

"Oh, I am so sorry. It's so icy out here," she said, feigning injury and reaching for her back.

"Here, we'll help you up."

"You're too kind." Gwynnie took hold of the hands reaching toward her. "Oh!" She slipped again, ending up on her knees and this time taking one of the guards down with her. "My apologies. I cannot find my feet on this ice."

"Perfectly fine," the guard said, wincing. He appeared to have cracked his knee on a particularly sharp-looking cobble.

"Here, I'll help." The other guard took Gwynnie's arm and steered her to her feet as the third finished collecting all the sheets.

"You are all so kind," Gwynnie murmured as the first guard managed to stand, flexing his injured knee. "I'm sorry to cause so much trouble."

"Where are you taking all this laundry at this time of night?" the guard who had watched the courtyard so keenly before asked.

"You will not tell, will you, sir?" she asked sheepishly. "It's Christmas, see, and the maids have been a little … distracted. I'm hoping to get this washed tonight, so none will know tomorrow that some took some time off today."

The two other guards laughed as the third's top lip stiffened.

"Ah, ignore Perkis," one of the guards said with a chuckle. "He works hard every day of the year. On your way now. Rest assured, we will not tell a soul."

Gwynnie thanked them profusely, curtsied and hastened off, making a show of walking much more carefully this time. She darted down a lane, heading out through the back alleys of the palace, until she saw a shadow moving ahead of her. It was not difficult to recognise Emlyn's tall figure, nor her limp. As Gwynnie caught up to her, she discarded the linen in a doorway.

"This way," Gwynnie urged. Together, they crept toward the orchard, flitting between the trees and toward the back of the chapel. As Gwynnie had suspected, this part of the estate was empty at this time of night. She led Emlyn through the cemetery, down a bank of earth and toward the curtain wall of the palace.

"How do you know this part of the wall is safe for an escape?" Emlyn asked.

"I just know," Gwynnie whispered, her eyes tracing the top of the wall and the tree beside it. Devlin had hidden above that wall, swinging up and down with ease from his hiding place in the tree. For a time, no one but she and Brynne had known he was there. "This way." Gwynnie moved toward the tree and started to climb.

"Miting…" Emlyn's tone was hesitant. "I told you, I'm not what I once was." She gestured to her bad arm and leg.

"Here, give me the rope." Gwynnie took the rope from Emlyn and wrapped it around her own shoulder, then began to climb. It was no easy feat; the tree was tall and this time, there was no Devlin to help her cross the gap from the branch to the top of the wall. She had to jump, listening as Emlyn gasped far below. Landing catlike on her feet, Gwynnie moved to stand straight, glancing toward Devlin's former hiding place.

She tried not to think about how they had sat there together, just a few nights before. Turning her back on the spot, her stomach tight, she tossed the rope over the nearest branch and fed it down to Emlyn, keeping a tight hold of the other end.

"Climb, and I shall help pull you up," Gwynnie called.

Emlyn hesitated, then nodded. She looped the rope around her waist, knotting it tight. Slowly, she started to climb, but it became clear that her bad arm would not allow her to cling onto anything for very long. As she gained height, Gwynnie threaded the rope through her hands, using her weight to keep Emlyn anchored to the tree. More than once, she feared she would drop her mother, but Emlyn managed to scramble to find footholds, aided by the little strength Gwynnie could offer.

When she reached the thick branch Gwynnie had walked along, she shuffled along on her rear instead, edging toward the top of the wall.

"Jump," said Gwynnie. "Jump and I shall catch you."

Emlyn smiled. "You're such a small one to catch me."

"I am not as weak as you think, Ma." Gwynnie held out her arms.

Emlyn took a deep breath and jumped. Her good foot landed on the side of the wall, just as Gwynnie caught her arm. Emlyn's foot slipped, almost pulling her off balance, but Gwynnie hung on, tugging Emlyn to safety.

The two of them fell on their knees on the boarded walkway, panting as they caught their breath.

"Hurry!" Gwynnie pleaded. "We don't have much time. Tombstone will be wondering where I am if I don't make it to his office soon." With the rope still tied around Emlyn's waist, Gwynnie looped the other end around one of the standing crenellations, so that she had a lever. "Go, Ma."

Emlyn hesitated, peering down at the ground below.

"Go!" Gwynnie urged. "I shall find you, I promise."

"The White Hart, in Shoreditch. That's where I'll be." Emlyn swung her good leg out over the wall. Gripping the rope with both hands, she started to move downward.

Gritting her teeth and straining to lower the rope a little at a time, Gwynnie thought only of her task. When she felt the weight lessen on the other end of the rope, she let go, her arms burning with the effort. She peered over the top of the wall, catching sight of Emlyn in the shadows at the bottom. Emlyn untied the rope from her waist and nodded, allowing Gwynnie to pull the rope back up again.

The wind picked up and made the branches of the tree behind her dance as she strained to keep Emlyn in sight. Gwynnie was just tying the rope back around her shoulder when her mother's shadow disappeared into the darkness. It was as if she had never been there at all.

CHAPTER 14

Gwynnie sat in Tombstone's office ten minutes later, leaning back in the Savonarola chair behind his desk. She nursed a glass of port she had taken from his buffet cabinet. She had lit a candle to keep her company, and the yellow flame danced back and forth on top of a thin stick of wax as she waited for Tombstone to appear. Her eyes were fixed on the flame as she thought of Emlyn and their hurried goodbye.

The door opened loudly, and Gwynnie's eyes snapped up toward the incomer.

Tombstone stood in the open doorway, breathless. He didn't even mention the fact that she had picked the lock to his chamber, yet again, nor that she had stolen his port.

He beckoned to her. "Come, quickly."

"What is it?"

"King Henry and Fitzroy. They've left the great hall and gone to the church. If we can hear what they are saying…" He broke off, panting.

Gwynnie was on her feet in an instant, the candle blown out. Tombstone led the way, Gwynnie rushing to keep up as they hurried toward the tiltyard and back into the courtyards. A guard stepped into their path, brows raised.

"Out of the way! Cromwell's business!" Tombstone barked. The guard stepped back in alarm and didn't question them.

Tombstone didn't slow down until they had reached the inner courtyard. He halted, a finger to his lips. Carefully, the two of them tiptoed through the garden toward Friars' Church. Gwynnie's chest tightened. She had seen much of the church recently. It was where Devlin had hidden for a while, and where he had confronted Queen Jane for the murder she had committed. She blinked hard, pushing away all thoughts of Devlin as she and Tombstone moved toward the church door.

"What did Cromwell say?" Gwynnie asked as Tombstone stopped to catch his breath.

"He didn't deny that Hereford was indeed Fitzroy. He told me without hesitation that I was to forget all that I remembered about Fitzroy." Tombstone shook his head. "To forget that Fitzroy is a murderer."

"Have you forgotten Queen Anne's fate, orchestrated by Cromwell as much as the king?" Gwynnie demanded.

"Shh!" Tombstone gestured to the church door. It was ajar. He pressed a finger to his lips and then moved to look through the gap. Gwynnie knelt down and peered through beneath him.

The church was a shadowy place tonight, the great ornate stone pillars oppressive and enclosing. Two candles had been placed on the altar, making the shadows on the stone faces of the gargoyles dance eerily.

King Henry stood before the altar with some difficulty. He had been kneeling, apparently in prayer. He put his weight on one leg as he turned to look at Fitzroy, who stood in the aisle of the church.

"Bow your head before God, my son."

Fitzroy did as he was told.

"Come." Henry held out his hand. "We shall pray together."

Fitzroy moved forward and knelt by the altar. Both men bowed their heads, silence descending upon the church.

"Are you going to let this happen?" Gwynnie hissed at Tombstone.

"What?"

"That man —" Gwynnie thrust a finger at the door — "killed someone you once claimed to love."

"I am well aware of that, thank you," he said sourly. "That relationship was over long ago."

"Do not pretend it doesn't hurt. I was there when we found Master Woodville, where Fitzroy had put him —"

"Gwynnie!" Tombstone held up his hand sharply. "I learned my lesson, believe me."

"What? You learned not to love?" Gwynnie asked, remembering what Tombstone had said to her when they had sat together on the docks a few days before, after Devlin had left. *We can't all have a life of love, Gwynnie.* "Can you so easily ignore the chance to love again, Tombstone? You seem to entertain enough men —"

"Pleasure without love. It's a way to live."

"Not a good one!" Gwynnie retorted.

"Forgive me if I do not take the advice of a woman who has probably never known that sort of pleasure."

Gwynnie stepped back, strangely hurt by the insult. It was true, she had never known the sort of experiences that they were talking of, but she had no longing to know them if she had no love for the man whom she could share them with.

Voices inside the church brought their argument to a halt.

"Does she know?" Fitzroy's voice practically echoed off the vaulted roof and stained glass windows.

"Who? The queen?" King Henry chuckled and took a seat in the front pew of the church. "No. Jane is a sweet soul. She sees what she is supposed to. She sees what I tell her. She scarcely saw you before you left. I have told her you are Viscount Hereford, and she believes me."

"A trusting soul," Fitzroy mused as he began to pace up and down in front of the altar, his heeled boots clicking loudly on the flagstone floor. "Are there any others of concern? Any you think may have recognised me?"

"None that need concern us," the king said with ease, sighing as he sat back in the pew. "I saw plenty of young ladies staring at you, my boy, but I think their gazes lingered for other reasons." He chuckled once more as Fitzroy turned away.

Gwynnie chewed her lip, knowing that Fitzroy would hardly be pleased by his father's suggestive comment. Like Tombstone, Fitzroy's interests did not lie with women.

"And Cromwell?" Fitzroy halted. "Can he be trusted?"

"Do you doubt it?" Henry's voice stiffened.

"You tell me, Father. You are the man who knows him best."

"He has facilitated your return, has he not? He is … useful. Do not disregard the man. He is no insect to crush beneath your boot."

"You think the man can bite, Father?"

"I know he can. I know the power he can wield," the king said, his voice low. "Keep the powerful men on your side, that's what my father told my brother and I. He was right."

Gwynnie glanced at Tombstone. "What does that mean?" she whispered.

"It means that we were right. Cromwell's position here is not set in stone."

"What of anyone else?" Fitzroy cast his hand over the fine ornaments on the altar. He lingered for a moment on a gold altar plate, even picking up one of the intricately carved silver candlesticks before returning it to its place.

"Who did you have in mind?" King Henry asked slowly.

"The lawyer, the one I saw tonight. Tombstone, that's his name, yes?"

"Do you mean that tall one? Copper hair? Works for Cromwell?"

"That's the one," Fitzroy said thoughtfully. "He was here in January. He knows … *all*." He avoided his father's gaze as he continued to pace. They both fell silent, neither one wishing to speak of particulars. "Do you think he would speak of it to anyone?"

"No." The king's answer came without hesitation. "Cromwell does as I say, and he will do as Cromwell says." He laughed softly. "Rather a neat chain, isn't it?"

"And the maid?" Fitzroy turned to face his father and the candlelight fell upon his scarred face. The skin looked puckered, almost as if it had been burned. "What of her?"

"The maid?" King Henry asked. "I cannot remember a maid."

"There was a maid. She saw something she was not supposed to see. She could tell another what happened."

"She's just a maid. Who would listen to a maid's word?" Yet the king did not sound as convinced now. "We need to keep whispers quiet, my boy. A lawyer going missing would certainly raise questions. Especially a lawyer in the employ of Lord Cromwell. A maid, on the other hand — well, maids come and go from the palace every day. Servants are like lice, aren't they? You get rid of one and another appears."

"Dispensable?" Fitzroy whispered, a wicked smile lifting the corners of his mouth.

"Just so."

CHAPTER 15

Gwynnie blew out the candle. The sun had risen above the windowsill in Tombstone's office and the morning light stretched across the room.

Gwynnie sat against the chimneypiece, a blanket tucked around her legs, the fire still burning softly. Tombstone sat in one of the chairs by the fire, his chin resting on his chest, his jerkin open and his copper hair ruffled where he had pulled at it throughout the night.

They had not listened to any more of Fitzroy and King Henry's conversation in the church. Instead, they had returned to Tombstone's office and had talked into the early hours of the morning.

"Maybe he didn't mean…" Gwynnie trailed off at a harsh look from Tombstone. "At least you're safe — I'm not!"

Tombstone sighed and slumped further into his chair, rubbing his tired eyes.

Gwynnie pulled the blanket tighter around her knees, trying to fight the chill that seeped in through the windows and doors. The air was icy, the grass beyond the window frosted white.

"I can't tell anyone, Gwynnie," Tombstone said after some moments of silence. "Cromwell and the king are the two most powerful men in the land, and they are protecting Fitzroy. If I were to tell anyone, a lawyer, a judge, even a constable, what had happened, what that man is capable of, what do you think would happen?"

"I think you'd find yourself locked in the Tower of London by the end of the day," Gwynnie replied miserably. "You never know, perhaps it's much more charming than we think. Perhaps Queen Anne enjoyed her last few days there before…" Yet she couldn't finish the jest and shrugged her shoulders.

"No one would believe me."

"I know." One thing brought Gwynnie comfort. It was the knowledge that Emlyn was no longer in the palace and could not be glimpsed by Fitzroy. She could survive the conspiracy to cover up what he had done. Knowing that Emlyn had escaped without even Tombstone seeing her made Gwynnie sigh with relief.

"I have a question for you." Tombstone sat up a little. "The pamphlets I let you read, the papers — why did you take one?"

"I'm sorry?" His words made her look sharply up at him.

"There was a paper missing. Did you think I would not realise it?"

Gwynnie thought of the paper Emlyn had taken. *The king's stolen jewels…*

"I didn't take a paper," Gwynnie said honestly. "You already let me read them. Why would I take it?" Tombstone stared at her. "I didn't take it," she repeated. "I left this chamber in a mess. Is it possible the paper was lost somewhere?"

"Perhaps." Tombstone sounded unconvinced and was watching her closely.

Gwynnie held his gaze, fearing that if she looked away too quickly, he would think she was lying. "I didn't take anything," she said evenly.

"Do you mind me asking what you made of what was in those papers?"

Now she looked away. Fixing her gaze on her lap, she fiddled with the blanket around her legs. "I didn't realise someone else had the name, before Ma and me."

"Any idea who they were, Gwynnie?"

"I have a suspicion as to who they could be," Gwynnie replied, praying he wouldn't see through this particular lie.

"There is something I've never understood." Tombstone paused, as if he were debating his words. "Why did your mother train you to become a thief in the first place?"

"Pff!" she scoffed. "That is a question from a man who has never lived on the streets." She knelt up. "Do you have any idea what it is like to have no money to buy food? No money for a roof over your head, unless you *take* that money?"

"Maybe I have a better idea than you think." Tombstone's voice was low.

Gwynnie frowned. "What?"

"My mother was no wealthy woman."

"She was a healer. You've always said as much."

"Yes, she was. And do you think healers are paid what a physician is paid? Do you think a *woman* is paid what a man is paid?" He shook his head. "I know what it is for a mother to struggle to feed her child, Gwynnie. I know well enough."

"Your mother had a vocation. She had a way to earn money. That is at least something. My ma…" She trailed off. Emlyn had been no seamstress, no great cook, nor even a particularly efficient maid when she had worked in the palace. "She was not trained for anything but thieving. We stole to eat, Tombstone."

"No, you didn't." Tombstone leaned forward. "Stealing to eat is one thing. Stealing jewels, taking on a name like the Shadow Cutpurses, creeping like cats across rooftops, in and out of people's houses, is an entirely different thing. Do you not see that? Do you not see what your mother raised you to be?"

"I see it. She trained me to be a cutpurse. That is what I am." Gwynnie held his gaze, unashamed.

Tombstone's lips parted then closed. He was clearly tempted to say more, but thought better of it. "I do not just see a thief when I look at you," he said after a moment.

"No. You see a shadow. Nothing of note." Her bitter words made him frown deeply.

"I call you a shadow, yes, but I have never treated you as if you were nothing, have I?"

Gwynnie could not deny it. Rather like Devlin, Tombstone had been one of the few to notice her in this palace. From the first day they had met, Tombstone had looked her in the eye.

"No, you haven't."

Tombstone stood swiftly from his seat. He rifled through his buffet cabinet then returned with more herbs and a manchet loaf wrapped in muslin. He deposited the bread on a pewter plate and placed it between them on the hearth, then began to boil water over the fire.

Gwynnie watched him work. She didn't bother to ask this time what he was adding to the hot water. She trusted he had learned the uses of all these leaves from his mother, long ago. When the mixture was ready, he added a small amount of honey to each pewter cup and passed one to her. They tore the manchet loaf between the two of them.

"Most men would not deign to serve a maid either," Gwynnie mused with interest. He paused before lifting the hot water to his lips.

"I'm not like most men."

"Well, that is a surprise," Gwynnie said. Her sarcasm brought a small smile to his lips. "No, Tombstone, you have not treated me as if I were nothing," she repeated after a moment or so.

"I'm glad you see it that way." He rubbed his face distractedly as he ate his bread. "You may not see it, Gwynnie, but I hope I am not so blind to the condition of every man and woman around me. Not as blind as some in my position are."

"Like Pascal?"

"At times, like Pascal," Tombstone admitted.

"You do not like hearing a bad word said against him, do you?"

"He's my friend."

"A very dear friend. Or maybe something more." She held up her hands when he glowered at her warningly. "I vow not to pry further."

"Good." He swallowed some more of his bread.

"You are rather different to Pascal in temperament, in manner, and in outlook," Gwynnie mused after a moment. "Lessons from your ma, perhaps?"

"I believe so." He paused with his food, staring into the fire beside her. "My mother had a unique soul. At least, that's the way Pascal used to describe her. She was no fool. She did not think that every person she met was a saint, but she treated everyone who came her way nonetheless. She once said that even Lucifer must have a chance to regain his wings." He shook his head. "She would have probably treated the Devil himself, as long as he had vowed to behave while he was under her roof."

Gwynnie smiled at the words. This was the most Tombstone had ever revealed about his mother. "She sounds like a formidable woman."

"She was. She did what she believed in. Stood up for what was just." Tombstone toyed with the bread in his hands.

"A little like someone else I know," Gwynnie murmured, eyeing him carefully.

"I'm not quite as honourable as her." Tombstone laughed, shaking his head. "I've known the identity of a murderer for a year, and have said nothing."

"You can't." Gwynnie felt empty at the thought but knew it was true. "Fitzroy is the son of a king. Illegitimate or not, King Henry will do anything to protect him."

"It angers me!" Tombstone stood abruptly. He marched around his chair, tearing the bread into small pieces. "To know that man will walk around the palace, as free as a strutting peacock, after he killed two men. With his bare hands, he killed two men!"

Gwynnie had rarely seen Tombstone lose his temper. "I know," she whispered. "And who's to say he will not do it again?"

Her words made Tombstone freeze. He reached out and grabbed the back of his chair.

"What did you say?"

"He has got away with murder twice." She shrugged. "He's already talking of me being dispensable. One of these days, you'll wake up and find me dead in the middle of the tiltyard. Or, better yet, dumped in the Thames, so no one will know what happened to me. And who is going to notice a missing maid?"

"I would. Samuel and Brynne would."

"It's not just me he could be a danger to," Gwynnie went on, watching Tombstone carefully. "If another lover threatened to reveal the secret of where his tastes truly lie…" She trailed off.

"Then I shall watch him," Tombstone said with resolve, gripping the chair tight. "I may not be able to see the man punished for what he has done, but I shall damn well make sure he never hurts another soul." His eyes flashed with anger as he looked at Gwynnie.

"What does that look mean?"

"Gwynnie…" He leaned forward over the chair. "You need to leave the palace."

"What?" she spluttered. "Leave the palace? Why?"

Tombstone raced around the chair, sitting down and leaning forward. "Gwynnie, Fitzroy as good as had his father's blessing last night to see you dead. In a house of God, no less. Are you just going to wait around for him to kill you?"

"No!"

"Well then," Tombstone said firmly. "It's time you left."

"You're ousting me?" Gwynnie stood up, her hands trembling. "After all I've done for you, you're throwing me out?"

"No." Tombstone stood too, towering over her. "I'm not throwing you out — I'm asking you to go. To save your life, Gwynnie."

"But I —"

"I will not wake up to see you dead in the tiltyard or bobbing along the River Thames."

Gwynnie turned on the spot, her hands over her face.

"I will not see him kill another." Tombstone caught her shoulders, forcing her to look at him. "I will not see him kill *you*. Leave the palace."

"This is my livelihood now. I have a roof over my head, food to eat." It took a moment to realise that what she felt was fear. Fear of going back to the life she had had before in the slums of London with Emlyn, stealing what she could each day to live.

"You must have some money you can take with you? I've paid you plenty."

"I have some, not enough to live on —"

"Gwynnie, listen to me." Tombstone bent down, so he could meet her eyes. "If you do not leave, how can we be certain that Fitzroy won't find you? That one of those two men who guard him won't find you?"

"If I go back to London —" she thrust a finger toward the latticed window — "I would become who I was again. I'd steal as easily as I breathe. My money wouldn't last, Tombstone. That's not the way the world works. You know it."

Tombstone marched across to his desk. He opened drawers, rifling through them and pulling out a purse she had never seen before.

"Where have you been hiding that?" she asked.

"Under one of the drawers. Necessary, when a thief is in and out of your rooms every day." He crossed the room and thrust the leather purse into her hands. "Take it."

"What?"

"This should be plenty to pay for food and lodgings for the next few weeks."

"Tombstone —"

"I'm not saying go forever," Tombstone said, his voice softening as his hands closed around her own. "I'm saying, run for now. It may be that Fitzroy is only here for Christmas, but we can't be certain. We need to *know*. And until we do, you can't stay here." He released her hands. "The possibilities are too unbearable to think of."

The room fell silent, the only noise the crackling of the fire in the grate. Gwynnie's stomach twisted. She could not believe she was being asked to leave the palace.

"If he were any other man," Gwynnie managed, her voice trembling, "he would have swung from a noose by now."

"But he is the man he is. You may be a shadow, able to hide, but you cannot hide forever, not if he is already looking for you." Tombstone's voice brooked no refusal. "The best place you can hide is far away from here."

She knew he was right. She gripped the purse tight, her palms sweaty despite the chilly air.

"The sun has not long risen and after the feast last night, not many will have risen from their beds yet. You should go today."

"What? You wish me to leave so soon?"

"Before Fitzroy can discover you're here. Gwynnie, you must leave within the next hour."

CHAPTER 16

Gwynnie stuffed the last of her clothes into her tapestry bag. Turning in a quick circle, she checked every inch of her chamber for something she may have missed, but there was nothing, just the bed, the small looking glass that hung from the wall and the basin.

Heaving the bag onto her shoulder, she made her way toward the door. It could just be a few days before she was back again, that was what Tombstone had said, yet it felt more like a lasting goodbye. If King Henry chose to keep his son at the palace, then this could be the last time she stood here.

"Goodbye, home," she whispered, almost laughing at her own foolishness. It was a small space, hardly bigger than a broom cupboard, but for the best part of a year she had felt safe within these four walls. Slowly, she stepped out of the room and closed the door behind her, letting it creak shut.

She hastened from the maids' lodgings, not wanting to be seen by others. It would not do to be questioned about where she was going and why she appeared to be leaving the palace at such an early hour.

In the courtyard, she looked across at the large palace gates that led out to the world beyond. The gates were open wide at this hour as carts rolled in, bringing the latest deliveries of grain, mead and claret. Gwynnie could slip out between those carts unseen, but she couldn't bring herself to leave yet, not without saying goodbye to two people in particular.

Turning her back on the gate, she made her way to the kitchens. She found Samuel hard at work kneading dough. Brynne was behind him, sitting on a large stone window sill and moulding some icing sugar into a fine creation, no doubt for the next Yuletide feast.

"Samuel —" Gwynnie stepped in front of his table. He was so shocked he jumped back, clapping his hands together and sending flour everywhere. Gwynnie blinked hard, wiping her eyes as the flour covered her face. "Well, it's a grand way to wake up in the morning."

"You know how to give a man a fright, lass." Samuel rubbed his chest and passed her a cloth to clean herself as Brynne slipped down off the windowsill and ran forward. Her eyes darted between Gwynnie's face and the bag on her shoulder.

"You're leaving?" she gasped, her Irish accent strong. "Why? How long for?"

"I don't know." Gwynnie glanced over her shoulder. The few cooks that had already risen at this hour were busy preparing the food for that day's feast, and no one looked their way. "I have to leave."

"When?" Samuel asked, his voice sharp.

"Now," Gwynnie murmured. "It cannot be avoided."

Brynne gripped her arm tight. "No, no. This is your life, Gwynnie. You can't turn your back on the palace —"

"Brynne —" Samuel cut in, but Brynne spoke over him.

"This is your life!" Brynne repeated. "Can you really walk away from it so easily?"

"Nothing about this is easy," Gwynnie mumbled.

"Brynne." Samuel tossed down the dough on the table, his eyes on Gwynnie. "I hardly think this decision is Gwynnie's. Am I right? It's that man. The one you work for. Tombstone, the lawyer."

"You are right," Gwynnie said with a sigh. "Though he makes the decision for my own safety."

Samuel sighed heavily. "I wish I could believe that."

"Samuel!" Brynne hissed.

"You have not seen everything I have seen within these palace walls," Samuel told his wife. "From the day Gwynnie arrived here, she has been beholden to someone. First it was that wayward mother of hers, now this lawyer. I fear who she will dance for next, whose call she will answer."

Gwynnie flinched at his words. Was that what she was? Just a puppet on a string? Regardless of what Samuel thought, she knew she had no choice. When she left the palace, there was only one place she could go. She would have to find Emlyn.

"You will come back?" Brynne asked Gwynnie, ignoring Samuel's last words.

"I hope so." Gwynnie squeezed her hand softly. "I have to go today, though — I have no choice." She glanced warily at the window where Brynne had been sitting a moment ago, fearing a face may already be peering in through the glass, hunting for her.

"Then you shall not go without food." Brynne was firm. She looked at Samuel, who nodded and took a canvas bag from a hook on the wall. He walked around the kitchen, filling it with provisions.

"Brynne, tell me one thing before I go," Gwynnie murmured. "Have you … heard anything? From…" She could not say his name.

Brynne smiled sadly. "Once. It was a verbal message. It came from a small lad who knocked at the gate and demanded that a guard fetch me. The boy refused to leave until I came." She sighed. "Connal left a message with a man who watched the ship, asking for it to be known that the ship left on time for Ireland. He'll be miles away now, on the open sea." She looked distantly through the window. "I may never see my son again, but I thank the lord above that he is alive." Her eyes filled with tears, and Gwynnie squeezed her hand tight. "I have you to thank for keeping him alive, Gwynnie. Thank you."

"There is no need to thank me." If Gwynnie had had her way, they would have proved Devlin's innocence. He could have walked out of the palace a free man, but such a task had proved impossible in the end.

Samuel returned and passed the canvas bag to Gwynnie. "Take it," he urged. "There's enough bread, pastries and fruit in there to last you a few days."

"Thank you." Gwynnie smiled and lifted the bag over her other shoulder. Samuel stared at her with an uncertain expression. "When you talked of my mother," Gwynnie began slowly, "it sounded as if you didn't like her."

Samuel shook his head. "I'm no fool, lass. I saw you running around after her when she was at the palace, trying to protect her from herself. In my experience, people like that don't want saving. Remember that."

"That doesn't help, Samuel." Brynne tapped his shoulder in quiet reprimand. She opened her arms wide and pulled Gwynnie into a tight embrace. Gwynnie rested her head on Brynne's shoulder, taking comfort from the hug, wondering when she would feel it again. "Come back soon," Brynne pleaded.

"I shall try," Gwynnie said as Brynne released her.

Gwynnie turned to Samuel. His hands, still covered in flour, hung at his sides.

"Goodbye," Gwynnie murmured to him.

"Take care of yourself, lass," he said with a heavy sigh. He clapped her on the shoulder, spreading more flour across her gown. Brynne tutted and brushed the flour off.

Gwynnie smiled and made her way to the door of the kitchen. She hesitated on the threshold, glancing back to see

Brynne waving eagerly, her smile full of a sadness she was trying to restrain. Samuel didn't wave. He just stared at her, his features etched with worry. Gwynnie waved at them once, then slipped out through the door.

"You have everything you need?" Tombstone asked, marching ahead of Gwynnie across the inner courtyard.

"Yes." She hitched the two bags higher on her shoulders, racing to keep up with his long strides.

More people had risen now. Ladies dressed in fine gowns were hurrying through the courtyards, men following behind with gifts wrapped in tissue paper and sprigs of mistletoe in their grasp. Gwynnie and Tombstone walked around them, taking as little notice of these merry groups as the latter took of them.

"Where will you go?" Tombstone asked.

"I don't know," Gwynnie lied. When Tombstone whipped his head around to look at her, she sighed. "The White Hart Inn. Shoreditch," she answered shortly. "If you need me, you'll find me there."

"Good." Tombstone nodded. "Will you take a wherry?"

"A wherry? Have you not seen the river this morning? It's frozen over."

Tombstone hesitated and moved back to the gate in Donsen Tower, peering toward the riverbank and the silvery water beyond. It looked like glass, the surface gleaming in the grey morning light.

"I'll go on foot," Gwynnie told him as they walked on through the courtyards.

"All that way?"

"Ha! The idea that a woman with such short legs could walk so far — baffling, is it not?"

"Oh, I know you're capable of more than people think, Shadow." They passed through the middle courtyard, where their pace slowed.

Lady Mary walked past them, her head held high and a train of ladies following in her wake. She glanced at them briefly, then moved on. She had worn black at the last two Yuletide feasts, but today she had dressed grandly, in purple.

"The king is clearly showing her great favour," Tombstone whispered with interest. "Purple is the royal colour, is it not? He is acknowledging her as family once again to allow her to wear such a gown."

Gwynnie's eyes swept over the richly decorated gown. There was gold embroidery at the high throat and the rather modern French hood she wore was decorated with gold and purple thread, with amethysts shining like periwinkles. Mary's dark eyes surveyed the yard as she led the way toward the great hall.

"Things feel like they're changing here," Gwynnie observed.

"That's because the king's mood can change quickly," Tombstone mused. "If you ask me, Lady Mary will not always be welcome at the palace." He paused. When Gwynnie continued to stare at him, he sighed. "How long does the king keep any woman at his side?"

Gwynnie huffed but said nothing as they walked on through the yard, heading toward the staff buildings and the large gate where fresh deliveries were still arriving by cart.

"The White Hart, Shoreditch," Tombstone muttered to himself, committing the place to memory. "If Fitzroy leaves, I shall get word to you that you can return."

Gwynnie adjusted the straps of the bags on her shoulders and turned to face the gate.

"Gwynnie, you have my word."

"I know," she said. It wasn't that she didn't trust Tombstone to tell her. She didn't trust the king to oust his son from the palace again. This could be the last time she walked through this gate. "It's strange. It's only now that I am leaving that I realise how much the palace has come to feel like home this past year."

"It is often the way. We do not realise what we have until it is gone."

"True." Gwynnie eyed him carefully. A wind had picked up. It ruffled his copper hair and threatened to blow off his bonnet. "How is Pascal?" He looked at her in surprise. "I only wish to know if he's continuing to recover."

"He is." Tombstone nodded slowly. "A message was left at the palace for me this morning. He is walking well and is enjoying the Yuletide celebrations with his family." His lips formed a tight line.

"No invitation to join them in their celebrations?"

"No." Tombstone faced the gate, indicating that this particular line of questioning had come to an end. "Time for you to take your leave, Gwynnie, before Fitzroy sees you."

"Very well. Then I suppose this is goodbye." Gwynnie shifted her weight between her feet. Tombstone stood like a statue, staring forward. "Tombstone? Will your cold heart not allow you to say goodbye?"

"I was otherwise engaged," he said, his voice tight. Gwynnie followed his gaze toward the gate.

Two men were standing on either side of the gate. One was Amaro, his hand on the weapons belt where his scabbard sat. The other was the second man who followed so readily at Fitzroy's heel, his name still unknown to Gwynnie. Today, he was clothed in a pink doublet, the ornate collar at his neck hanging down in great ruffles that were reminiscent of clouds.

Despite the softness of his clothes, he called out harshly to every cart that passed by.

"What business have you here, sirrah?"

"Mead, sir," grunted one driver. "For the king."

Tombstone took Gwynnie's arm and turned her around. "We'll need to find another way out of the palace."

As Gwynnie glanced back over her shoulder, Amaro's eyes slid over them. Then his head jerked back around, his gaze fixing solely on her.

"Tombstone! Amaro has seen me."

CHAPTER 17

"Go!" Tombstone hissed. "Run, Shadow!"

Gwynnie didn't hesitate. Amaro was already moving away from his place at the gate, his hand tightening around his weapons belt.

Gwynnie hitched the bags higher over her shoulder and ran through the courtyard. When she reached the inner courtyard, it was now so full of the ladies and gentlemen of the court, who had gathered to wish each other another merry day, that she had to dart between the groups, trying not to bash into anyone or knock them over. One or two glanced her way, before returning to their happy chatter.

"Did you see the king last night?"

"With his daughter? Oh, I did. How lovely it is to see the Lady Mary returned to her rightful place."

"The credit must go to the queen, to be sure."

Gwynnie raced on toward the far edge of the courtyard, only glancing back when she reached the archway under Donsen Tower. Amaro stood under another arch, peering over the heads of the crowd.

"Gwynnie, why are you here? Shouldn't you be in the laundry room today?"

Gwynnie turned to see Ricard beside the entrance to Donsen Tower. The friendly guard stared at her flushed face and the bags on her shoulders.

"I should be," she muttered hurriedly. She glanced back to see that Amaro was now pushing his way through the crowd toward her.

"Goodbye, Ricard." She clapped him on the shoulder as she ran past him, toward the riverbank.

"Goodbye? What? Who is that? Is someone chasing you? Hey!"

Gwynnie didn't turn to see what had happened, though she heard a scuffle behind her. Hoping Ricard had intercepted Amaro for long enough to give her a head start, Gwynnie raced across the riverbank toward the docks.

She could run across the ice. If it was frozen enough, she might just make it all the way. But even in the dull grey light, she could see watery patches. The memory of her recent plunge into the icy water, the feeling of the cold leeching into her skin, made her shudder and step back.

"I don't fancy dying today," she said to herself, choosing instead to sprint along the riverbank in the direction of the boathouse. She chose another archway, leading back into the body of the palace, pausing just long enough to see that Amaro hadn't yet made it onto the riverbank. Perhaps he was still tussling with Ricard.

Seeing an opportunity, she cut back toward the staff quarters. Walking now, so as not to draw attention to herself, she made her way toward the laundry rooms with a plan forming in her mind in case Ricard was not able to stall her pursuer for long.

Stepping inside, she found the laundry alive with activity. Steam was rising in great swirls from hot water that bubbled in cauldrons on fires. Sheets and linen had been draped across lengths of rope, hanging from wall to wall, creating a white maze of cloth. The maids whom Gwynnie had so often worked alongside all had their heads down, working hard, sweat beading on their brows and running down their noses.

"Did you see? He was not in *her* chamber."

"Well, judging by the red spots on *these* sheets," one maid said, holding up some linen, "I think I know where he was last night!"

As the maids all laughed, Gwynnie slipped between them, ignoring their gossip. They were too busy with their tasks to take much notice of her, though one or two raised a hand in greeting. At the back of the laundry room, she waited, huddled between a great fireplace and barrels of lye, her eyes pinned on the door.

If Amaro had heard what Ricard had said about the laundry room, then this was where he would come next. It was the obvious place to come searching for her, and that was what she wanted now, to be found. If she could lay a trap for him, she might just be able to incapacitate him enough to stop him from chasing her altogether.

She waited with bated breath, her palms sweaty. Tucked away at the back of the long building, none of the other maids glanced her way.

The door eventually opened. Gwynnie held her breath, watching through the maze of hanging sheets and the billowing steam as the unmistakable figure of Amaro entered.

"You can't be in 'ere," one of the young maids barked at him. A linen sheet was flapped in his direction.

He leapt back. "I'm looking for someone." His voice was gruff.

"Who?" another maid asked.

"Young maid."

"Can't move round 'ere for one of those," the first maid said, prompting all the others to laugh. "Look round, then leave. We've got work to do, and you're getting in our way."

Amaro stepped forward between the sheets.

Gwynnie slowly lowered the bags from her shoulders, the sound muffled by the loud splashes. She placed the bags on the floor and stepped behind a long sheet that hung from the ceiling.

She could hear Amaro moving amongst the maids, though they paid him little heed, hurrying to get their jobs done and gossiping all the more about what they had seen in the palace.

"Aske? Oh, 'e left at first light. Not as welcome as per'aps 'e thought."

"I thought he was staying for the whole of Christmas, as part of the king's wish to show the north he wanted peace."

"Well, 'e's done all 'e needs to, 'asn't 'e? You mark my words. That peace won't last long. Peace in this palace is all for show, isn't it?"

Footsteps grew nearer. Beneath the sheet, Gwynnie glimpsed a pair of boots. They were particularly well made, studded and embroidered with fine black thread. The boots halted, the toes turning to face Gwynnie.

"What about the queen?" another maid asked. "How long will this one last, do you think?"

"Shush. You shouldn't ask such questions."

"If you ask me, the king will be rid of her next. He didn't keep Queen Anne long, did he?"

Gwynnie's heart raced as she stared at the boots. The sheet began to bulge in the middle as a hand reached toward her.

Gwynnie acted fast. With her hands braced on either side of the sheet, she pulled it down and thrust it forward in one swift movement. The sheet tangled around Amaro's head and arms. Gwynnie squeezed tightly, wrapping Amaro up so he couldn't pull out the dagger in his scabbard.

"Mmff!" Whatever he had tried to shout was muffled by the linen.

Gwynnie threw her full weight against him and they fell in a tangle. Amaro's head knocked against the hard brick wall and his cries halted.

He no longer fought against her. His flailing arms had stilled, his body limp on the ground. Gwynnie sat up, tore the sheet from his face and stared down. His eyes were closed, his lips parted, and though there was no obvious wound, the strike to his head had clearly been enough to knock him out.

"Dear God, Gwynnie," one of the maids gasped nearby.

A sheet hanging from the ceiling had been swept aside to reveal three maids peering at her, their jaws slack.

"What did he try to do to you?"

"What all men want when we say no," Gwynnie said, pretending to shudder.

"Then go quickly," another maid said. "We've got some rope for him."

Gwynnie jumped back as the maids got to work. Amaro's wrists were soon tied together, his ankles too, as Gwynnie collected her bags. As she thanked the maids, they waved her on her way and she slipped out of the laundry.

Keeping to the walls of the courtyard, she crept around the edge, heading toward the main gate which she and Tombstone had approached before. Tombstone was nowhere to be seen, and she didn't have time to look for him now.

The gate was busy with people, carts lining up to enter or leave the palace grounds. Every one of them was stopped by Fitzroy's well-dressed man, in his fine pink doublet.

"I need to know your business here," the man demanded, facing the cart drivers.

"By who's order?"

"The Viscount Hereford's."

"Who's he?"

"What does it matter, other than the fact he's a viscount?"

"His word don't count for much when it's the king's palace," one of the cart drivers said as others chuckled around him. "What's your name?"

"Miles Humphrey," the man declared, fussing with his elaborate collar. "Now, state your business and you can be on your way."

All at once the cart drivers started talking, shouting out their deliveries which ranged from mead and claret to fresh chickens. One driver pulled back a canopy to reveal crates full of geese. They honked noisily, their beaks pressing against the wood.

Humphrey wrinkled his nose in distaste. "One at a time!" he barked, peering between the carts, clearly looking for his partner, Amaro.

Gwynnie waited until he turned his back on the carts, calling to one of the guards who sat lazily beside the gate, yawning, having left his pike against the stone wall.

"Aren't you supposed to be monitoring who goes in and out of the palace?" Humphrey snapped at him.

"There's no man here by the name of Connal Devlin. That's who I'm looking for, sir. Besides, they say he's headed north already. He won't be here."

Humphrey shook his head, and while his back was turned, Gwynnie took her chance. She tiptoed toward the cart carrying the geese. Raising the canopy, she slipped into the back, hunkering down between two large crates. She pulled the canopy back over herself, so that she was completely hidden.

The stench of birds made her nose wrinkle. A goose's face pressed closed to hers and honked loudly, yet Gwynnie forced herself to stay silent, ignoring the din and keeping as still as possible.

"On your way!" someone barked.

The cart moved forward, rocking from side to side on the cobbles. Gwynnie braced her hands against the crates, splinters digging into her skin as she felt the cart move beyond the palace gates.

Gwynnie prayed that the cart would take her into the city. Humphrey and the cart drivers' voices faded away, replaced shortly by the cries of market stall holders pushing their wares, the smell of fresh fish filling the air. She could smell spices too, cinnamon and cardamom.

Gwynnie stared at the geese beside her in the crates. Some had settled down now; others still honked at the wooden slats caging them. It was clear that the cart was destined to make a delivery; soon the driver would pull back the canopy to find her there. She needed a diversion.

Reaching toward one of the crates, Gwynnie turned it to face the back of the cart. Then she lifted the peg holding the latched door in place.

There was a flurry of feathers as the geese scrambled to escape.

"Hey — carter! You've lost your cargo!" a passerby shouted.

The cart came to a heavy halt as more shouts followed. Some must have been trying to help the driver to round up the geese, as the sound of honking and shouting grew to a frenzy.

Under the cover of the commotion, Gwynnie slipped off the back of the cart, pulling her bags over her shoulders as she looked around, blinking in the daylight.

She was in a busy London street, stalls lined up along one side of the road, tall buildings on the other. Raw lamb and beef hung from metal chains attached to the wall of a butchers shop. Next door was a confectionery shop selling marzipan and sweetmeats, and on the other side was a cobblers.

Gwynnie peeled a grey feather off her lips as she looked back at the stallholders, who were all laughing as the cart driver chased his geese. Beyond the stalls was the gleaming River Thames.

Hurrying away from the cart, Gwynnie hopped up onto a ledge behind the market stalls and peered out across the frozen river.

She was on London Bridge. To her right, she could see Greenwich Palace, the yellow stone building just a smudge on the horizon. From this distance, she could see no human being on that riverbank, no guard patrolling the battlements. To her left was London city. The timber and thatched buildings were squashed together, smoke billowing out of the tall chimneys that pierced the cloudy sky. The roads were full of people, some dancing and singing, celebrating Yuletide, others hurrying to their business. Horses rode back and forth, some dressed in fine livery, others wearing the poorest of reins. Huddled beggars ran between fine gentlemen, who clutched their leather purses protectively.

In spite of her apprehension, Gwynnie smiled as she looked around. "I'm back," she whispered. The wind suddenly whipped up from the frozen Thames, making her shiver as she stood on the wall of the bridge. It was either a greeting or a warning, she wasn't sure which.

Jumping down, she headed past the cart driver — who had just caught one of his geese — and the stallholders. They were all so busy watching the geese that neither the apple-seller nor the cloth-weaver noticed her pinching their wares. She bit into the apple as she tucked her hair beneath the new coif.

Gwynnie paused just long enough to examine the roads around her. The streets bled out in multiple avenues. She knew these roads well. She had grown up in the slums of London and made this place her hunting ground. She and Emlyn had walked these streets most days, for London Bridge had always been fruitful. The stallholders frequently didn't notice one or two items going missing, and the fine ladies and gentlemen were too concerned about the beggars to notice Gwynnie or Emlyn slipping past them to steal loose purses. Gwynnie's eyes tarried on a road that led to the right, along the riverbank.

Of all the taverns and inns where she and Emlyn had rested their heads for the night, she could not recall the White Hart. But Emlyn had said it was in Shoreditch.

Gwynnie glanced back across the river. She caught sight of Greenwich Palace before it was lost behind a horse and cart carrying strips of leather, then she walked on.

CHAPTER 18

Darkness had fallen by the time Gwynnie had found the White Hart Inn. Finsbury Fields stretched out to the left. To her right, thatched buildings were pressed tightly together, as if battling for space. Amongst these buildings was one much larger and squatter structure, with a sign bearing a painting of a white stag. Its eyes gleamed silver in the light that shone from the inn's windows.

It didn't seem to matter that it was past the city's curfew and at this time of night, watchmen should be patrolling the streets. The inn showed no sign of hurrying its customers home for the night. Gwynnie even spied two watchmen leaning on the wall of the inn, both too drunk to march the streets. Both wore uniforms of gold and blue, their customary staffs at their sides.

Gwynnie walked toward the inn, peering in through the bright window. Beyond the yellow glare of the candles, Gwynnie saw crowded tables and settle benches. Drunken customers either fought over seats or were out cold, their mouths hanging open. Courtesans walked between the tables as men made a grab for their skirts. There were a few men too whose shirts were open low. Judging by the way other men reached for their collars, they were also selling themselves for the night.

The air was full of laughter and the smell of ale and vomit. With a wrinkled nose, Gwynnie opened the door of the inn and stepped inside.

It was a cramped space with low timber beams. Rather like a rabbit warren, there were various adjoining rooms. Gwynnie peered past men's shoulders as they drunkenly swayed, trying to get a glimpse of Emlyn.

"You cheating me, boy?" a woman's voice snapped.

Gwynnie froze, her stomach clenching.

"N-no," someone stammered in response. "I … I was just trying to —"

"You don't cheat a lady!"

"Pah! You think you're a lady?" A third voice joined the argument.

Gwynnie followed the voices into a room at the back of the inn.

Around a table sat five people. Emlyn was wearing men's clothing, her hat slipping to the side, her dark hair loose about her shoulders. Next to her was a very young lad, his wrist clutched tightly in her hand. He had a coin in his palm. Three other men at the table were watching the exchange, their eyes wide. On the table were cards, though they lay forgotten.

"Let it go," Emlyn warned the lad.

At once, he dropped the coin. He sat back in his seat, his face pale despite the raging heat in the room.

"I won't be conned by a boy a quarter of my age," Emlyn spat at him. "You should have more respect for a lady."

"Still see no lady here," an old man said. He sat hunched over the table, his shoulders rounded, his cheeks gaunt.

"Oh, do you not?" Emlyn abruptly turned to face him, her back straight, her chin lifted just enough to reflect the bearing of a lady. Gwynnie was oddly reminded of Lady Mary's posture that morning as she'd walked through the courtyard. "But a lady takes many forms, does she not, sir?" Emlyn asked in a refined accent.

"Where'd you learn to talk like that?" the man asked, waving his cup of ale at her. He took a sip, realised his cup was empty, then waved it at a nearby barmaid to fill it up for him.

"Don't ask questions you don't want to know the answers to, old man." Emlyn's voice had returned to normal. "Here. We playing cards? I won't play with this boy no more. I don't play with cheats." As she said the words and one of the men dealt out fresh cards on the table, Gwynnie watched Emlyn closely. She switched one of the cards in her hand for one she had up her sleeve. The move was smoothly done. Only Gwynnie, who had watched her perform such a trick for years, would have seen it. All Emlyn ever had to do was convince a group to watch elsewhere, to give her the time to pull her own trick.

Gwynnie leaned back against the wall of the inn, observing her mother as she played the hand of cards. It was a game of noddy, a game played for high stakes. They all added their coins to the centre of the table, Emlyn watching with a hunger that Gwynnie had not seen for some time. When the round ended, Emlyn's coin pile was higher than all the rest.

"You cheated," a man said from across the table.

"You accuse a lady of cheating?" Emlyn declared, once more adopting that fine tone. She adjusted the hat on her head. "I do not think I shall drink at this inn anymore." She sniffed haughtily. "Too common for my tastes."

Gwynnie stood up straight, her stomach tightening as she sensed what was coming next.

"I'll bid you goodnight, gentlemen." Emlyn stood at the same time as the man who had accused her of cheating. "How kind, a man wishing to wave me on my way."

"What you about, lad?" the elderly man asked, but the other said nothing. He glowered at Emlyn, his eyes so wide they appeared to be bulging out of his head.

"Don't trust her," he grunted. "She sits down, demands to play, accuses the lad here of cheating and then she wins. Just like that. When did you last see a woman win at this game?"

"Insult me all you like, but do not insult my sex," Emlyn said, counting up her coins and adding them to a leather purse she attached to her doublet. "You do them all a disservice. Believe me."

"I want my money," the man spat under his breath.

"Then you should work harder to hold onto it," Emlyn replied with ease. "I wish you all goodnight. Again." She inclined her head and stepped away from the table. She'd barely taken two steps before the man's hand closed around her wrist and jerked her back.

The other patrons at the inn halted their conversations, watching keenly.

"Do not make an enemy of me," Emlyn murmured, looking down at him, for he was both younger and shorter than her.

"I said, I want my money." A knife flicked under her chin, the blade nearly scraping her skin.

"Lad!" the elderly man cried. "What use is blood over a few lost coins? Where's your pride?"

"In my pocket with his coins," Emlyn said with a smile.

Gwynnie's heart fluttered. She stepped away from the wall, gradually making her way toward the group, though none noticed her. All eyes were on Emlyn and the man.

"Hand over my money," the man warned, his teeth gritted, "or I cut your throat here."

"No. You don't have the stomach for it." Emlyn's voice was curt. "Or you would have done it already."

Gwynnie surged forward, watching as the blade came dangerously close to Emlyn's throat. There was a well-dressed man beside her, so busy watching the scene that he didn't notice Gwynnie slipping the leather purse from his belt as she walked past him.

Emlyn grabbed her assailant's wrist, bending it back, though it was not enough to make him drop the blade. When the man elbowed Emlyn in the stomach, there was a roar of outrage from those watching on.

"You'd hit a woman?"

"He hit her. You saw it."

"I hit a cheat!" he cried to those now closing in around him.

Gwynnie used the cover of those moving nearer to step up behind him. When she trod on his toe, he cried out in pain. As he mistakenly turned to face Emlyn, believing her to be the source of the pain, Gwynnie swiped the blade from his hand.

"Have your money," she said simply, and emptied the leather purse she had taken onto the floor. The coins rolled away across the boards.

The man was not the only one to sink to his knees, scrambling to pick up the loose coins. Gwynnie dropped the leather purse, grabbed Emlyn's arm and marched her through the building.

"Miting!" Emlyn gasped, still rubbing her stomach as the two of them left.

They stepped past the well-dressed man, whose eyes were widening in realisation.

"That's my purse. Hey, that's my money!" He leapt forward to join the fray.

Gwynnie glanced back to see a brawl ensue. Men tussled with one another for the coins as the true owner of the money crawled around on his hands and knees, trying to salvage what he could.

Gwynnie led Emlyn all the way through the inn and out through the front door. They stepped from warm light into cold darkness. Gwynnie forced a smile for the two watchmen outside, who merely tipped their caps to the two of them in parting.

"You're here, dearest."

"None of that now." Gwynnie dragged Emlyn down the road, only releasing her when they reached a stile beside a fence. To one side, Finsbury Fields opened out before them. On the other were the dark lanes of London, leading back to lodging houses and inns. She could see shadows lurking, people wandering back and forth even at this late hour. "Is this what you do now?" Gwynnie asked. "You go from inn to inn, starting brawls?"

"I didn't brawl." Emlyn sat down on the stile and reached into her pocket, holding up the coins. "I won, miting."

"That is a matter of opinion." Gwynnie took Emlyn's chin and lifted it a little higher. "He did scratch you."

Emlyn chuckled. "I have survived to tell the tale. Don't you worry about me." She counted up the coins and returned them to her pocket. "My lodgings are there for the night. We shall have to go back."

Gwynnie glanced in the direction of the inn with reluctance. It was just a speck of light in the distance now, innocuous, yet she knew what danger could lurk there. "Do you enjoy living in disarray?"

"What good's your bed if you haven't fought to get there?" Emlyn smiled, though there was sadness in her eyes. "We have to earn our beds."

Gwynnie sighed and leaned against the fence. She dropped her two bags and slumped down beside Emlyn.

"Why are you here?" Emlyn asked after a moment of silence. "Have you come to help me after all? Help me find the loot?" She took hold of Gwynnie's arm with excitement.

Gwynnie opened her mouth to refuse, but found the words wouldn't come.

What did she have before her? If Fitzroy didn't leave the palace, then she was stuck here in London. All she had were the two bags at her feet — one with food that would not last beyond a few days, the other with a few items of clothing. It wasn't much to show for a life. She rubbed her face tiredly.

"If I were to help, Ma —" she watched a spark of hope appear in her mother's eye — "then I need you to tell me again why we are doing this."

"I have already told you."

"And I want to hear it again," Gwynnie said, harsher now. "Why do you want the loot?"

"Because I want to know once and for all why your father had to die." Emlyn stood. "I want to know the secret. What it was that Titus coveted so much, he would blackmail someone and see his old friend dead in his grave." Her voice broke. "I have to know."

Gwynnie rubbed her face once more. She could remember the last time Emlyn had left the palace. Gwynnie had pleaded with her then to start a new life away from thieving, yet Emlyn hadn't done so.

"If we find the loot, then you have to promise me you'll start that new life we always spoke of. I need that vow, Ma. I need to know you'll keep your word."

Emlyn sank down onto her knees. She took Gwynnie's hand, gripping it tightly in her own. "I give you my word. I will turn my back on this life, and I will forge a new one, far away from London, and far away from thieving."

Gwynnie felt a lightness to her shoulders. It took her a moment to recognise what that feeling was — hope.

"We can go to France together, as you always talked of. Or anywhere else you wish to go. The world will be open to us." Emlyn smiled with excitement.

A wild idea entered Gwynnie's head. She thought of going to Ireland, of seeing the land that Devlin called home, of seeing him again. But the thought had no sooner alighted than she let it slip away, as if the cold breeze had sent it on its way. She pulled her shawl tighter around her shoulders.

"Maybe France," Gwynnie whispered.

"Just so." Emlyn drew her to her feet. "So, will you help me? Will you help me do what I can no longer do?" She nodded down at the bad arm that hung awkwardly at her side.

"I will help you." The moment the words left Gwynnie's lips, Emlyn hugged her, nearly knocking her off her feet. "Careful, Ma. If you need my help, then you need me in one piece."

Emlyn set her firmly on her feet again. "Then we have our plan. Come, come. We'll sneak back into the tavern, to my chamber, and tomorrow we shall follow the trail. This time tomorrow, we may have our hands on that loot at last." She was already hurrying down the road, urging Gwynnie to follow. Gwynnie took her time pulling her bags onto her shoulders and adjusting her shawl before she followed.

On reaching the White Hart, Gwynnie and Emlyn stood outside, staring at the candlelit windows.

"I'm not following you back in there for a brawl." Gwynnie nodded down at Emlyn's bad arm. "You are hardly in a fit state to hold your own these days."

"I wasn't planning on finding my way back through those fools." Emlyn gestured for Gwynnie to follow her around the back of the building. "When I said I had a chamber, miting, I was a little … loose with that term." She halted beside a stable door and pushed it open.

The door swung inward and three horses, their heads just visible in the moonlight, turned to look at them.

"This is your chamber?" Gwynnie whispered.

"It's better than paying for a room. Come, let's get some sleep. In the morning, we go hunting."

CHAPTER 19

"Here it is." Emlyn reached into the open neckline of her doublet and pulled out a neatly folded piece of parchment. She laid it on the beams between them, flattening it out so that the morning sunlight shone brightly upon it.

Gwynnie leaned forward to peer more closely at the parchment. They had spent their night in the rafters of the stable, sleeping on hay. Gwynnie had barely slept a wink, due to the occasional loud snort from the horses, while Emlyn had slept peacefully, her arms flung out wide. Gwynnie missed her bed in the palace, and most of all, she missed the locked door, being able to shut out the world.

Yawning, she let her eyes trail over the parchment. It was the map Emlyn had shown her at the palace.

"Well, if this is a map to some buried treasure, it is scruffily done. They weren't exactly worried about finding it again, were they?" Gwynnie muttered, prompting Emlyn to laugh, though she herself could find no reason to smile.

On the paper was a series of lines, a box, and various arrows. There were no numbers, no words. Perhaps Titus, like her mother, had been unable to read? Then Gwynnie remembered that her father could. It was he who had taught Gwynnie to read and write as a child.

"What do you make of it?" Emlyn asked.

Gwynnie frowned as she examined the parchment. It was clear that the map led to some sort of a building. The drawing consisted of just one building with small paths drawn around the edge of the thick walls and a myriad of corridors within. Without any other buildings drawn, it was impossible to tell where exactly it was. Beside the drawing, there was an emblem that looked rather like a lion, its claws outstretched, its mouth wide. Leading past this emblem were arrows. They trailed a path through various rooms: left, right, straight, down. The arrows ended beside a square that had been coloured black. Above the square was another, smaller emblem, which resembled two sticks crossed together.

"As clear as mud," Gwynnie mumbled.

Emlyn sighed and snatched up the parchment, folding it neatly once more and returning it to her doublet. "All will become clear, I am sure. Once we find where to begin." She opened the canvas bag Gwynnie had brought with her and divided up a manchet loaf.

Gwynnie nibbled as she fussed with her hair, pulling out loose strands of hay. "And where *shall* we begin?" she asked.

"Marie remembered where Titus went the day they hid the treasure. In the morning, he went to work as usual, carrying the crates with him, then he and John-Louis were to meet at one of their favourite haunts — The Devil's Tavern."

"Well, that name bodes well."

Emlyn ignored the comment. "After leaving the tavern, they went to Billingsgate guildhall to watch one of those performances they liked so much, a comic play." She waved her hand dismissively. "By the time they returned to Titus's lodgings, Marie said they no longer carried the crates with them. They must have hidden the loot in one of those two places — the tavern or the guildhall."

"You think they used the cover of a play to hide the loot in the guildhall?" Gwynnie asked. "People are in and out of such buildings every day. Anyone could have found the jewels since."

"Perhaps." Emlyn shrugged. "Or perhaps they hid it in the cellar of their favourite tavern, and they simply went to the guildhall afterwards to celebrate. That map showed an arrow leading *down*, didn't it?"

Gwynnie nodded. It was possible, yet nothing on the map had immediately made her think of either a cellar or a tavern.

"Where is the Devil's Tavern?"

"On the Thames — Billingsgate. Where the fish markets make the air smell ripe." Emlyn swallowed the last of her bread and wiped the crumbs from her fingers. "I suggest we visit there first."

Gwynnie held out a hand to see the parchment again. Emlyn hesitated then reached into her doublet and handed it over. Gwynnie turned the parchment over. It was blank on the back, save for a small *SP* in the bottom corner. She showed Emlyn.

"What do you think this means?"

Emlyn shrugged. "Titus couldn't write."

"No, but my father could." Gwynnie laid the parchment on her lap. Was it possible that John-Louis had written these initials on the map?

A memory surfaced. She was sitting in their lodgings on a tall chair, her legs swinging back and forth as beside her, John-Louis read from a text.

You should know how to write, he had whispered to her. *There's power in words, little one, power for those who have the ability to use them.*

"The Devil's Tavern it is, then." Gwynnie sighed. "It will be closed at this time of day. How do you expect to get inside and look around?"

"Oh, we'll think of something, I'm sure," Emlyn said with a smile.

*

Gwynnie's nose wrinkled as the smell of rotting fish filled her nostrils. Hastening behind Emlyn, the two of them trailed through the early-morning market in Billingsgate. The buildings were squat and tightly packed here, with tiled and thatched roofs bumping against one another. The dockyard stretched out far ahead of them, reaching into the Thames itself, where the half-frozen water glistened in the cold morning light. Some stretches were hard and glacial; other patches were liquid, lapping against the dock and the sloops which had brought goods ashore. They wandered between stalls laden with sturgeon, pike, trout, cod and eels, their silvery scales shimmering like ice. Women were busy salting the fish, rubbing their raw hands against the freshly cut flesh.

The air was filled with voices as the stallholders called and shouted, announcing fresh fish for sale. Fishmongers walked amongst them, dragging small carts, errand boys loading up baskets full of fillets. Behind the stalls were trenches filled with fish guts, blood and fermented flesh, ready to be swept away into the Thames later.

"This is where they came for a drink?" Gwynnie asked, trying not to inhale too deeply.

"They were fond of it," Emlyn replied. She had donned her maid's gown and coif, and pulled on a thick woollen shawl like Gwynnie's. She walked proudly, not shivering in the cold. "Your father used to say there was nothing like a busy tavern. Everyone was so concerned with their own business."

"Easier to hide in plain sight," Gwynnie murmured, an old lesson her mother had taught her long ago.

"Exactly." Emlyn tucked her injured arm into her woollen shawl and carved a path through the market and down to the dockyard, where the wooden struts moved dangerously beneath them. She stood in the middle of a plank and pointed. "There!"

A tall building of white plaster and blackened timber stood on the riverbank, the windows warped at strange angles. A wooden sign swinging from a timber strut depicted a red devil, its horns as black as the night sky, its feet like a pig's trotters and its tail raised like a goat's, as its long-fingered hand raised a tankard to its lips. The Devil's Tavern.

"Well, who could blame them for visiting such a cheery place?" Gwynnie muttered as someone opened the door of the tavern, cursing loudly.

The man had a bucket in his hand. He returned inside, before reappearing and tipping the bucket out into the icy Thames.

"The place is flooded," Gwynnie observed.

One of the windows opened and an old woman started tipping more water out.

Emlyn laughed and clapped Gwynnie on the shoulder. "Time to see the place for ourselves."

Gwynnie took Emlyn's elbow before she could stride off. "And how do you expect to get inside if the place is flooded?"

Emlyn looked around the dockyard, before her gaze settled upon a small sloop that had broken up the icy river. Men still prodded at the ice around them with thick oars, as women clambered onto the docks. Some were dropping their skirts from where they had been tied high around their thighs, offering a momentary glimpse of pale legs mottled with red welts. One woman carried a large jar in front of her, leeches bobbing inside it.

"Time to tie up that skirt of yours, Gwynnie," Emlyn said, her voice full of cunning. With no other explanation, she walked along the dock toward the tavern, Gwynnie racing behind her to keep up.

"No, no," Gwynnie muttered, fearing she knew exactly what her mother was thinking. "You cannot seriously mean to —"

"Morning, sir!" Emlyn called brightly, talking over Gwynnie as she approached the doorway of the tavern.

The man had just finished tipping out another bucket of water. He turned to face them. Broad-faced and broad-shouldered, he looked like a thick plank of wood, his face notched and wizened with age. His nose was rather bulbous too, as if it had recently been broken.

"What do you want?" he drawled, watching them warily.

"My friends here —" Emlyn nodded at the ladies clambering out of the sloop with their leeches — "say you've been flooded. Ah, mighty shame that." She had adjusted her accent to match his.

Gwynnie bit her lip to stop herself from laughing. She had seen before how Emlyn could ingratiate herself with anyone she met. One of her finest tricks was adopting their accent, to show she was like them.

"Shame? You could say that. Damned devil has been at it again." He let out another string of curses and spat into the Thames. "They named this place after him for a reason."

Emlyn grimaced. "I take it the whole place is flooded? Cellar and all?"

"Every inch!" the old woman leaning out of the window suddenly screeched. "It's 'is fault." She pointed at the old man. "The great prune. Won't do nothing 'bout it. I told 'im we needed sandbags. We won't be eating for a month now, thanks to 'im."

"I can't control the tide!" the man spat. "Bad-tempered old crone."

"Watch that mouth of yours."

"Devil has a lot to answer for," Emlyn cut in, clearly trying to head off their argument before it could escalate. "I have an offer for you, stranger, a way you could still make some money out of this mess."

He barked a laugh. "You think anyone could make money out of a drowned cellar? You should see the mess that's been swept in here. Stools floating in river water, old boots, fishbones and dog shi—"

"'Ear the woman out, you fool," the old woman snapped. She leaned out of the window. "What you offering?"

"We're leech women by trade," Emlyn said, gesturing toward Gwynnie. "Well, my daughter here does the hard work now. Leeches love her legs, see?"

"Leeches, eh?" the old woman said with interest.

"Ha! You think a few leeches can make much money?" The tavern owner shook his head.

"It's something, stranger." Emlyn shrugged. "A way for you to make a few shillings. Whatever my daughter and I can catch in your cellar, we will split with you. Mighty fine profits you can make here on Billingsgate market."

"You think it's worth my time, standing there all day shouting about fresh leeches?"

Yet the old woman had scrambled back inside. She made her way to the door, splashing loudly through the flooded tavern as she reached the man's shoulder and pulled on his arm. "Look out there." She thrust a bony finger toward the market. "Look!"

Amongst the stalls was a woman selling jars of leeches. She didn't have to shout or catcall as others did. Many found her. The tavern owner stalled, his protests fading.

"Your blind ways won't be sending me to the grave," the old woman told him, then turned to face Emlyn and Gwynnie. "Come in. Bet there's enough leeches in our cellar to fill Billingsgate market!"

CHAPTER 20

"I feel sick," Gwynnie murmured. She stood at the top of the wooden steps leading down into the flooded cellar. The smell of stale water, rotting fish and excrement turned her stomach.

The cellar was cold and dark, their only source of light a candle given to them by the old woman. She had wished them luck and then closed the door behind her.

"In you go." Emlyn gestured toward the water.

"What?"

"We'll need some leeches to take back to them, won't we? Or they'll think we're not keeping our word. We don't need them following us home or mentioning us to a constable. Come, girl, skirt up and in you go."

"Why don't you go in? I don't fancy pockmarked legs!"

"I've already said you're the one with the tasty blood. It will have to be you, dearest."

"Calling me 'dearest' does not make this any better!"

"Finding jewels will," Emlyn said softly.

"God's blood!" Gwynnie huffed and clambered down the steps toward the water. She slipped off the woollen shawl and laid it over the banister, then raised her skirt and tied it high around her hips. Her eyes danced over the cellar.

It was a small space, the ceiling held up by wooden pillars, the stone walls scratched and marred from years of use. On one side, barrels were stacked together. Whatever was in those barrels would now be spoiled by the river water that had rushed in. On the far side of the room, Gwynnie could just see the top of a doorway.

"There's more than one room." She pointed at the wooden frame peeking above the water.

"Well spotted." Emlyn balanced the candle in a nook in one of the nearest beams and gestured toward the water. "In you go. Catch those leeches and I'll see what I can make of this." She reached into her doublet and pulled out the map.

Gwynnie slipped off her boots and stockings, then took her first step down into the watery depths. The water was ice-cold, sending a shooting pain up her calf.

"Argh!"

"Don't make a fuss, miting."

"Then you bloody well do it!"

"Language, dear."

Gwynnie gritted her teeth and placed her other foot into the water. Her whole body tightened as she took the final step down into the cellar, finding the stone floor.

"Now, look for a lion. Well, it looks like a lion. What else could it be?"

Gwynnie didn't bother answering Emlyn. She waded across the cellar floor, holding her arms high above her head. She inched toward the doorframe, intent on searching the room beyond. When the first leech attached to her leg, she gasped and danced on the spot in the water.

"Women do this for a living?" she asked through gritted teeth.

"You of all people should know how desperate we can all be to buy food," Emlyn reminded her distractedly, her eyes on the map.

"I'd rather steal than do this," Gwynnie hissed as a second leech found its way onto her thigh. She was no longer sure which was worse, the cold of the water or the feeling of the leeches on her skin. But after the initial sting of each bite, the pain quickly passed.

Gradually, she approached the doorframe, holding the wood tightly as she peered around the first room.

"Any sign of a lion?"

"No." The walls bore no decoration, no carving of a lion, only the marks of barrels being tossed against the stones over the years. "If they had hidden the loot here, wouldn't they have drawn a picture of a devil on the map, rather than a lion?"

"Too obvious," Emlyn muttered. "What's in that other chamber?"

Gwynnie inched her way forward into the next room, where the ground gave way beneath her. Unprepared for the sudden steps, she plunged into the water, her head disappearing beneath the icy depths. Her arms thrashed about as she reached for the doorframe, her feet finding the top step as she pushed her head back above the water, gasping for air.

"Careful, miting."

"Oh, what a good idea! If only I had thought of that!"

"Hush now — do you want them to hear?"

"I don't care who hears." Gwynnie leaned against the doorframe, still catching her breath. Clearly, there were stairs leading further down into the next chamber. The candle offered such a feeble light that she couldn't see beyond it to the next wall, let alone if there were any more doorways.

"If this is the right place," Gwynnie gasped, her teeth beginning to chatter, "where should I go?"

"The map says…" Emlyn paused. "Go straight through a doorway, then it curves to the left. It could be through a door or an archway — it's not clear."

"Is there anything on the map that looks like steps?"

"No."

"So, no lion and no steps. Ma…" Gwynnie gripped the frame tightly. "I don't think we're in the right place."

"We don't know that yet." Emlyn looked up from the map. "Trust me, we need to go a little further."

"We?"

"You, then." Emlyn wore a faint smile on her lips. "I promise, all will be well. If you freeze up with cold, I'll be wading in there to pull you back out again."

"What a comforting thought."

"Come along, miting. Best to be quick."

Gwynnie cursed, then, taking a deep breath, she plunged forward into the next room. She kept her chin just above the water, her feet kicking wildly beneath her.

"Left, miting."

Gwynnie turned as best as she could, her hands outstretched, praying that the room would not extend forever. She had not expected the wall to be so close. Her hand hit solid stone, and she grunted with pain. Latching her fingers onto a thin ledge, she wedged her toes against the wall. "No door," she called back to Emlyn.

"What?"

"There's no door!" Gwynnie called, louder. "Only a wall."

"Are you sure? Search the length of the wall."

Dragging her body along the wall, Gwynnie first went left, finding only the corner of the room, then moved right. The wall was longer than she had expected, but there was no opening, no doorway.

"Nothing!"

"What about under the water? The door may be beneath you."

"Then you come and swim amongst the sh—"

"Gwynnie, you're already the wet one."

She took a deep breath, then plunged her head under the water. She pulled herself slowly down, amazed at just how deep this second chamber went. Her fingers traced notches in the wall, but nothing gave way. Made of solid stone, there was nothing to discover. As her feet hit the floor, Gwynnie used her legs to push herself back up. Her head broke the surface and she inhaled deeply.

"Did you find anything?"

"Yes, hear me cheer with delight. I think I just found a diamond."

"Not the time for your sarcasm, miting."

Gwynnie moved along the wall and plunged underwater again. She repeated this three times along the length of the wall, but there was nothing to discover. Finally, she swam back to the doorframe, her eyes adjusting to what felt like the sudden brightness of the lonely candle over Emlyn's head.

"Nothing," Gwynnie muttered, putting her feet down at last and walking toward Emlyn. "This is not the right place."

"Are you sure?"

"Would you like to go and check?"

"Gwynnie —"

"There is no way through that wall. It's made of stone — ceiling to floor." Gwynnie stepped up onto the stairs, rivulets of water running off her body as she shivered.

Emlyn's eyes widened, looking eerie in the candlelight.

"What is it?" Gwynnie demanded.

"Don't look down." Emlyn reached for her legs, but Gwynnie did exactly what her mother had just told her not to.

"Jesus Chr—"

She couldn't count how many leeches were on her legs, from the tops of her feet to her thighs. Tears sprung to her eyes as

Emlyn pulled them off with scrambling fingers, dropping them hurriedly into a jar the old woman had given them.

"Get them off," Gwynnie begged.

"Just hold still," Emlyn said gently. Fortunately, Gwynnie was so numb with cold that she didn't feel much. "Turn around. I'll do the backs of your legs."

Gwynnie held her breath as she felt Emlyn tear the leeches from her skin.

"I think they're all gone now. Quick, turn around, let me check. Yes, yes, they're all gone."

Gwynnie scratched her stomach, meeting Emlyn's gaze. "Could they be…?" She pointed at her gown.

"Clothes off, miting. We need to make sure we've got every single one." Emlyn glanced up at the cellar door to ensure it was shut.

With shaking fingers, Gwynnie pulled off her kirtle, stays, and then the shift, dropping the clothes on the steps. She looked down to see there were indeed leeches across her stomach. A strangled cry escaped her lips and she hastened to help Emlyn pull all the leeches off.

"Next time, you're the one going swimming."

"That's fair enough, dearest," Emlyn said softly.

They checked every inch of Gwynnie's skin. Only when Gwynnie was sure there were none left did she reach for her wet clothes. Emlyn pulled out another two leeches that had been hiding in the shift, then helped her to dress again.

"This has to be your worst idea yet," Gwynnie muttered, pulling the wet kirtle on over her head as she shivered.

"It was worth a try."

"When I have welts from leeches and I'm about to freeze? Oh yes, definitely worth a try!"

"Hush. Do you want them to hear?"

Gwynnie was still shaking as she pulled on her dry boots and the woollen shawl. She followed Emlyn up the stairs, squeezing out the dregs from her hair and stuffing it under her coif.

Emlyn pushed her way through the door, carrying the jar of leeches. She smiled brightly, approaching a table where the old woman sat.

"Ah…" The woman winced when she saw Gwynnie. "Should have told you there's a drop into that second room."

"That may have helped," Gwynnie muttered, glaring at her.

"She's an old hand at this now," Emlyn said with a big smile. "Mighty good at her job. Look!" She presented the jar to the woman, whose eyes widened.

Gwynnie didn't pay attention as Emlyn and the woman divided the leeches between them. Instead, she hastened to the door leading out onto the docks, shuddering as the cold breeze whistled up the Thames and buffeted her wet kirtle. Emlyn appeared a moment later, a sealed jar in her hands.

"Well done, Gwynnie. They didn't suspect anything."

Gwynnie nodded but felt she had lost the power of speech. Emlyn took her shoulder and guided her back through Billingsgate market. Gwynnie was only dimly aware of Emlyn dropping the jar down onto a stallholder's table. If the woman was startled to find more leeches on her table than she'd had before, she didn't call out as they passed.

"Gwynnie? How are you doing?"

"I feel … weak." Gwynnie's legs gave way.

"Woah!" Emlyn caught her under her arms. "Not to worry, sweetheart. I've got you."

Gwynnie sat huddled by the fire in the White Hart. She was dressed in dry clothes, a blanket around her shoulders. It was very like the night that Tombstone had taken care of her after she had fallen in the Thames, only this time, she had her mother watching over her. Emlyn thrust a large plate of food under her nose. Gwynnie felt a little nauseous as she stared at the pigeon pie.

"How are the legs?" Emlyn asked softly.

"Sore." Gwynnie rubbed at her legs, desperately trying to stop the itchiness. It was strange, how she had barely felt the leeches bite after the first few had latched on, but since then, she could not stop wanting to scratch where they had been. "But I don't feel as cold as I did." Gwynnie stretched her fingers toward the fire. "I can feel my fingers and toes again."

"Good." Emlyn glanced around the pub, but tonight, it was quiet. Most of the pub's customers were hidden in different alcoves. Gwynnie wondered if they were avoiding Emlyn on purpose, not wanting to cause trouble. "You need to eat." Emlyn pushed the plate forward once more.

Gwynnie nibbled at the pastry, mostly poking the food around the pewter plate.

"You did well," Emlyn said. She dragged two more candles onto the table where they sat. With the glow of the fire, the air was warm and filled with yellow light.

"Well?" Gwynnie huffed. "We've only discovered where the loot *isn't*, Ma. And I've got wounds to show for it."

"Exactly! That means we know where it *is*. Tomorrow, we go to the guildhall." Emlyn slid off the bench and tucked the blanket tighter around Gwynnie's body.

"It's been a long time since you looked after me like this," Gwynnie murmured, a warm feeling blooming in her stomach.

"You may try to take care of me, but I'm still the mother here." Emlyn smiled. "Remember that." She affectionately brushed a loose strand of hair out of Gwynnie's face, then returned to her seat.

"How are we going to gain access to the guildhall?"

"It depends on what's happening there." Emlyn leaned back on the bench, staring thoughtfully into the fire. "Billingsgate Guildhall is used as a courtroom when the assizes are in town. It can be a meeting place for merchants. And it hosts plays." She nodded decisively and reached into her bag, which was old and patched in multiple places. With one hand, she lifted out a fine red gown. "I think I must go as something grander than a maid tomorrow."

Gwynnie sighed and reached for the cup of ale that Emlyn placed down beside her. "Let's just hope the guildhall isn't flooded."

CHAPTER 21

"It's quite the centre of activity today, isn't it?"

Gwynnie and Emlyn stood before Billingsgate Guildhall. The doors, atop a flight of white stone steps, were flung open, and many gentlemen were wandering in and out. The walls were hatched white and dark brown, the eaves hanging low over the street, and the great windows revealed people inside.

Every man was dressed grandly, either in a fine doublet and hose, with an ornate cloak hanging from his shoulders, or in black clerical or lawyer's robes.

"At least we don't look out of place," Emlyn said, adjusting her fine headdress.

Emlyn had indeed dressed for the occasion. She wore her fine gown, made of a rich ruby-red silk and embroidered with silver thread. The voluminous skirt sat over a farthingale that limited her movements but ensured no one could stand too close to her. The headdress, in the French fashion, was tucked neatly over her ears and pinned back her dark hair. She had tucked her bad arm into an ermine muff, to keep her fingers warm.

"There is only one problem," Gwynnie whispered. She had worn her usual maid's gown and was careful to stand behind Emlyn, playing the part of a ladies' maid for the day. "If you go inside, you will be the only woman in that crowd."

"Indeed, I will be," Emlyn said, adjusting the gown and clearly doing her best not to shiver in the cold. "Well, only one thing for it. Come along, miting."

Before Gwynnie could respond, Emlyn walked straight up the stone steps to the entrance. Men stepped out of the way of her large farthingale, allowing her inside. Not a single person moved to intercept her or ask what she was doing there. Gwynnie hastened on behind her.

As they stepped inside, they passed through a small antechamber.

"Look for a lion," Emlyn urged over her shoulder, though Gwynnie had already been doing so.

There had been no lion on the front of the building, though it had borne the shields of merchant guilds on wooden plaques over the door. Now, in the antechamber, Gwynnie saw those arms again, small wooden shields pinned high on the wall above dark mahogany panelling. One plaque bore two silver fish, crossed like swords, and another three silver goat heads, for the cordwainers. Gwynnie searched those plaques, but she didn't see a single lion amongst the emblems.

Emlyn walked on into the main hall, Gwynnie following. The panelled walls opened up wider here, revealing a tall ceiling that was heavily beamed. Flags and more merchants' emblems hung from the beams.

Men talked together in small circles, their heads bent low. Some glanced Emlyn's way, yet only one showed any interest in talking to her. He broke off from the main group and walked toward her. He was a tall and imposing man with jet-black hair streaked with grey. He ignored Gwynnie, his eyes fixed upon Emlyn.

"My lady." He bowed his head.

"A gentleman indeed." Emlyn adopted a fine accent, inclining her head.

"You startle us. It has been some time since a woman walked amongst us."

"Ah, forgive me. It was imperative I came." She offered a sorrowful look. "My new husband, a merchant from the

Netherlands, has just moved to London. He is intent on joining you. I confess…" She stepped toward him and whispered, "He has sent me on as something of a scout."

"How cunning of him." He smiled at her.

"Cunning indeed. Though, of course, I must be careful in what I reveal. I would of course be grateful for a tour?" She extended her hand toward him, her charming smile making the stranger lift his hand to take hers at once.

"Then allow me to offer to be your guide. Master Zacharia la Mare."

"French?"

"By heritage, yes. And your name?"

"Lady Emiline Van Der Hoek."

Gwynnie bit her lip to avoid smiling at Emlyn's inventive name.

Soon enough, Master la Mare was showing them around the guildhall. He first took Emlyn on a tour of the hall itself, where she enquired diligently into every guild that came here. When they returned to the antechamber, she asked after every plaque.

"Goodness, just look at how many animals are represented in the emblems. One would not be surprised to see a lion amongst them."

"A lion? No indeed, there are no lions here, my lady. Come, let me show you more."

Gwynnie caught the flicker of a pained expression on her mother's face, though she smothered it quickly and followed their guide. Gwynnie trailed behind as they entered a hallway on the far side of the hall. La Mare gestured toward a set of stairs, explaining that they led to a minstrels' gallery and offices for clerks when the courts were in session, then he led them around the back of the guildhall. They descended a flight of stairs to a lower level.

“What is this room?” Emlyn asked, trailing at her escort’s side with her hand on his arm.

“This used to be the guildhall before we had the finer one built,” he explained. “As you can see, there are many doors from this room. These are mostly used now as storerooms for the guilds. Come, let me take you back to the main hall. I’ll be sure to answer any questions your husband has left with you, though of course I shall seek to maintain my own guild’s secrets.”

Emlyn offered him a flirtatious smile and acquiesced readily. Gwynnie was careful to curtsy by the door, her hand loose at her side. Emlyn surreptitiously slipped the map into Gwynnie’s hand as she passed. Gwynnie didn’t raise herself up until she was certain the pair were long gone, a distant door closing behind them.

Unfurling the map, she eyed it carefully. Rather like the drawing on the parchment, there was indeed a door to the left where there should be one. Only there was a problem. When she turned to look at the wall behind her, there was no lion, no emblem or guild shield that could refer to such a creature. Cursing, Gwynnie turned back and followed the map regardless. She turned left through the open door, finding herself in a small storeroom. There was nothing here except sheets of wool, bound up with string and pushed into a corner. She turned right next, following the map into an adjoining chamber.

She should have been able to walk through yet another door or archway, this one leading to a staircase, yet she found herself staring at a blank wall. Gwynnie sighed, her hand trailing across the wall for some sort of secret notch, but there was nothing, only plaster and timber.

Gwynnie returned to the old hall. She tried orientating herself differently, hoping that a shield on the wall which bore a dog could have been mistaken for a lion. She turned left, then right, but each time she came up against a blank wall. Cursing, she tucked the map into her gown and left the room.

She found her way back to the main hall. Without Emlyn to accompany her, she drew attention. More than one clerk dressed in black looked at her, not with curiosity but plain suspicion. Gwynnie searched the crowd for her mother and Master la Mare. She found them, sitting together on the far side of the hall, only Emlyn had attracted something of a crowd now. There were another three men, hanging on her every word.

"Not the time, Ma," Gwynnie muttered under her breath. She hovered for so long in the doorway that a man approached her.

"This is no place for women," he warned and held a hand out to the door behind her.

"I'm waiting for my mistress." She bobbed a curtsy and gestured toward Emlyn across the room.

"You should wait outside."

"But I —"

"Outside." He grabbed her arm.

Shocked by his tight grip, Gwynnie acted on instinct, grabbing his wrist and twisting it back so he was forced to release her.

"Argh!" he cried out in pain, wringing his sore wrist and staring at her in alarm. "Out. Now." He marched toward her, his arm outstretched as if he would strike her.

"What is this?" Emlyn's voice called loudly from across the hall. The man approaching Gwynnie stilled, his hand raised.

"Would one of your clerks strike my maid? My maid who waits so dutifully by the door like a mouse?"

Some of the men shifted uncomfortably. An older merchant with white hair waved his cane at the young man.

"What are you doing?" he hissed.

"Women are not allowed in here, sir."

"So you would strike her?"

Slowly, the man lowered his hand. Gwynnie was relieved that he didn't speak of the fact she had hurt him. It could have got her thrown out on her ear.

"Well, I do not think I wish to encourage my husband to work with a guildhall that would accept the striking of a woman. *Any* woman," Emlyn declared, standing up. Master la Mare tried to apologise, but she spoke over him. "I suggest you teach your clerks some manners, or how can my husband and I possibly return here with our staff in tow? I cannot guarantee their safety." Imperiously, she marched past the young man who had raised his hand, looking down her nose at him. "You have cost your masters business today. Learn from your mistake. No woman is yours to strike." She turned to Gwynnie and flicked her fingers at the door. "Away," she ordered, like a true mistress.

"Now, quickly, before they see we did not come with horses or a carriage," Emlyn hissed, taking her arm and leading her away from the building and down a narrow lane. Had anyone followed them out, they would have been too slow to see them take cover in the alleyway. "Why was he going to strike you?"

"For nothing more than being a woman — a maid in a building full of clerks and merchants." Gwynnie shook her head and took the map out of her gown, handing it back to Emlyn. "It didn't fit."

"What?" Emlyn took the map, her mouth falling open. "But it has to be here. The map has to fit."

"It didn't."

"It has to!" Emlyn said in panic. She opened the map once more, as if she could somehow make sense of it in a way she had been unable to before. "These were the two places John-Louis and Titus went that day. There is nowhere else. Nowhere!" She glanced into the main street, then apparently thinking better of it, walked quickly away, further down the narrow lane, in danger of snapping the wooden hoop of her farthingale in her agitation. Gwynnie followed her. "This doesn't make sense. Did you find a lion?"

"No lion."

"It could have been taken down. The main hall —"

"It couldn't have been a map of the main hall," Gwynnie interrupted, "because there were no doors at the sides. As for the old hall, I tried various different ways to make the map work, but I came up against a solid wall every time."

"There could have been —"

"No trick walls. No hatches. Nothing, Ma. Nothing." Gwynnie sighed. "Whatever this map is, you don't know that it relates to the loot. Titus could have drawn this about anything."

"Then why keep it?" Emlyn shook her head, walking on with purpose. "There was no reason to keep it among his papers. If they had hidden some other loot, drawn a map and gone back to find it, they'd hardly keep the map, would they? No, Gwynnie. It doesn't make sense!"

They strode out of the lane and into a small square. Horses and carts rushed back and forth, people hurrying about their business. There were few signs that it was still Christmas. Only a few people walked with sprigs of evergreen shrubs in their hair and on their clothes.

Emlyn halted and turned angrily on the spot. "I cannot be wrong."

"Maybe Marie Duffield was wrong."

"She was clear," Emlyn said, turning to face her. "She knew exactly where Titus had been that day. After going to work, he met John-Louis at the Devil's Tavern. They went on to the guildhall and then back to Titus's lodgings. They no longer had the loot with them. They must have hidden it somewhere." She turned and walked on again, heading toward Shoreditch and the inn. But Gwynnie had halted.

"Ma!" she called after Emlyn.

"What?"

"You said Titus went to work. Where did he work?"

"Oh, he was a curate." Emlyn shrugged. "He hated the position. Insisted he was never paid very much for it, but he kept it up. Said it gave him an honest appearance. He rather liked being thought of as an honest man, despite his other line of work."

"*Where* was he a curate?" Gwynnie asked, hurrying to Emlyn's side. "He went there that day. What if John-Louis went with him?"

"Oh…"

"Yes, oh!" Gwynnie repeated, nodding quickly. "Ma, where was he a curate?"

"St Paul's Cathedral."

CHAPTER 22

Gwynnie and Emlyn soon found the road to St Paul's Cathedral. After a long walk, they came to a stop in the square in front of the cathedral, pausing under the eaves of a nearby building.

The square was full of people. Many had gathered for another religious service to mark the days of Christmas. Gwynnie peered over the heads of the crowd, looking at the curate who stood on the steps in front of the giant double oak doors of the cathedral. Dressed in a black smock, with a white band at his throat, he read a service in Latin for the poor who had gathered. Gwynnie supposed it was only the wealthy who were allowed inside to pray.

"A curate?" Gwynnie whispered as she caught her breath. "Titus was a curate! A man who turned out to be a…"

"A killer? Yes." Emlyn's voice was cold. "I am not sure he had much space in his heart for God. He certainly liked the appearance of goodness, though. I heard him speak of this place with scorn. He hated the richness of it — the sheer amount of money spent on those who worshipped at the altar." She laughed without humour.

"So, if he had no respect for the place," Gwynnie mused, "he would have no qualms about hiding something he had stolen here."

"You think it possible?" Emlyn asked.

"Where else is there? You said it yourself. Marie claimed they went nowhere else that day." Gwynnie nodded at the building. "Is it not a perfect hiding place? Who would think to look for stolen loot in a house of God?"

Emlyn fidgeted with her ermine muff and stared at the doors. "Well, we are hardly going to be allowed to look around inside during a service."

"No, we'll have to come back when it's quieter," Gwynnie agreed. Her eyes traced the building, looking for another way in beside the front doors. She supposed there would be side doors to a cathedral of this size — perhaps a door to a vestry or other apartments within. As she stared, some of the crowd shifted, tired from standing and listening to the curate preach for so long. Through the new gap in the crowd, Gwynnie saw a stone figure beside the steps. Sitting back on its haunches, the lion's jaws were open wide, its front paws lifted.

"Ma, look!" She grabbed hold of Emlyn's shoulder.

Emlyn followed Gwynnie's gaze, looking through the crowd. She too saw the lion and breathed in sharply. "We're in the right place." Her voice was barely above a whisper. "Can it be possible? Can it have been here, all this time?"

"Perhaps." Gwynnie continued to scan the building. On one side were wooden struts of scaffolding. There were tables erected for stonemasonry too, and signs of other work. "They're working on the building."

"We could come back disguised as workers tomorrow," Emlyn suggested. "We'll wear men's clothes."

Gwynnie shook her head. "No, that won't work."

"Why not?"

"Because I'm too small for anyone to mistake me for a stonemason." She laughed at the thought. "And you have a bad leg and an arm that can't even lift a pebble, let alone anything heavier."

Emlyn frowned. "Do you have a better idea?"

"We'll come back at night," Gwynnie said firmly, "when all is quiet and there's no one to see us."

"You want to break into St Paul's Cathedral, miting?" Emlyn's tone was teasing.

"I do," Gwynnie replied. "We'll find a door to force, something smaller than those." She nodded at the giant oak doors. "Then we'll search."

They fell silent, both deep in thought. Gwynnie's eyes traced the lion again, staring at the outstretched claws. After a moment, a small laugh escaped her lips.

"What is so amusing?" Emlyn asked.

"My father did write on that map," replied Gwynnie, thinking of the letters that had been on the back of the parchment. "SP — St Paul." She gestured to the white stone figure of a man far behind the lion, on the wall. Saint Paul, clothed in robes, stared impassively back at them. "Then we are in agreement? We come back tonight?"

"Tonight." Emlyn didn't hesitate. She turned and walked down the street. Gwynnie cast one glance back at the cathedral and then turned to follow.

Gwynnie caught up with Emlyn by the river, where she was staring out across the water. Gwynnie followed her gaze, then blinked. The glistening surface was frozen solid. Gwynnie pulled her woollen shawl tighter around her shoulders, watching her breath cloud the chilly air.

"Frozen over. All of it," Emlyn murmured in awe. "Look." She pointed down to the bank, where children were stepping out onto the ice. They'd strapped antlers to their shoes that they must have bought from a nearby stall and tentatively skated on the ice. Two children tumbled together, landing heavily, but the ice did not break beneath them.

"They are not the only ones," Gwynnie replied, nodding across the river.

As if encouraged by the children's bravery, women and men were stepping out onto the ice, some carrying tables and chairs, turning the frozen river into a place to banquet. Others carried their stalls out, with their friends following behind, bearing their wares. People began to stream onto the ice, hurrying down a flight of steps in the riverbank wall beside them, clinging to the stones to avoid slipping. Gwynnie thought she saw a flash of copper hair and a neatly trimmed beard, but she quickly dismissed the thought. Tombstone would not be amongst the crowd here today.

"It's a long time since I've seen such smiles," Emlyn said with a contented sigh. "The river froze in my youth once. For days it was impenetrable, as though the angels had trapped the watery demons beneath the surface and made it impossible for them to rise."

"As always, Mother, your piety astounds me," Gwynnie muttered, her sarcasm eliciting a chuckle from Emlyn.

"Once upon a time … in my youth, I believed, Gwynnie."

Two men carrying a stall passed by, their voices audible.

"Is it true?" asked one of the men.

"I just told you it is. You got cabbages for ears?" replied his companion.

"Nah, I don't believe you. Why would the king walk here?"

"It's Christmas, isn't it? I'm only telling you what I heard. It's parade day tomorrow, and the king and queen will parade down the river if it's still frozen over."

Gwynnie and Emlyn exchanged glances. Gwynnie shifted uneasily, pulling her shawl tighter around her shoulders.

"Ah, you're telling lies."

"I'm not! You wouldn't know the truth if it bit you on the nose."

Gwynnie didn't hear the rest of their argument. They slipped down onto the ice with the others, gesticulating as they set up their own stall of mussels.

"It could be true," Emlyn whispered to Gwynnie. "I remember the king before old Henry now. He used to parade on the ice too."

"He did?" Gwynnie looked up and down the frozen river. "It's a risk. What if the ice broke?"

"Does it look like it's going to break, dearest?" Emlyn laughed and pointed down at the children who were chasing one another. They frequently fell down, hitting the ice hard, but it didn't crack.

"I don't know. It hasn't yet been tested by a man of the king's weight."

Emlyn let out a bark of laughter as she jumped down onto the steps of Paul's Wharf, hurrying toward the river.

"What are you doing?" Gwynnie hastened to follow her.

"What does it look like? I'm going out onto the ice." Emlyn gestured toward the frozen expanse before them. "I want a good look at the rooftops, miting, in case we need to make a quick escape. Not a bad view of St Paul's from here, I'll bet." She scuttled out onto the ice as Gwynnie slowly followed.

In the middle of the river, they halted. The wind was stronger here, for they were not sheltered by the timber buildings. Gwynnie's heart thudded, for despite other people's ease, she could not stop staring at the ice around them. If it were to crack beneath them all now, she wondered how many would make it back to the bank before the cold water claimed them.

"What do you think?" Emlyn asked.

Gwynnie followed her gaze toward the spire of St Paul's. It was clearly visible, being just two roads away from the riverbank. It towered over the surrounding timber buildings, which looked rather like a nest for the tower.

"It's tall," Gwynnie said as she stared up at the spire. It was topped by a crucifix. She shivered. A fall from such a height would mean certain death. Even the roof of the knave and apse was far taller than the roofs of the houses nearby. "A fall would kill us both. To jump from there to the nearby roofs … it cannot be done. No, if we need to run, we escape through a door, Ma."

"It might be done —"

"With your arm and leg?" Gwynnie nodded at Emlyn's injured arm, cradled against her stomach.

"Very well. Then we find another way out other than the roof. With all the scaffolding and building work, it must be a rabbit warren of pathways. There will be many places to hide."

Gwynnie said nothing. She was looking at the expansive churchyard around the cathedral. Should they need to run across that yard, they would be easily seen, all too easy to chase.

"We will need to disguise ourselves," Gwynnie said with a sigh.

"Then we go as men." Emlyn pointed down at Gwynnie's skirt. "No fine gowns for you anymore, miting —"

"This is hardly fine!" Gwynnie protested, gesturing toward the elaborate gown Emlyn was wearing.

"I was never given a maid's gown as fine as the one you are wearing now."

"I bought it with the money Tombstone paid me," Gwynnie said defiantly.

"Shame you didn't buy a hose and doublet too."

"Ma!"

"No matter, we'll find some in the laundry of the inn this evening. The drunkards are fond of throwing their soiled clothes in there before they head to bed."

"Soiled hose and doublets. You paint a pretty picture indeed, Ma."

Emlyn didn't respond. She was staring over Gwynnie's head into the crowds on the ice, her lips pursed.

"What is it?" Gwynnie asked, turning to follow Emlyn's gaze.

She didn't see him at first. There was a tangle of doublets, cloaks and shawls, men holding onto felt bonnets in the wind and ladies clutching at fine hoods. Stalls were decked with fresh fish and spices as children skated between them, nearly knocking over some of the older folk, who shouted as they passed. Then she caught a glimpse of copper hair once again.

It was Tombstone. It had not been wishful thinking before. He was talking to some clerks who looked familiar to Gwynnie.

"Who is he with?" Emlyn whispered.

"Cromwell's clerks." Gwynnie watched as they gestured toward the ice before them. "They're making plans," she surmised, watching as Tombstone gave instructions to the other clerks.

"Then that stranger must have been right. The king and queen will parade on the ice tomorrow."

"Hmm." Gwynnie watched Tombstone. He hadn't noticed her, far too caught up in what he was doing.

If Tombstone and the king and queen, along with the rest of the court, would be here tomorrow on the ice, there was every chance that Fitzroy would be there too. Gwynnie chewed her lip. She couldn't risk walking on the Thames tomorrow, in case he saw her.

"If you're thinking of speaking to that man —"

"Tombstone, Ma. His name is Elric Tombstone. You should remember that, considering how he has never chased you for your crime —"

"You cannot speak to him." Emlyn was firm, though the icy air was making her teeth chatter. "We don't need anyone recognising us, Gwynnie. No one must see us in the vicinity of the cathedral."

Gwynnie nodded, though her eyes remained on Tombstone. He smiled at one of the clerks, who must have made some jest. She suddenly ached to be back in the palace.

"You have a soft spot for that man?"

"Pah! Clearly, you have forgotten his tastes, Ma. He is my friend."

"He is your employer. Have you forgotten this is the man who sent you out of the palace?"

"To protect me."

"Or to be rid of you," Emlyn scoffed. "Do not think of him anymore." She turned on her heel. "Come, miting. We must prepare for tonight."

Gwynnie glanced once more at Tombstone's back, then turned and followed Emlyn off the ice.

CHAPTER 23

The bells chimed midnight. Gwynnie peered up at the belfry tower. In the darkness, the grey and white stone looked black, the structure only distinguishable from the night sky because of the white stars that dotted the clouds beyond. Gwynnie stood in the shadows of Old Change and Cheapside, hidden under the eaves of a thatched house. Even though the hose and doublet she had taken from the inn's laundry was itchy and so long that she had to hitch up the sleeves, she fought the temptation to scratch and stood as still as the timber beams.

"All will be in bed now," Emlyn breathed beside her. "Not a soul to see us."

Gwynnie continued to stare at the cathedral and its compound. On its northwest side, she spied the roof of the Bishop's Palace. Even at this time of night, she knew someone could be awake in the palace. It was why they had agreed not to enter the cathedral from that side. Gwynnie peered through the gate standing at the north-east entrance. The stone structure — carved with grotesque gargoyles and shadowy crucifixes — was not particularly high, but the wooden door forbade any entrance at this time of night.

"We are agreed?" Gwynnie whispered to Emlyn. "We enter through this gate and cross through the cemetery. None will walk there at night, too fearful of men walking again after death. I'll try the side; they must have a vestry door somewhere. If I have no luck, I'll search the scaffolding and look for a way in."

Emlyn nodded silently.

Gwynnie left her mother in the eaves of the building. Pulling the bonnet low over her brow, she approached the gate. She cast a look over her shoulder, but all was quiet in the dark street; there was not even a watchman to see what they were doing. Carefully, Gwynnie leaned on the gate, but it refused to budge. Checking around once more, she reached into the sleeve of her doublet and pulled out the thin metal rod that she usually kept hooked in the sleeves of her gowns. Feeding the rod through a tiny gap in the wooden doors, she slowly moved it up and down, finding a latch that prevented it rising any further. She inched the rod up a little, loosening the hook which kept the door bolted. Eventually, metal scratched against metal, and the hook lifted out of place. She let the hook fall away then pressed on the door once again. It swung open.

Breathing deeply, Gwynnie poked her head inside.

Before her, St Paul's Cathedral stood ghostly and intimidating in the moonlight. Its grey stone appeared black in places, while other parts shone white in the moonlight, as if the whole structure was an iridescent ghost. The spire disappeared into the clouds, and the wooden scaffolding on one side of the building was muddy brown hatches. On the ground sat tombstones, squat and fat, like crouching men ready to attack. Gwynnie's eyes flitted over each stone, checking for movement.

A shadow stirred behind a stone. Gwynnie's hand tightened on the wooden gate, her heart in her mouth. She was ready to run, to let the wooden gate swing shut, when the shadow moved again. It was only a cat, pouncing at something in the undergrowth.

Gwynnie's heartrate slowed. She took two steady breaths then stepped into the cemetery, holding the gate open behind her. Emlyn soon followed, closing the gate with her good hand.

They both stood and stared at the tall spire and the gargoyles that looked down malevolently. There were dragon-like stones, faces morphed into something almost human, though the eyes and cheeks were far too large. There were human faces, too symmetrical to be real, their lips parted in round 'o's, and demons, with wings curled on their backs and oversized talons clinging to the walls.

Emlyn nudged Gwynnie, urging her on. Gwynnie's eyes tarried on a gargoyle a moment longer. Its curled horns and the way it stared at her made her shiver.

Inching slowly through the cemetery, Gwynnie hardly dared to breathe. She saw the cat flitting between the stones, a mouse in its jaws, then it too melted away.

They sank into the shadows near the cathedral. In the northern transept was a door, half hidden beneath towering scaffolding. Finding the door firmly locked, Gwynnie once again slid out the rod from her sleeve. Pressing it carefully into the lock, she turned it back and forth, but there was no satisfying click. Retrieving the rod, Gwynnie bent down and pressed her eye to the keyhole. All was black, suggesting the key was in the lock on the other side.

Cursing, she returned the rod to her sleeve and stepped back, looking up at the scaffolding struts. She was no great climber, though she had done it many times in her life, especially when it had been necessary to flee nightwatchmen after a theft. She tested a wooden strut with her foot. It creaked a little under her weight. She shifted, choosing another spot that was much quieter, and began to climb.

Her shoulders soon burned with the effort of lifting her body up the struts. She rested on wooden boards, and took the opportunity to peer through the stained-glass windows.

In daylight, these windows would be full of glorious golds, reds and greens. At this time of night, however, the colours were muted to dull shadows. Gwynnie pressed her face to the cold glass and peered through. There was just enough moonlight for her to make out a few pillars and a dark altar. No candle had been lit inside the church. It was empty.

Gwynnie returned to climbing. It was hard work and her palms grew sweaty, making it difficult to cling to the wooden struts. Sweat dripped down her back and her hair slipped out from beneath her hat. At the top of the scaffolding, she stuffed the strands back under her hat and sat crouched on the boards, so none would see her from the street.

She was now level with a balcony that circled the central tower. There were not just windows here, but doors. Crouching low, she inched stealthily along the boards toward the doors. A board creaked beneath her, but she was so high up it didn't matter.

She reached for a door handle, only to find it was locked. Once again, Gwynnie pulled the rod from her sleeve and pressed it into the lock.

A sharp caw made her spin around, her back flat to the door behind her.

A raven had landed on the scaffolding, eyeing her warily, its black beak glinting in the moonlight. Heart pounding, Gwynnie returned to her task. She felt strangely unnerved by the raven, as if it somehow knew she was breaking the rules.

The lock eventually popped out of place. As she opened the door, the raven flew off. Gwynnie watched it go, its black feathers merging with the darkness, then she slipped inside and closed the door.

Patches of silver moonlight lit her path toward a narrow spiral staircase. Descending into the darkness, Gwynnie reached out and ran a hand along the stone wall as she navigated her way down the stairs.

She thought they would never end and grew breathless in her haste to descend. When she eventually reached the bottom, she stumbled in the darkness, struggling to find her balance and clinging to a door which barred her way. Reaching out, she found the handle and turned it, inching the door open.

Sudden moonlight made her blink, the scents of incense and candle wax making her nose tingle.

The great apse of the cathedral opened out before her. Huge pillars reached high overhead, elaborately decorated with gargoyles and jewel-encrusted crucifixes. The altar was decorated with fine plate and candlesticks, while the pulpit was topped with a golden eagle, its wings spread wide to hold an enormous bible. Gwynnie crept past as she inched toward a door in the north side of the apse.

The door was locked from the inside, the key thrust into the lock, explaining why Gwynnie had been unable to pick the lock from the outside. Turning the key, she opened the door, poking her head out.

Emlyn crept toward the door, her face emerging from the darkness of the cemetery. Gwynnie stepped back to allow her inside, then locked the door again behind them.

"Anyone?" Emlyn whispered.

"No one. And in the cemetery?"

"None." Emlyn turned to face the apse. Her lips parted at the sheer grandeur as her hand reached into her doublet and pulled out the map. When she showed no sign of looking at the map, too busy staring around in awe, Gwynnie snatched it from her.

Gwynnie proceeded toward the great oak doors of the cathedral, at the far end of the long nave. She hastened past thick pillars and long pews, heading across polished flagstones, then turned around so that she was facing the aisle and the breadth of the cathedral's grand interior.

Outside, behind the double doors, was the statue of the lion she and Emlyn had seen earlier that day. Gwynnie's finger traced the lion on the map, then followed the path of the arrows. She began to move, Emlyn hurrying to catch her up.

Gwynnie walked down the nave and turned left, into the north transept, the pillars bathed in moonlight. She followed the arrow to the right. Between two white pillars was a narrow gap. A curtain had been drawn across to hide this part of the building. Gwynnie began to carefully pull the curtain aside, before Emlyn impatiently swept it away.

Behind the curtain was a tiny chamber which could have been a vestry. It contained coffers and buffet cabinets. On one side of the chamber was scaffolding and excessive amounts of building dust on the floor.

The arrow on the map pointed straight ahead, toward a little door. It was so short that even Gwynnie had to bend down as she reached for the handle. This door was not locked. She swung it open and stepped through, Emlyn practically having to fold herself in half to fit through the gap.

Before them was a flight of steps, leading down into darkness.

"A crypt?" Gwynnie whispered.

"It's possible." Emlyn nodded.

Gwynnie held the map tight and started down the steps, one hand skimming the stone wall. Emlyn stayed close behind her, her quick breaths practically in Gwynnie's ear.

When they reached the bottom, a thin strip of moonlight shone across the floor, bringing them both to a stop. It came from a tiny gap in the wall, no bigger than the palm of Gwynnie's hand. It was set high, almost into the ceiling. The light shone onto a small ledge in the stone wall beside Gwynnie, revealing a tinderbox and a fat beeswax candle. Reaching for the candle, she tucked the map under her arm and lit the wick using the iron wool from the tinderbox. The wool smoked, offering a small flicker of warmth before it faded. The candle flame glowed orange as Gwynnie held it high over her head.

A subterranean chamber opened before them, deeper and wider than Gwynnie had been expecting. The short pillars reached just above Emlyn's head, holding up an arched ceiling. As they moved forward, the candlelight revealed plaques engraved with Latin words, effigies of soldiers and knights bearing shields, and tombs made from smoke-grey stone.

"It is a crypt," Gwynnie whispered. "They hid their treasure amongst the dead."

CHAPTER 24

"Where do we go now, Gwynnie? Concentrate, dearest. Where does the map say we are to go next?"

Gwynnie tore her eyes away from the effigies all around them. Their vacant stone eyes stared past her and up to the ceiling. It was almost as if *she* were the ghost walking amongst them, unseen as they contemplated the heavens.

She passed the candle to Emlyn and flattened out the map. The arrows on the parchment snaked their way through small squares, toward one square in particular.

"These squares — they must be the tombs," Gwynnie whispered, following the path of the arrows as Emlyn held the candle high over their heads. "Look." She pointed at each tomb in turn, which matched the rough illustrations on the map. "They drew this quickly."

"They were probably afraid of being disturbed, or raising suspicion if they lingered too long. No doubt there would have been plenty of others in the cathedral at the time."

Gwynnie passed two plaques engraved with Latin words that she couldn't read, then came to a wall that blocked their path. To her left and right were more tombs, names carved into stone and bronze. Yet on the map just one more square was drawn, shaded in black ink. Above this was another tiny emblem, resembling two sticks crossed together.

Gwynnie ran her finger over the drawing, raising her head toward the tombs. Amongst all the names of the dead was one plaque written in English. At the top of the bronze plaque, an emblem had been carved into the metal. Two swords, crossed together.

"Crudely done," Gwynnie mused as she held the map up beside the emblem of the swords and Emlyn inched the candle closer.

"It's … in the tomb," Emlyn whispered.

"So it would seem."

Gwynnie squinted at the plaque. The name read, *Regalis Monk, Vicar of this Parish.* The death date shone in the flickering candlelight: *1522.*

It was the year Gwynnie's father had died. Now, she knew it was also the year that John-Louis and Titus had stolen a king's fortune, Titus had murdered John-Louis, and Emlyn had taken revenge on Titus.

Gwynnie glanced at her mother, but Emlyn didn't notice. She had placed a hand on the stone and was staring hungrily at the tomb.

"Think of it," she whispered. "Just behind this could be the king's jewels. A *fortune* just waiting for us."

Gwynnie felt an old tingle of excitement run up her spine as Emlyn rested the candle on a nearby effigy. "It's time, miting. We need to open this thing up."

It took some minutes for them to return soundlessly to the main part of the cathedral and find what they were looking for. Amongst the scaffolding and building works, they found tools. Between them, they took hammers, chisels, a couple of staffs and a coil of rope, then returned to the crypt, still bathed in the light of the candle.

Gwynnie placed a chisel where the bronze plaque met the stonework and began to hammer it into place, nudging the bronze away from the wall. Emlyn started on the other corner, but her injured arm made her wince, and soon enough, she let the chisel and hammer drop, her face pale.

Gwynnie directed Emlyn to hold the candle closer.

It was hard work. The plaque had been set firmly into the stone and though Gwynnie had strength, she knew she lacked the power needed to prise the tablet away fast. She ground the chisel further and further into the stone, until eventually the corner of the tablet lifted away, then she shifted to the other corner. She had to throw off her hat and roll up the sleeves of her doublet and shirt. Despite the cold air in the crypt, beads of sweat were soon running down her back as she worked.

When the second corner of the tablet lifted away from the stone, Gwynnie took the rope and fed it through the back of the plaque. Taking both ends, she sat back and pulled.

Nothing happened.

Grunting, Gwynnie heaved again, her arms shaking with the sheer effort, but still, it would not shift.

Dropping the rope, she went for one of the staffs, feeding it into the side of the plaque and trying to prise it away from the stone wall. Moving her grasp to the end of the staff, she gave herself a longer lever and pushed again. This time it jolted.

She and Emlyn looked at each other. Emlyn raised the candle higher.

"Take the other staff," Gwynnie said. "Come, you can do that."

Emlyn balanced the candle on an effigy and took the second staff, threading it behind the tablet on the other side. She pushed with her good hand and once again, the tablet shifted, the bronze scraping against the stone.

Gwynnie left her staff in its place, balanced against a nearby pillar, and returned to the rope. This time when she pulled, using her whole weight, it toppled forward.

Emlyn leapt out of the way as the bronze plummeted to the flagstone floor and Gwynnie fell back. There was a cloud of stone dust, a sudden stench that made Gwynnie cover her mouth with both hands, and the deafening ring of metal on stone.

For a moment, neither of them spoke. As the cloud of dust billowed, danced, then settled, they waited with bated breath to see if anyone would come running. Yet there were no echoes overhead in the cathedral. There was no flicker of another candle joining them.

Emlyn was the first to move. She stood in the opening, peering into the tomb.

"Is that...?" Gwynnie could not finish the question as she gagged on the foul air.

"The stench of death," Emlyn answered. Hurriedly, she thrust her head through the gap. "God have mercy!"

It was so rare to hear Emlyn curse that Gwynnie hastened to join her mother, ignoring the stench.

A long, narrow stone box was before them, erected on a wooden platform. The stone was dappled, as if the carver had not taken too long to complete his task. It wasn't even properly sealed, which was why the smell had carried toward them. Yet it was not the coffin Emlyn was staring at.

Two wooden crates sat on the platform in front of the coffin. They were small enough for a single person to carry, about the span of Gwynnie's arms. They had been pushed together in the small space between the coffin and the tomb entrance.

"Is that the loot?" Gwynnie whispered.

"It must be." Emlyn reached inside and tried to grab the first crate, but her injured arm protested at the odd angle.

Gwynnie took her place and lifted the crate out through the hole they had made, placing it down by their feet. Reaching for the second, she pulled that through too. Beside her, Emlyn was running her fingers over the first crate, her eyes wide. She lifted a chisel and began trying to break the padlock which kept the lid shut.

Suddenly a sound reached Gwynnie's ears. It was distant, muffled, but enough to make her chin jerk up.

Emlyn pressed down hard on the chisel as Gwynnie took a hold of her shoulder.

"Ma?"

"I need to see, Gwynnie. I have to *know*."

Another thud followed. Was that a door, or perhaps someone's heavy tread? The sound was certainly closer than it had been before.

"Ma, we do not have time to open these now."

"I have waited so many years." Emlyn's voice trembled with emotion. "I need to know what's in them. Why it happened. Why John-Louis…"

At any other time, Gwynnie would have comforted her mother, but there was no time now. Instead, she shook Emlyn's shoulder.

"Use your ears, Ma!"

"What?" Emlyn wasn't paying attention. She struggled with the chisel, jamming it into the padlock once again.

Gwynnie stepped away from Emlyn and grasped the candle on the effigy, making the light dance around the crypt. There was no doubt in her mind now. She could hear footsteps and the creak of the door at the top of the stairs. Someone was about to discover them.

"What is it?" Emlyn looked up at last. The chisel was still in her hand, though she no longer tried to break open the crate. She stared past Gwynnie toward the crypt steps. "Someone is coming."

"They must have heard." Gwynnie nodded at the heavy bronze plaque, face-down on the flagstone floor. If someone had been in the building, or in the Bishop's Palace next door, the crash could have rung out loud enough for them to hear.

Footsteps sounded on the stairs. Gwynnie glimpsed a pair of boots, the leather well worn, then she blew out the candle in her grasp, plunging them into darkness.

CHAPTER 25

"Cursed graverobbers," a voice croaked through the blackness. It was a man's voice, though it was impossible to discern his age from the raspy tone. "You won't rob my master's house. No, you won't. Roast on the spits of Hell, you will."

Gwynnie didn't dare put down the candle in case the bronze holder clinked and drew the man's attention. She couldn't see him in the darkness, but she could hear him inching into the crypt.

Gwynnie reached back for Emlyn's shoulder. She grasped the doublet and steered Emlyn to stand. The movement was painfully slow, the two of them trying not to make a sound.

"Damned graverobbers," the man rasped again. His voice was closer now.

Gwynnie tried to pull her mother backward, but Emlyn refused to move away from the crates at their feet.

"You'll be whipped for this!" The man smacked his lips with evident pleasure at the idea. "Put in the stocks. Flogged through the streets!"

Gwynnie strained to peer through the darkness. She could just make out his silhouette. The man no longer blocked the stairs. If they could pick up the crates and carve a silent path through the effigies, they could make their escape. She pulled on Emlyn's doublet, wondering how to communicate this plan.

"Larceny's still a *hanging* offence!" the man spat, so close now that Gwynnie could have sworn she felt his spittle upon her face. She didn't dare raise her hand to wipe it from her cheek, in case he caught the movement in the darkness. "They'll kill you for this! I tell you — argh!"

Gwynnie saw only a flailing of arms in the gloom and heard the bloodcurdling cry.

There were no more rasping threats. No more scuffling feet. Gwynnie could just make out Emlyn raising her arm again, clutching the chisel.

"No!" Gwynnie gasped, dropping the candle and scrambling to catch Emlyn's arm. She jerked her mother's elbow back. "What did you do?"

"Hanging! That man was ready to see us hanged from the neck until dead."

"Did you…?" Gwynnie couldn't say any more. She took her mother's shoulders and pushed her away. Emlyn stumbled, breathing heavily. Gwynnie crouched down. Reaching into the darkness, her hands found the man. He was breathing, the sound shallow, but on his head was something wet and warm. *Blood.*

Gwynnie scrambled to stand, wiping the blood on her hose as she turned to face Emlyn in the blackness. Unsure where she was, she accosted the shadows.

"You trying to kill him? You want to be a murderer again?"

"He's alive. I didn't hit him that hard."

"There's blood, Ma. Blood!" Gwynnie hissed, her heart thudding.

"We have to get out of here. Now." Emlyn's voice came from somewhere near Gwynnie's feet. "I can lift one. Gwynnie, you need to take the other."

Gwynnie didn't move. She was thinking of the man on the floor who lay bleeding.

"Gwynnie! You want to be caught and hanged for this?"

The fear made her active. She reached down, picked up the second crate and hurried toward the crypt stairs. Unable to see where she was going, she bumped into multiple effigies and tombs on her way. Bruised, she reached the steps just after Emlyn, who hovered on the bottom step, waiting for her.

"It was necessary," Emlyn said plainly.

"You may yet have killed him."

"He'll live. I know what it is like to kill a man. It takes more than that." She hastened up the steps, struggling with the crate.

Gwynnie stared back across the crypt. Unsure what she could do to help, she climbed the steps, following Emlyn back into the cathedral.

Silently, they made their way to the side door in the northern transept and stepped out into the cemetery. As they reached the gate, Emlyn slipped out without a sound. Gwynnie hesitated.

When Emlyn was far enough away, disappearing down a darkened street, Gwynnie took the opportunity to kick the wooden gate shut as loudly as she could. A dog barked, disturbing the peaceful night air, and voices soon followed.

She ran, swinging the crate across her chest as she caught up with her mother. Emlyn's face was wild in the moonlight as they hid down an alleyway.

"Did you do that?" Emlyn demanded. "Why, Gwynnie? Why?"

"Because I am not you, Ma," Gwynnie shot back. "I won't leave a man to die alone without help."

Emlyn's cheeks were flushed with rage, but nothing more was said between them. They took off down the road together, Gwynnie sprinting and Emlyn limping on behind her.

"Quick, get inside." Gwynnie was breathless as she nodded at the door of the White Hart's stable.

She held the door open with her foot, allowing Emlyn in first, then hurried inside herself. She put down her crate, bolted the stable door shut, then picked up the crate and moved toward the mezzanine level where they had made their beds the last two nights. Emlyn had dropped her own crate at the foot of the ladder and was now struggling to clamber up, her exhaustion and aching limbs slowing her down. Gwynnie pushed her up the last few rungs, then scampered back down for the crates. When she was done, they were both on their knees, staring at one another and panting.

Gwynnie looked down to see blood on her hose and doublet. With a strangled cry, she stood and marched across the boards, tearing the clothes off her body.

"Miting, it had to be done —"

"Do not say a word to me."

"Have you never done what had to be done? Never hurt another to survive?"

Gwynnie didn't answer. She could remember all too vividly the way she had hurt Daundelyon, the Spanish spy, to save Tombstone's life. She was capable of violence. But what had happened tonight had not been necessary.

"We could have crept out of that crypt," she insisted, her voice shaking. She threw off the bloodied clothes and reached for a bucket of water they had placed there earlier that day. She washed her body, her face, the back of her neck, getting rid of all signs of sweat and blood. "We could have escaped him without shedding a drop of blood." She dried herself on a cloth then reached for a woollen shift, pulling it over her head and praying it would offer some warmth.

Emlyn had lit candles and was placing them around the wooden boards, filling the space with a pale, creamy light.

"Ma? Are you listening to me?" Gwynnie found a thick blanket and pulled it tight around her shoulders, turning to face her mother.

Emlyn had a small plank of wood and had pressed it into the gap between the lid of the crate and the base, trying to prise it open. "This isn't working. I need that lock pick of yours. Come, Gwynnie. Quickly!"

Gwynnie stared at her mother. Emlyn was no longer the woman who had pulled leeches off her and nursed her by the fire. She was a woman possessed. Her face was flushed, her dark hair wild about her ears. She didn't even look away from the crate.

Gwynnie reached for her discarded doublet and pulled out the rod hidden inside the sleeve, then handed it to Emlyn. "You didn't have to hurt him."

"One day, you'll see how necessary it was."

"I hurt a man once, Ma. *That* was necessary, but what you did…" She broke off.

Emlyn glanced her way then quickly returned to her task. Driving the rod into the loop of the padlock, she pressed down on her good hand. The padlock broke apart. She inhaled sharply and lifted the lid. Her eyes practically glowed as she stared into the crate.

Gwynnie hid her face in her hands. She told herself she did not want to see, that the jewels and treasure in that crate had no pull on her, but they did. A yearning grew in her stomach, a desperation to see.

"Oh my," Emlyn gasped. "What jewels! Gwynnie, you know what this is, don't you? *This* is the sort of hoard we were hunting last year. A hoard that could mean we'll never have to steal again." She laughed; it was delirious and full of excitement. "There's gold, such gold — Spanish gold, by the look of these crucifixes. Rubies, too. And is that … a sapphire? Ha! A medallion — the king's medallion. You need to see this, miting."

Gwynnie sank down in a corner of the stable. The treasure may have meant that Emlyn never needed to steal again, but at what cost? Would that man live or die?

"This could easily buy us our new lives, Gwynnie," Emlyn exclaimed. "We could reach France. Buy a house. Imagine that! We could *own* our own lodgings! Such things have been but cloudy dreams." She lifted the rod and moved to the second crate. This one was more difficult to get into, the padlock being smaller and more neatly hewn. In the end, Emlyn's bad arm made it too difficult, and she approached Gwynnie with the crate, placing it by her feet. "Help me, dearest."

Woodenly, Gwynnie took the rod from Emlyn. She placed the rod into the padlock and pushed her weight down upon it. Abruptly, it broke apart with a shattering of metal.

Emlyn turned the crate back toward herself, lifted the lid and reached inside. There were coins, such gleaming coins that Gwynnie's eyes hurt to look at them. Each one was marked on one side with an image of the king's head. Emlyn let them dance across her palms and between her fingers.

"Think of the food we can eat," she whispered. "The banquets we'll have."

"You said you'd only take what you needed. You're not going to keep all of it, are you?"

"Of course not," Emlyn said dismissively. "I'll only take what I need."

Gwynnie wanted to believe her. Underneath the coins, she spied some papers. They looked like letters, their red wax seals broken.

Emlyn lifted out the letters and passed them to Gwynnie.

"What do they say?" she asked as she continued to toy with the coins. She looked up, her brows knitting together when she saw Gwynnie had not moved. "Read them, miting. If there's a reason Titus killed your father, it will be in those letters."

Gwynnie sighed. "Ma, have you ever thought that he may have just killed my father to have this treasure to himself? Look at it all." Gwynnie motioned toward the jewels that glistened like liquid sun and the coins in Emlyn's grasp. "You're giddy with excitement. Is it so mad to think that it went to Titus's head? That he longed to be like a king himself, to banquet and feast, and never worry about money again?"

"That's not what happened." Emlyn shook her head. "I told you, Titus talked of something they had discovered. Something they could use to make someone pay them, so their coffers would never run empty again. He was speaking of blackmail, Gwynnie. But blackmail over what?" She nodded down at the letters. "Please, I have to know. What do they say?"

Gwynnie looked down at the papers, uncertain what she was searching for. She saw a letter from Cromwell that was written in such elaborate cursive script that it would need deciphering. There was a letter from the late Queen Catherine too. Gwynnie shuddered. She did not want to read that letter any more than she wished to read Cromwell's. As she unfurled another letter, something fell out and landed in her lap. It was a necklace, with a diamond in the centre and thin gold wiring in the shape of a fleur-de-lis emblem. She and Emlyn stared at the jewel before Gwynnie turned her eyes to the letter. Oddly, it was not signed with a name, merely an initial — *G.*

CHAPTER 26

"What does it say?" Emlyn asked.

"It's dated 1521," Gwynnie whispered. The handwriting was rushed, but legible all the same. Gwynnie read the first two lines. A creeping sense of unease made the hairs on her neck stand on end.

"Dearest? What is it?" Emlyn asked, concern in her voice.

Gwynnie read aloud from the letter. "*Your Majesty. I have carried out what you have asked of me. Rest assured that what passed shall never cross my lips. It shall never be spoken of to another, nor shall this quill write of such things again, only now do I write to confirm that it is done. Valeriana Moreau will not breathe again. Her treacherous heart was stopped today by these two hands. None saw me. Even Moreau was unaware of the face of the man who took her life. It was done as you asked, though. I told her why she died as I took the last breath from her. I strangled her…*" Gwynnie trailed off and looked at her mother in shock as Emlyn stared back at her.

"Go on, Gwynnie," Emlyn urged. "Read the rest."

"*I strangled her,*" Gwynnie continued, "*and I whispered that it was revenge for her betrayal of you. That no English king would allow a French spy to infiltrate his bedchamber and live to tell the tale. She clawed to survive. It's true; I bear the scratches. I believe she would have begged to live if she could have spoken in those final few moments. I enclose as proof of her death the diamond that King Francis of France bestowed upon her. I hear it is worth a fortune, but may it be a lasting treasure of your victory over the King of France and his spies. Valeriana Moreau will not spy on the English or your good self again. Today, I watched from the shadows as she was interred in her coffin. The King of France deigned to attend the service himself. He shed tears for her. If the rumours I heard today are indeed true, then your suspicions were well-founded, my lord, for she was as much his bedfellow as she was your own. Now, she will not betray your secrets to your enemy again. I await your payment. I shall remain in Dover until I hear from your envoy. Once I have the money you promised me, I shall be gone. I shall flee from this land, and as I vowed to you before, you shall never see my face nor hear of this sorry tale again. It was my honour to carry out this task for you. I do it in the name of God, in the name of the one he anointed our ruler on earth, in your name, Your Majesty.*"

Gwynnie dropped the letter into her lap. "He signs off with merely an initial, G."

"A letter … from a murderer?" Emlyn's voice was low.

"He is no ordinary murderer, if you could ever use such a phrase," Gwynnie replied. "He is an assassin." She gestured toward the letter. "He carried out this killing in the name of *King Henry*." She shivered, thinking of the unctuous, flattering words and how the killer had described the murder with relish. He had enjoyed the death.

Reluctant to think of it, Gwynnie brushed the letter from her lap and let it drop onto the boards. Emlyn scrambled to pick it up.

"The person Titus wanted to blackmail was the king — to demand more money to keep this murder a secret," Emlyn murmured.

Gwynnie frowned. "It can hardly be the first time a king has ordered the assassination of a spy."

"Yet this woman was not just a spy but the King of France's *bedfellow*. How much more of a betrayal is that?"

Gwynnie thought of the king, then pictured her father — the gentle man who had taught her to read and write, who used to dance with Emlyn in the evenings at their lodgings, his laughter filling the rafters. *He* had died at Titus's hand, and for what?

Because the king had ordered the murder of a woman. And because of the scrap of parchment that was now clutched in Emlyn's hand.

"This is why John-Louis died." Emlyn held the letter out, her hand shaking. "Because of *this*."

Gwynnie felt her breath quickening as she stared at the parchment. "Greed," she muttered darkly. "All because of Titus's greed."

Emlyn folded up the letter and returned it to the crate. She looked rather ill, her skin grey and her shoulders hunched forward.

"That is the best place for it." Gwynnie nodded at the crate. "Better yet to destroy it."

"Destroy it?" Emlyn's head jerked up.

"Ma…" Gwynnie searched her mother's eyes. "What good can come from keeping that letter? Better to be rid of it. It has already caused two deaths, Pa's and Titus's."

"It's proof of what the king did. Of murder," Emlyn said, her voice dark.

"The king is responsible for much murder. Adding another to his name will hardly do much good."

Emlyn didn't answer. Gwynnie noticed that she hadn't released the crate.

"Ma, tell me you are not thinking of blackmail of your own? Tell me you do not intend to use that letter?"

"Of course not!" Emlyn spluttered. "There are enough jewels and coins here for a happy life, without such tactics."

Gwynnie sat forward, a new fear rippling through her. "You agreed to give away what you did not need, Ma. Surely you will not keep all these coins and jewels for yourself?"

"No, no. You are right." Emlyn sighed. "As tempting as it is, miting, even I know I do not need such a fortune." She chuckled and reached back into the open crate full of jewels. "Quite something, though, is it not? To stare at such riches?"

Gwynnie looked down, finding Valeriana Moreau's diamond brooch still in her lap. She picked it up, her fingers running delicately over the shining stone. There was a longing deep in her gut when she thought of the food such a jewel could purchase, the home too. Slowly, she lifted the lid of the crate and placed it down on top of the incriminating letter it accompanied.

"It is tempting," Gwynnie admitted, her eyes falling upon the other crate. "Yet sense prevails. A quarter of what is there could set you up for life, Ma. They are not half-cut stones or poor imitations. These are *real* jewels."

"I know, dearest, I know." Emlyn released the crate and stood, moving across to the basin of water. Slowly, she changed, dropping the man's clothes she had worn beside Gwynnie's. "In the early hours, I shall drop those bloodstained clothes in the river. We do not want anyone to find them."

Gwynnie screwed her eyes shut as she thought of the man that they had left injured in the crypt of St Paul's Cathedral. Surely someone had found him by now. Perhaps they had taken him home, to a wife and children who were terrified for his safety, praying that he would survive his wounds.

"You need some sleep," Emlyn whispered as she passed Gwynnie, patting the top of her head. "Come, let us hide these. Then we can rest."

The clothes were bundled into a bag, ready to be dumped in the morning. The crates they pressed into the wall of the stable, high up near the rafters. Their wooden frames matched the wall so well, it would be hard for anyone to notice them who did not know they were there. Eventually, Gwynnie laid her head down on a hay bale to sleep. She heard Emlyn's soft snores as she drifted off, but Gwynnie could find no such peace.

She stared at the rafters, glimpsing spiders weaving webs in the darkness. Every now and then, she glanced at the crates nestled in their hiding place. She had no wish to peer inside them again, knowing that the contents had led to her father's death.

"Pa," she whispered aloud, closing her eyes tight. She was tempted to rise early in the morning and drop the whole lot in the River Thames, so it could never cause any more bloodshed. Yet what good would it do? At least now, the jewels could pay for a new life for Emlyn.

As Gwynnie eventually drifted off to sleep, she pictured the life Emlyn would have, somewhere in France in a little thatched cottage. It would be a simple life, one where Emlyn could buy food from the market like everyone else, and she wouldn't have to steal bread and apples just to survive.

There was a noise in the darkness. Gwynnie heard it distinctly. She lifted her chin just an inch, her ears straining.

Feet scuffled softly on the wooden boards. Whoever was there was trying not to make a sound, perhaps walking on tiptoe.

Gwynnie opened her eyes. It was still dark, the sun not yet risen, yet as her eyes adjusted to the gloom Gwynnie could see a figure moving about. It was Emlyn. She had dressed in the garb of a fine woman once again, the red silk shimmering in the poor light, and she had donned a large, wide-brimmed headdress to hide her face. She turned and Gwynnie shut her eyes, pretending to still be asleep.

Emlyn continued to tiptoe around the boards, inching back and forth. Gwynnie supposed she should have sat up and declared herself awake so that Emlyn didn't need to creep about anymore, yet something kept her flat on the floor.

There was the crackle of parchment and the creak of wood, perhaps coming from the lid of one of the crates. A clink, maybe jewel on jewel, or coins falling together. A second creak of wood, then all was quiet.

Gwynnie dared to open her eyes.

Emlyn had inched forward. She stuffed something into a small tapestry bag and pulled it over her shoulder, moving carefully toward the ladder. Any thought Gwynnie might have had that Emlyn was leaving early to dump the bloodstained clothes in the river was proved wrong, for the tapestry bag was far too small, barely bigger than the span of Emlyn's hands.

Emlyn turned to descend the ladder, forcing Gwynnie to close her eyes again. She listened, waiting until Emlyn had reached the floor below, then she opened them. Emlyn was creeping out of the stable, the door creaking open and shut behind her. Gwynnie sat up.

She acted fast, pulling on her maid's gown, tying the kirtle around her waist and snatching up her coif from the floor. Her boots took the longest, and she tangled the laces in her haste. As she stood, ready to dart toward the ladder and follow Emlyn, she glanced back at the crates they had hidden by the wall. Dashing toward them, she lifted the lid to the crate of jewels. It was still full, though if any were missing, Gwynnie had no way of knowing. She moved to the second crate, lifting the lid to find the coins and letters stacked together. However, the letter about Valeriana Moreau and her diamond brooch were not on top, where Gwynnie had left them the night before. She searched the crate, moving the coins back and forth, but could not find the brooch. She even sifted quickly through the other letters, to be certain the assassin's note was not there.

"What are you up to, Ma?" Gwynnie whispered to herself. She let the lid of the crate drop and ran toward the ladder.

CHAPTER 27

Gwynnie caught sight of Emlyn as she walked around the White Hart Inn, heading into the back roads of Shoreditch. Pulling her coif low over her head, Gwynnie followed at a distance, careful not to get too close to her mother. The grey light was starting to lift, the first rays of sunlight shining upon the frosted rooftops. As they walked, the streets came alive. People left their houses, yawning and hurrying about their business. Horses rode up and down, pulling carts behind them. Gwynnie barely heard the distant cries of 'Merry Christmas' and 'Yuletide greetings'. Her attention was fixed on Emlyn, watching her as an eagle would its quarry.

They soon left the streets of Shoreditch behind, heading into the city of London itself and toward the river. They had been walking for at least an hour when they neared London Bridge and the iced river.

Today, there were not so many stalls set up on the bridge. Instead, the market was being erected on the ice itself. There were great cries of 'Frost Fair!' as the early-morning risers descended the bank and began their tasks. Stalls were set up in great lines, a path between them cordoned off with ropes and small wooden stakes. Already there were heralds carrying the king's standard, though they yawned and leaned on their poles.

Emlyn barely cast a glance at the preparations for the Frost Fair and the royal parade. Instead, she crossed London Bridge, to the southern side of the river. Gwynnie followed her, careful to keep a distance between them.

Crossing into the southern streets of London, Emlyn headed along the bank, walking purposefully toward the very place that

Gwynnie had fled just a few days before — Greenwich Palace, its red roof and spiral chimney pots standing tall in the white morning light.

They had now been walking for two hours. The sun had firmly risen, the day had begun, and the streets were full of people. Emlyn glanced over her shoulder, and Gwynnie fell behind a group of milkmaids who were distributing pails between them. Without looking up, one of them passed a pail to Gwynnie, mistaking her for one of their group in her coif. She moved the pail to her shoulder, concealing the side of her face as she followed Emlyn.

As they neared the palace, Emlyn smoothed down the skirt of her gown and halted to peer into a nearby window, adjusting her headdress to ensure there were no loose curls. Gwynnie was waylaid by a passerby, who asked for some milk to be poured into the pail he carried. Gwynnie completed the task, taking the few coins offered to her while keeping Emlyn firmly in sight.

Soon enough, Emlyn carried on, and Gwynnie followed once again. Emlyn headed toward the main gate on the west side of the palace. She stood straight, adjusting the bodice of her fine gown as she approached the gate, guarded by two yeomen. Gwynnie walked down the street a little, watching as Emlyn talked to the guards. She could not hear their conversation, nor the reason Emlyn had for entering the palace. Though she had the appearance of a fine lady, she came without a horse or a carriage, surely suspicious, yet the soldiers laughed at something she said and they stepped aside, allowing her through the gate.

Hurriedly, Gwynnie walked back toward the gate. She smiled at one of the soldiers, pretending to be a little distracted by him for too long. He smiled back, rather startled by her attention, then Gwynnie forced herself to stumble, digging the toe of her boot into the cobbles beneath her.

"Oh!" she cried as the pail of milk catapulted through the air. The milk cascaded over the soldier's companion, running down his cheeks and off the brim of his hat. "You must forgive me, sir," Gwynnie called loudly, adopting a rough accent. "Don't know what I'm doing most the time. My ma says my head will fall off if I don't take better care of it."

The other soldier was chuckling away, moving to collect the bucket and help Gwynnie up.

"Clear off!" the soldier covered in milk cried.

"Oh, but you must let me help, sir. What will they say when they hear I've spilled all the milk?"

"You look a right mess," the first soldier said to his friend, offering him a cloth.

"Give me that!" The second snatched the cloth from his hand. "I'll stink of sour milk all day now."

In the midst of their argument, it was all too easy for Gwynnie to slip in through the gate, carrying her pail. She glanced back once, but neither man noticed her. The first soldier was too busy laughing as the second tried to wipe the milk from his face.

Gwynnie hurried forward, her eyes scanning the garden of the palace. There was no sign of Emlyn. Cursing under her breath, she headed past Friars' Church. She pulled her coif low around her face, nervous that Fitzroy or one of his men, Amaro or Humphrey, might glimpse her.

She was about to head toward the courtyards in the main body of the palace when she caught a glimpse of the fine red skirt of Emlyn's gown. It had flicked past one of the gravestones, heading in the direction of the orchard and garden. Carrying the empty pail in front of her to give herself an excuse for walking about the palace, Gwynnie hastened to follow. Soon enough, she caught sight of Emlyn again, marching through the orchard. Gwynnie halted behind the frosty trees, ensuring Emlyn had ample time to enter the tiltyard before she dared to follow.

Peering through the gate into the tiltyard, Gwynnie saw Emlyn step through the door leading to the lawyers' chambers.

"Ma," Gwynnie muttered darkly under her breath, "tell me you are not here to do what I think you are."

She took off at a run, no longer caring if she was seen. She sprinted to the door, dropped the pail outside and bolted inside. She ran down the corridor just in time to see the door of Tombstone's chamber closing. Emlyn must have gone inside.

Gwynnie skidded to a halt, breathing heavily. She reached out, her hand hovering over the door handle, when the sound of voices reached her from inside.

"Do you not remember what I vowed before?" Tombstone's voice was clear and firm. "If you walked this palace's corridors again, I'd have to arrest you."

"Oh tush, we have other things to speak of now."

"Emlyn…" Tombstone huffed angrily. Gwynnie pressed her ear to the door. "We had an agreement. I made a vow to your daughter not to go after you if you stayed away. I have kept your secret and ensured that none but I know the identity of the Shadow Cutpurses. You risk all that now by just walking into my office chamber. Why?"

"Because we have matters to discuss," replied Emlyn. "Come, look at this." There was the crackle of parchment. "It makes for quite an interesting read."

"I thought you couldn't read?"

"Another read it for me."

Tombstone didn't answer.

Gwynnie shifted soundlessly by the door, praying that Tombstone would not jump to the conclusion that it was *her* who had read the letter for her mother.

"God have mercy," Tombstone hissed after a few moments.

"It's quite something, is it not?" Emlyn replied. "Is it true? Was Valeriana Moreau a French spy?"

"That is not something I can know." Tombstone's words were quick. "This was before my time here in the palace, but I have heard the name."

"What do you know of her?"

"She was mistress to the King of France. I had heard a rumour that she was mistress to King Henry too, though it had merely been gossip. She was at the Field of the Cloth of Gold with King Francis in 1520. It's said that this was where King Henry met her."

Gwynnie had heard of such an event. Samuel had spoken of it once, and had said a painting of the magnificent summit in France between the two rival kingdoms existed somewhere in the corridors of Hampton Court Palace. The two courts of King Francis and King Henry had come together for feasts, tournaments and religious services to celebrate their alliance, though nothing formal was ever written down. Samuel had chuckled, saying he'd heard that the show of friendship had been somewhat soured when the two kings had wrestled, and King Henry had lost.

"And?" Emlyn asked now. "What more do you know of her?"

"Very little. I heard that she died. I did not know she had been killed."

"By an assassin. On the *king's* orders."

The room fell silent. Gwynnie itched to grasp the handle and fling open the door, to accost Emlyn and beg to know why she was doing this, but curiosity prevented her. How far was Emlyn willing to go in this venture?

"So it would seem," Tombstone said, his voice grave, "if the information in this letter is true. It could be a forgery."

"And this? Is this jewel not proof of Valeriana Moreau's death?"

"What is it you want, Emlyn?" Tombstone's voice had taken the dangerous tone Gwynnie had only heard a few times before.

"Money."

"Money?" Tombstone spluttered. "You think the king would pay a thief and murderer to keep quiet about this?"

"You think he would not?"

"The king would call it a matter of politics."

"Would he now?" Emlyn said, her voice rising. "Because the last I had heard, there was peace between England and France. The war of ten years ago is over. Do you truly believe the King of England would want it known that he had arranged the death of the mistress to the King of France?"

A tense silence followed.

Gwynnie's heart thudded hard. All the jewels, all the coins in those crates hidden back at the stable, they were not enough for Emlyn after all. Just like Titus, she had been tempted into seeking *more*. For all her talk of justice, of wanting to know why John-Louis had died, she had proved herself to be no different from the man she had killed.

"You would risk peace for a few coins? If war broke out, hundreds of men could die. Thousands!" Tombstone spat angrily. "Yes, you should flinch at such a thought. Or have you not thought that far ahead?"

"I do not believe it would go that far."

"Listen to yourself!" Something was slammed down with a thud. "You are considering blackmailing a man who is accustomed to ordering the death of women. A man who last year ordered his own wife's head to be cut from her body. Do you think he would be willing to pay a woman so wholly unconnected with him to stay quiet? Or do you think he would resort to the more dangerous means referenced in this very letter with which you threaten him now?"

"I think he would opt for the more convenient route. Your employer, Lord Cromwell, certainly would."

"Oh, now I see your game." There was a pause. "You do not wish this to even reach the ears of the king. You think Cromwell will pay you himself to keep quiet."

"In exchange for the letter and my silence. I hear he is an educated man. From what I saw of him last year, I know he is not afraid to bend the law, or to keep his king in ignorance, if it means the safety of his throne. Now, sir, am I wrong?"

The silence stretched. Tombstone could not refute her argument.

"You have accepted the inevitable, I see," Emlyn said, breaking the silence.

"How is it that someone like Gwynnie could come from someone like you?"

"What do you mean?" Emlyn's voice was tight.

"Gwynnie has a good heart. A thief she may be, and her underhandedness is remarkable. Yet she'd do anything for the welfare of another. She'd do anything for *you*." His words hung in the air for a moment.

"She is my daughter. I would do anything for her."

"Would you now?" asked Tombstone. "From what I see, you'd do anything for *yourself*, Emlyn. Nothing for *her*."

"I have lived my whole life for her."

"You led her into a life of thievery!"

"What else was there, when we had nothing to live on?" Emlyn's voice grew louder. "Judge me if you dare from your palace of good fortune, lawyer, but you do not know what we have been through. You do not understand the difficult decisions a mother must make so that her child may survive."

A chair moved on the other side of the door, the legs scraping against the floor.

"Gwynnie would do more for you than you would for her," said Tombstone, his voice quieter. "Of that, I have no doubt."

"You know nothing of our relationship."

"I know Gwynnie."

Gwynnie expected Emlyn to argue, but all was quiet. She could hear the sound of someone fumbling, the heavy clod of boots being put on.

"Your threat is not something I have the power to concede to," Tombstone said. "If you want money, then I shall have to take you to another to decide."

"Cromwell?"

"Cromwell," Tombstone confirmed. "He will be at the Frost Fair on the river by now. He has gone to oversee the final preparations for the king's parade." More scraping of furniture inside the chamber followed. "If you are determined to proceed with this course of action, then he will be the one to decide."

"Then I'll hold on to the letter." There was a fumble of parchment. "And I'll keep this jewel close. If Cromwell wants to protect his king, he will pay to have them from me."

"Where exactly did you find them?" Tombstone asked.

"That is my business."

"And Gwynnie's, I don't doubt," Tombstone muttered, his voice moving closer to the door. "Who else could have read the letter and told you what was in it?"

Emlyn made no attempt to hide the truth.

Gwynnie didn't bother to stand back from the door. She stood with her arms folded as it was flung open. Tombstone stood there, holding a cloak.

"Good morning, Shadow," he said with interest.

Behind him, Emlyn's eyes were wide as she and Gwynnie stared at one another.

"Good morning, Tombstone," Gwynnie responded in a level tone. She didn't take her eyes off Emlyn as she spoke. "I see my mother has come to see you. No need to tell me what was discussed. I heard every word."

CHAPTER 28

Tombstone tugged on the reins of the horse, pulling the cart to a stop on the icy cobbles that lined the riverbank. Gwynnie drew her shawl up around her neck as she looked down at the frozen river.

Much had changed since she and Emlyn had walked past that morning. The whole breadth of the river had now become a fair. There were dancers on the ice, and minstrels and pipers singing songs and waving boughs of holly. Stalls served spiced wine and mead from great pewter tankards as children ran back and forth, carrying sweetmeats and dried orange segments. In the middle of the ice was a parade on horseback. King Henry led the way, clothed richly in gold and magenta, while behind him rode Queen Jane, in a sumptuous gown that matched her husband's attire. An entire train of courtiers followed them, and crowds of people stood on either side of the ropes, waving their hands and shawls enthusiastically, and craning for a glimpse of the royal couple.

Amongst the courtiers, Gwynnie spied Fitzroy. He hardly seemed pleased by the parade, a heavy frown on his brow. Ahead of him rode Lady Mary, given pride of place in the entourage, while he had been demoted to the rear.

"Quite a sight," Emlyn said with interest from the back of the cart.

Gwynnie exchanged an uncertain look with Tombstone. "Tell me you are not going to do this," she hissed at Tombstone as Emlyn jumped down off the back of the cart.

"Do what?"

"Pay her."

"You do not wish me to give in to your mother's blackmail?"

"Has the sky begun to rain pigs? No, I do not!"

He pressed a finger to his lips, urging silence as Emlyn walked around the cart, within hearing distance.

"Yes, a sight indeed," Emlyn declared with a smile. "I imagine Lord Cromwell frequently enjoys such festivities. No doubt he wishes to maintain his position at court. He wouldn't wish for the king to be rid of him, if he were to allow a scandal to break out."

"Enough, Ma," Gwynnie snapped, jumping down from the cart and facing her mother. Emlyn's smile vanished.

"Do not look at me like that, miting."

"And do not call me that."

"It is for the best," Emlyn said in hushed tones as Tombstone paid a boy to mind the horse and headed toward the river.

"There is enough money in those crates to last many lifetimes, Ma. For what reason could you want more?" Gwynnie demanded, stepping closer to her.

"Jewels are not easy to move and sell. You know that. You always receive less money than you hope for."

"And the coins? Are they so difficult to move? Or is it just greed —"

"It is not greed."

"That is exactly what this is." Gwynnie turned her back on Emlyn and hastened to follow Tombstone. As they reached the ice, he turned to face her, shrugging off his cloak. "What are you doing? It's freezing."

"I know. Put this on." He nodded toward the court, riding between the flags that flapped in the strong wind. Fitzroy still stared forward, his brow deeply furrowed. "Hide your face as best as you can."

Gwynnie inclined her head in thanks and pulled the cloak tight around her shoulders and face, following him down onto the ice as Emlyn fell into step on her other side.

The first steps onto the ice were slippery. It took them all a few moments to find their balance, leaning forward into the wind as they made their way into the Frost Fair. Gwynnie glared at her mother, wondering what had become of the woman she had known and loved her whole life. A woman willing to plunge them all into war with France, all for the sake of a few more coins.

Tombstone led them toward a group of well-dressed men on one side of the rope. As they fell behind, Gwynnie gripped Emlyn's arm tight.

"Why are you doing this?" she hissed.

"What do you mean?"

"I mean, when did you allow greed to dominate you so?"

"You do not understand, miting."

"What do I not understand?"

"We all have our reasons, Gwynnie. Mine is not greed."

Gwynnie huffed. Perhaps Emlyn craved some sort of power over men like Cromwell and King Henry.

Gwynnie hurried to catch up with Tombstone and pulled on his arm. "Do not give in to her demands, Tombstone," she said firmly.

"I am pleased to see you do not have your mother's greedy heart."

"Of course I do not!"

"Then give me the benefit of the doubt, Shadow," Tombstone said, with the smallest of winks. "Perhaps I have another motive here."

"What are you up to?" she whispered, following as they approached Cromwell's party. Cromwell stood amongst the lawyers and council members, his back to them.

Before they reached them, Tombstone halted and turned his head. He was looking at a group of women standing by the rope. Ladies of the court, they were dressed excessively finely, with rich furs around their shoulders, elaborate headdresses, and jewels that glistened as if they too were covered in frost. There were necklaces of pearls and diamonds and earrings that dripped with emeralds. The ladies were not guarded, for all the yeomen were manning the rope, ensuring that no one advanced too close to the royal party.

"Wait over there, with the other ladies," Tombstone ordered Emlyn. "I need to talk to Cromwell alone and persuade him away from the other councillors. I'd be wary of walking up with you beside me — he may yet remember your face from when you last met."

"A fine hiding place," Emlyn replied sarcastically, but she turned to join the other ladies. She hesitated at the back of the group for a moment, before striking up an easy conversation with one of them. Soon enough, she was accepted as one of the group. Together, they waved at the royal party. The younger women pointed animatedly at the king and queen, as those of Emlyn's age tittered at their enthusiasm.

"You must have a plan," Gwynnie hissed at Tombstone. "What are you doing?"

"You shall see, soon enough." Yet he showed no sign of moving toward Cromwell and the other councillors. He simply watched Emlyn from a distance, his jaw taut.

The noise became clamorous as the royal party drew alongside them. King Henry was beaming, his mouth spread almost impossibly wide. Queen Jane sat rather demurely in her own saddle, waving softly and pulling at the rich gold cloth on her shoulders every now and then. The people thronged forward, straining against the ropes. The yeomen stood their ground, one or two thrusting their pikes forward.

"There!" Tombstone suddenly whispered.

Gwynnie followed his gaze. Unlike the other ladies in her group, Emlyn was not gawping at the king and queen. Instead, she appeared to be assisting one of the younger women, warning her she was about to lose her headdress. As she reached out, adjusting the gable hood, Emlyn's fingers dropped lower, toward the clasp of the woman's necklace.

"No, no, no," Gwynnie muttered desperately under her breath. "She has everything she needs. Why steal now?"

Tombstone let out a bark of cynical laughter. "Do you remember what I told you once, Gwynnie? There is no point in trying to save a woman who does not want to be saved." He motioned to two yeomen nearby. "You two, with me. There is a theft underway."

"You wouldn't…" Gwynnie stepped back, tripping on the hem of her cloak.

"I have no choice." The two yeomen had hurried toward him. "I need you to arrest a thief."

Gwynnie whirled around. Emlyn was pocketing the necklace, a string of pearls and rounded gold crosses on a thin wire chain. There was a flicker of gold as it was slipped into a pocket of Emlyn's skirt, vanishing from view.

"Who?" one of the yeomen asked Tombstone.

"That lady, over there." Tombstone pointed directly at Emlyn.

"No!" Gwynnie cried. She moved away, stumbling so much on her cloak that she had to throw it down on the ice to be rid of it. One of the yeomen tripped on it, landing on his knees and scrambling to stand once again. Gwynnie tried to run, her boots slipping beneath her.

At the sudden commotion, a few people turned to look, but not Emlyn. She was now applauding along with the other ladies, her eyes firmly fixed on the king and queen, a victorious smile on her lips.

"Gwynnie!" Tombstone called, moving toward her.

She dug her toes into the ice and bolted forward. She scampered across the river, reaching the group of ladies and skidding to such an unwieldy stop that she ploughed headlong into Emlyn and two of the other ladies, who yelped and fell on the ice.

"I am being attacked! Who is this? Someone call for a guard!"

"What are you doing?" Gwynnie hissed angrily above the lady's calls, clinging to Emlyn as they steadied themselves together. "Is it a compulsion? An addiction? A need?"

Emlyn didn't answer, though all traces of her smile had now vanished as she stared at Gwynnie.

"He saw!" Gwynnie continued. "It was a trap. Tombstone led you here to make you steal and now..." She looked over her shoulder. The yeomen had recovered and were catching her up. "Go! Now!" She pushed at Emlyn's good arm, urging her to flee.

Emlyn spun around, but more yeomen were approaching from the other side of the ropes, rallied by the ladies' cries. Panicking, Emlyn darted under the ropes and into the middle of the royal parade. Gwynnie watched, dumbstruck, as Emlyn careered into the path of the king's own horse.

The king bellowed a curse, pulling on the reins to stop his steed from ploughing straight into her. Emlyn cowered back, arms raised, as the horse whinnied and reared up on its hind legs.

"Down, down, you beast!" the king barked, as the horse tried to throw him from its back.

The horse landed heavily on its front hooves, forcing Emlyn to scuttle back. Then it reared again.

Gwynnie couldn't hear the cracks, not at this distance, but she saw them as the horse bucked and reared repeatedly. The cracks snaked through the ice beneath the horse's hooves, spreading outward like cobwebs. They extended beneath the royal party, and under Emlyn, who had frozen to the spot, her eyes on those fractures.

"Get to the king!" cried a voice as the ice broke apart and the horse's front hooves dropped into the water.

King Henry was thrown from the animal's back in a cascading display of gold and magenta cloth.

Gwynnie ran forward, pulling herself over the ropes, though she was not heading for the king. She spared but one glance for the royal party.

Queen Jane was surrounded by yeomen who were escorting her away, as another tried to calm her now bucking horse. Behind them was Fitzroy. He was calling to the king in panic, then his eyes slid away.

Through the chaos of wild arms and screaming faces as the ice shattered beneath the crowds' feet, Fitzroy's eyes met Gwynnie's. There was a shift in his expression. The fear vanished, replaced by something altogether more menacing. His horse inched forward, in her direction, before it was met by a wall of people, all trying to run to safety.

Gwynnie knew she should do the same, or she might just plunge through the ice. But instead, she scurried forward, squeezing through the tiny gaps she found between yeomen and fine ladies who were struggling through the crowd in their large farthingales.

The ice around Emlyn was now breaking more quickly. She stared down and took a step back. There was an almighty crack, then Emlyn dropped through the ice like a stone and vanished into the water.

CHAPTER 29

"Ma! Ma!" Gwynnie screamed as she scrambled to the edge of the hole. Sliding down onto her knees, she peered into the belly of the River Thames. Without thinking of the cold, she plunged a hand into the freezing water, reaching desperately for her mother.

"Ma!" Gwynnie cried again, but no hand gripped hers, and no one came to her aid.

All around her, people had fallen through the ice. There were flailing arms and piercing screams, as soldiers threw aside pikes and dived into the water to pull people out. Horses bolted, their hooves scattering freezing powder behind them as they threw riders from their saddles. The ice had split down the centre of the river, forming one long, thin crack.

"Get the king to the palace!" someone barked nearby.

King Henry was shivering. He too had dropped through the ice, though only his legs looked wet. He cursed at everyone within ten feet, and demanded to be given another horse at once. He was limping toward the riverbank, yeomen and the court fussing around him.

Gwynnie could no longer see Fitzroy or the queen, or even Tombstone. Without knowing what else to do, she plunged her arm further into the water.

"Please, please," she begged under her breath, wishing with all her might that Emlyn would somehow hear her, that she would swim to the surface in that heavy gown and be able to break free.

There was a thud beneath Gwynnie's knees. She pulled her arm out and looked down to see what was moving against the ice beneath her.

It was Emlyn, her face deathly white. She was driving her fists repeatedly up against the ice, trying to break it.

Gwynnie lay down on the ice. Reaching into the water and under the sheet of ice, she grabbed hold of Emlyn's shoulder. With a groan of effort, Gwynnie pulled Emlyn toward the opening.

Emlyn was much taller and bigger than her. It was no easy feat to heave her up through that gap. The heavy gown was streaming with water as Emlyn landed on the ice, coughing and spluttering. Her headdress and the outer layer of her skirt were gone — probably now at the bottom of the Thames.

"It won't hold our weight," Gwynnie said, grasping Emlyn's hand.

The ice was still cracking. She could hear it now, like a hissing whisper spreading beneath them.

"Move!"

Emlyn scrambled forward on her hands and knees. Gwynnie didn't know how far they travelled. There were too many legs running for the riverbank, too much shouting. With so many people in the way, Gwynnie couldn't even stand. She just kept urging Emlyn on, when she felt the ground shift beneath her.

She didn't even look down as the ice cracked around her. As she plummeted into the water, the sudden cold stole the breath from her body.

It was like the night she had fallen into the Thames at the boathouse, only much worse. The shock of cold was so paralysing that she could not move her limbs. She tried to breathe, and water shot up her nose.

Suddenly, she flew upwards. Her head broke the surface of the water and she inhaled fresh air. Someone's arm was around her waist, carrying her away, as if she were nothing more than a tapestry bag.

They were at the edge of the river, and she was tossed onto the riverbank. She landed on her hands and knees on the frosted grass, coughing and retching.

"Gwynnie!" It was Emlyn's voice. She was wiping the water from her mouth and holding her hair back.

Gwynnie lifted her head. Behind her, on the ice, stood Tombstone. He was splattered with water, his arm drenched from where he had reached in to pull her out, his cheeks pink with the effort.

"Tomb—" She halted abruptly as the ice cracked beneath Tombstone and he too started to slip into the water. The second crack threw many who stood at the edge back down into the icy depths. Some scrambled for safety; others disappeared.

Someone reached past Gwynnie, pushing her aside. Winded, she raised her head.

Beside her, Emlyn's arm was outstretched. She had grabbed Tombstone's hand just in time to stop him from going under. His eyes were wide as he clung on to Emlyn, climbing to safety on the bank. When he let go, they just stared at one another.

Gwynnie retched again, the water rising up her throat. When she felt fingers in her hair, she thought it was Emlyn again, holding back the tendrils for her. The sudden jerk of her head showed her how mistaken she was.

Her neck twinged painfully as she found herself looking into Fitzroy's eyes.

His face was red with rage. Behind him stood his men, Amaro and Humphrey. He dragged her to her feet by her hair, as if she were a dog grabbed by the scruff of its neck.

"What are you doing?" Emlyn shouted. "Release her at once!"

"Enough!" Tombstone grabbed Gwynnie's arm and jerked her out of Fitzroy's hold.

She stepped behind Tombstone and looked around quickly, but no one had noticed their altercation. Most were too busy pulling their friends and family out of the water. Yeoman guards swam out, trying to rescue those who were struggling. Others were scrambling up the banks and, in the distance, Gwynnie could just see the heralds of the royal party, leading the way back to the palace.

"Hand her over," Fitzroy growled, his voice deep. "Lawyer, you will do as you are instructed."

"No more secrets, no more pretending." Tombstone stood between them. "Your father may be content to try and fool the whole court, but that does not change who you really are."

"You don't know me —"

"You think I would forget your face? It is the face of a murderer," Tombstone hissed.

Amaro and Humphrey surged forward, but Fitzroy held up his hand. He was breathing heavily, his shoulders shaking. It was rather like the moment Gwynnie had first seen Fitzroy, on the cusp of losing his temper and lashing out.

"Hand her over and this ends!" Fitzroy barked, spittle forming at the corners of his mouth.

"Lay a hand on her and I'll ensure that you face the noose for what you did to Florian Battersby and Jerome Woodville."

"You forget yourself." Fitzroy stepped forward, his face a few inches from Tombstone's. "As you say, no more secrets… You think you can see the son of a king hang from a rope?"

"And you forget yourself," Tombstone said evenly. "You are not the son of a king, *Lord Hereford*, are you?"

Fitzroy stared at Tombstone.

"Hurt her, and I'll see those crimes are laid at your door and that you swing for them. You have been warned." Tombstone's voice was full of quiet malice.

He turned on his heel and reached for Gwynnie's arm, helping her up the riverbank and toward the path. She was only too happy to go, Emlyn close behind them. She glanced back, watching as Fitzroy held up his hand, giving the silent order for Amaro and Humphrey not to follow.

"Do you think he'll listen?" Gwynnie asked as they hurried along behind the others heading back to the palace.

"For now. But when he collects himself, when all is calm again and he remembers he still has the power of the king behind him, he will come after us. Quick. Let's get you hidden."

There was much commotion in the palace grounds, and none looked their way as they slipped toward the lawyers' chambers. They entered Tombstone's office, where he lit a fire and told them not to leave as he departed.

Gwynnie sat by the fire, extending her hands toward the flames. Emlyn hovered by the window, shivering in her sodden gown and looking tempted to flee.

"You want to die of the cold?" Tombstone's voice disturbed them a few minutes later. "Flee now without warming up and you will." He dropped a small coffer he had evidently gone to fetch from his chamber. "These are spare clothes. Put them on while I send for some food." He left once again, closing the door behind him.

Emlyn crept toward the coffer and lifted the lid nervously. When she found only clothes inside, she passed some to Gwynnie and they changed. Gwynnie had to roll up Tombstone's long sleeves and hose to make them fit her arms and legs. She didn't bother with a doublet but pulled on a thick fur cloak, huddling as close to the fire as she could. The clothes fitted Emlyn much better. She sat in one of the two caquetoire chairs by the fire, pulling her dark hair over her shoulder to dry it near the flames. Gwynnie watched her closely.

"Why did you do it, Ma?" she asked. "Two crates, one full of jewels, another full of coins, and you were about to blackmail the king. Why take a woman's necklace as well?"

Emlyn blinked. For the first time, she looked uncertain. She stared into the fire, the flames reflected in her eyes. "Desperation and hunger became a way of life. You feed off the possibility of *more.* I can't always stop myself, miting. It's just who I am."

"It's an obsession," Gwynnie snapped. She tutted and looked away. They sat in silence until the door eventually opened.

Tombstone was not alone. Samuel was behind him, carrying a trencher of bread and steaming soup.

"Thank you, Samuel," Tombstone said. He moved a small table nearer to the fire, so the trencher could be placed down.

Samuel hesitated when he saw Emlyn. Tombstone took the tray from him, placing it down on the table. When Emlyn said nothing, Samuel moved to Gwynnie's side and laid a hand on her shoulder.

"You all right, lass?"

"As well as I can be," she whispered.

"Tombstone and I have arranged it all. For the next few nights, you shall be in the chamber beside Brynne and me. He says someone is looking for you." He glanced in Tombstone's direction. Gwynnie knew that Samuel didn't entirely trust Tombstone, though over the last few weeks he had learned that he was a good man. "We'll make sure they don't find you."

"Thank you, Samuel." Gwynnie placed her hand over his. He promised there was more food if they needed it, then moved to leave.

In the doorway he glanced back at Tombstone, who was laying a cauldron of water on the fire.

"They'll be safe here," Tombstone assured him, acknowledging his concern. Samuel nodded then left, his footsteps echoing down the corridor. Tombstone made the same warming tea he had made for Gwynnie before. She hurried to eat the soup and drink the tea, but Emlyn was much slower, picking at her food. Tombstone sat in the opposite chair by the fire, watching Emlyn. "Why did you do it?"

"I have just told Gwynnie," Emlyn said, sounding tired. "It's who I am. I'm a thief."

"Not that." Tombstone's words made Emlyn look up from her food. "Why pull me out of the water?"

Gwynnie paused with the tea halfway to her lips.

"I may have killed a man in my time, but it doesn't mean I'm fond of death."

"You might have just saved my life," Tombstone remarked, his voice light.

"And you saved Gwynnie's." Emlyn pointed at him. "I watched you do it. With no concern for yourself, you stood on the very edge of the ice to reach in and pull her out. It could have broken beneath you, but you did it anyway."

"Well, I owed her that." Tombstone smiled a little at Gwynnie.

"Ah, that's the only reason you did it, is it?" Gwynnie said wryly. "A debt repaid?"

"I would have done it anyway."

Emlyn nodded slowly, returning to her food.

"Emlyn, I cannot speak to Cromwell nor the king about Valeriana Moreau." His level words made Emlyn's shoulders rise a little. "I know enough about their ruthlessness, most of all of the king's. You'd be dead before any money was paid to you. I will not see you dead because of something I have done."

Emlyn sat back in her chair, staring at him. "You are a curious man. You value life. Not every man is like that."

"Nor every woman." Tombstone rubbed his face. "You are still a murderer, Emlyn. You admitted that much to me once before. I am a lawyer. It is my duty to see you arrested for such a crime, and yet…"

Gwynnie stopped chewing her food, watching with parted lips.

"I have given you food, clothes and warmed you by my fire. Tell me what happened."

"What happened?" Emlyn spluttered.

"If you do not want me to arrest you for murder, then I need to know why you did what you did."

CHAPTER 30

Gwynnie had drained the bowl of soup by the time Emlyn had told the first part of her tale. She had informed Tombstone that her husband, John-Louis, and Titus were the Shadow Cutpurses. She had told the story of their visit to Southampton, where they had spied the king's ship and stolen aboard one night when the royal party were on land. She had described how John-Louis had gone missing, how Titus had shut the door in her face and refused to help find him.

"You searched for him?" Tombstone asked. He glanced momentarily at Gwynnie, but she avoided meeting his eye.

It felt strange, cold and oddly distant, to have her father spoken of in such a way.

"I wandered the streets for hours." Emlyn's voice was hollow. "I found him, eventually, in a back street near London Bridge. He…" She looked briefly at Gwynnie. "He had been stabbed. Left to die."

Gwynnie carefully placed the spoon in her bowl and slid it away. She felt rather sick and wished she had not eaten so much.

"What did you do?" Tombstone asked.

"I … I tried to make him stand. I talked of taking him to a physician, an apothecary, or someone. He could barely talk, but he kept muttering how cold he was. He could not stand up." She stared down at her lap. "I sat there in a silent street, my husband's head in my lap as he bled to death. He became heavy as a stone in my arms. I don't know how long I sat there."

Gwynnie felt tears prick her eyes. She didn't dare lift her head to look at either of them, in case she gave way and let her tears slide down her cheeks.

"Before he died, he said that Titus had done it. Titus was the one who had killed him."

"So, you went after Titus?"

"I did. When I knocked on his door, but he wouldn't even open it. The next day, all was quiet in his lodgings. I broke in and found Marie and all her clothes had gone. She had left him." Emlyn paused. "I watched his lodgings. Eventually, Titus left in the middle of the night. At the time, I didn't know where he was going, though now I think I do. He was heading in the direction of St Paul's Cathedral. I think he was going to retrieve the loot. He stole across the rooftops at first. He was being followed by a nightwatchman. Maybe he had stolen again that night, or the nightwatchman was wary of him. I just don't know." She turned toward the fire, watching the flames dance in the grate. "I followed him along the Thames at a distance. I was in men's clothes. It was easier to sneak through the shadows. I had thought he'd lost the nightwatchman when I finally caught up with him. He ended up in a corner of the dockyard, looking out over the water. The damn man was smiling. That's what broke me." She shuddered. "You can never understand rage and the desire for revenge until it engulfs you. It's like fire spreading through your body."

She breathed out heavily. "I approached him, demanded he speak to me. I told him I knew that he had killed John-Louis — that I had watched his old friend die, held him as he'd bled his last. Titus showed no emotion. He didn't *care.* The man who had professed to be John-Louis' friend never really had been, had he? It was all about the loot," she hissed as angry tears slid down her face. "I shall never forget the way he looked at me. He tried to march away. He told me to let things lie, that everything was for the best. *The best!*" she spat sharply. "He had lost nothing. I had lost *everything.*"

Gwynnie struggled to hold back her own tears. She had never heard her mother talk of this moment.

"I asked to know what it was all for, if it was just about the loot. He shook me, then thrust me away from him. I hit my head on a wall and nearly fell into the water. The victory in his eyes made me sick." Emlyn's hands fell limp between her knees. "He tried to walk away then. All I could think of was John-Louis. How his eyes had grown still, staring back at me. And then … it happened."

"What happened?" Tombstone whispered.

"He had a blade in his belt. I took him from behind, wrapping my arm around his neck. I … I didn't want him to escape," Emlyn stammered. "I couldn't bear the thought of him walking away after what he had done. We were almost the same height. It made it difficult for him to throw me off. He staggered back against me, and I reached around, grabbing the dagger from his belt. I brought it up, threatening him. There was a moment where it just hovered in the air by his throat … and then…"

Neither Tombstone nor Gwynnie said anything. They both stared at Emlyn.

"Then he threw his body back against me. We landed on our backs on the docks. I kept trying to wrestle the blade free from him. We ended up on the riverbank, covered in mud, then I…" She lifted her hand, the fingers pointed together like a blade. "It went into his stomach, but still he didn't stop. He was screaming in pain, saying he'd kill me."

Gwynnie held her hand over her mouth, not daring to make a sound.

"There was only one way I could think of stopping his cries. To stop him from killing me as he threatened to. We were by the river. I pushed his head under…" She trailed off, closing her eyes as she turned her head away.

Gwynnie could barely breathe.

"It took a long time," Emlyn said eventually. "A part of me thought that I could run, that all would be fine if I did, then I remembered the look in his eye when he said he'd kill me. What if I had let him go and he did catch up with me? And God forbid, what if he only caught up with me when I was with you, Gwynnie? What would happen to you then?" She paused, shuddering. "I couldn't take the risk."

"You call that self-defence?" Gwynnie gasped, her whole body turning cold.

"It was." Emlyn's voice was quiet. "I didn't know what else to do. He had already killed your father, and now he was threatening me. I had every reason to think he would follow through. I kept his head pushed down. I never knew how much breath a man could hold inside him. He stopped moving. When I realised what I had done, I didn't feel guilt. Isn't that strange?" She looked at Tombstone. "No guilt at all. Not after what he had done to John-Louis." She sat upright in her chair. "I tipped him into the river. His body drifted down into the depths, carried away by the tide. I never saw him again. I picked up the blade, threw it into the water, and my hands … they were bloodstained from the dagger. I was going to wash them in the river when the nightwatchman who had followed Titus earlier appeared. He was calling out to me, running toward me. I suppose he had seen it all happen from a distance. It took no great leap of the imagination to know that I was facing a noose if he caught me."

"Have you *ever* felt guilt?" Tombstone asked after a moment of silence.

"No." Emlyn stared back. "Justice was done that night."

"Revenge. Not justice," Tombstone said suddenly, moving to stand.

Gwynnie watched Tombstone as he walked around the room, apparently unable to find a place to stand or sit.

"Are you going to arrest me?" Emlyn asked, as she wiped the last tears from her face. "See me hanged?"

Gwynnie moved to kneel by Emlyn's chair, as if she could somehow protect her from such an eventuality.

"No."

Gwynnie and Emlyn looked at one another.

Emlyn sat forward in her chair. "You are a lawyer who has a murderer in his chambers, and yet you will do nothing?"

Tombstone turned to face her. "The loot you have recovered, the jewels, the coins, all of it — you will return it to me."

"What?" Emlyn spluttered.

"Unless, of course, you'd like me to arrest you for murder?" Tombstone went on, as Emlyn gaped like a fish. "Gwynnie, you will bring the loot here. I will keep Emlyn under watch until then. Once I have the loot and it is returned to the king, Emlyn will walk free."

"You would do that?" Gwynnie asked, moving to stand. "You will let her go?"

"One life for another." His expression softened. "Mistress Wightham, you pulled me from the river. It is something I cannot forget. I'm no swimmer, and as you two saw today, that freezing water was enough to drown a man. Consider this the repayment of a debt. Your life for mine." He nodded. "Gwynnie, bring the loot here today. Whilst you are gone, there is something more I must discuss with your mother."

Gwynnie glanced between them. "What are you going to speak of?"

"I shall make the facts plain to Emlyn here, that if she were to continue with her attempt to blackmail the king, she will end up dead. Probably dumped in the Thames with a knife in her, much like Titus."

Emlyn flinched at his words.

"Now, Gwynnie," Tombstone said, his voice quiet but firm, "let today be an end of this. Find the loot and bring it back here."

Gwynnie had to pay for a cart to bring the crates from Shoreditch to Greenwich Palace, unable to carry both on her own along with Emlyn's bags, which she had found in the stable. When she reached the palace, she enlisted a servant boy to help her carry the second crate to Tombstone's lodgings.

By the time she returned to Tombstone's office, darkness had fallen. He'd lit rushlights and he and Emlyn were still sitting on either side of the fire. Emlyn looked tired and she clutched her bad arm, nursing it against her chest. Tombstone sat very still, his hands on the arms of his chair. He stared at Emlyn, much as a kestrel watches its prey.

The servant boy dropped the crate and bags at Gwynnie's feet. She thanked him and he turned to leave. Once the door was shut, Tombstone stood, moving toward the crates and helping Gwynnie to place them on the desk. Popping open the lids, Tombstone cursed.

"So much for me being the one with the rude tongue," Gwynnie murmured.

Tombstone shook his head as he stared at the jewels. "A fortune," he whispered. "Had the king known it had been found, he would have probably ordered a guard to run you both through at once." Gwynnie flinched as Tombstone calmly closed the lid. "We have an agreement then, Mistress Wightham?"

"What?" Gwynnie said. "What agreement?"

Emlyn had stood from her chair. "As you wish." Her voice was matter-of-fact now, with no hint of emotion. "I shall not bother you with this business again."

Tombstone lifted the letter from the assassin off his desk and wrapped it around Valeriana Moreau's jewel, placing it in a pocket of his doublet. "I shall return these crates to the king. We shall say they were found by local constables who brought them to the palace. A good Samaritan, that sort of thing."

Emlyn hung her head, her shoulders slumping just an inch.

"However…" Tombstone lifted the lid of the crate of jewels. He chose one, seemingly at random, a golden cross engraved with fine curling swirls, and edged with pearls and tiny diamonds. He turned, holding the jewel out in Emlyn's direction. "I shouldn't think the king would notice if one jewel were to go missing."

Gwynnie stared, open-mouthed. "What are you doing?"

Tombstone didn't answer.

"You would do this?" Emlyn stepped forward, but she didn't reach out to take the jewel, clearly mistrusting him.

"Use it to pay your way. Gwynnie tells me you always dreamed of giving up this life. That you both talked of living quietly, somewhere in France." Tombstone took Emlyn's hand and turned it, placing the jewel in her palm. "Take it and live that life. I never want to hear from you again." Turning away, he walked toward his desk, sitting down in the Savonarola chair, his manner unemotional as he drew the crates toward him.

Emlyn smiled, turning the jewel over in her hand. "It's a fine thing," she whispered.

"It is," Tombstone agreed. "So take it and be gone." He lifted parchment from a drawer, along with ink and a quill. "I can continue to give your daughter a life here. I have it on good authority from Cromwell that Fitzroy is leaving at the end of Twelfth Night, so I believe she'll be safe after that. But I cannot extend that protection to you."

Emlyn turned to Gwynnie, the jewel cradled in her palm. "You are going to stay?"

It had always been the deal that as long as Gwynnie stayed at the palace, Tombstone would not arrest Emlyn. Now, there was a choice. Tombstone was letting Emlyn leave for saving his life that day. Gwynnie could follow Emlyn too, if she wanted.

She thought of all that had happened over the last few days — hiding in London with her mother, hunting for a treasure that had caused so much bloodshed.

"I don't like the danger of that life, Ma."

"And it's safer here, is it?" Emlyn asked, her brow creasing.

"Not particularly," Gwynnie had to acknowledge. Tombstone looked up momentarily from what he was writing. "But it is a life I like more," she confessed, her words barely audible.

Emlyn moved toward her. Gwynnie thought her mother might shake her, beg her to come away, but instead Emlyn wrapped her good arm around Gwynnie and pulled her into an embrace.

"You've found a place for yourself, haven't you, miting? And it's no longer at my side."

Gwynnie said nothing, but held onto her mother tightly, knowing that soon enough she would have to let go.

CHAPTER 31

So many carts and horses were passing out of the open gate of the palace, that the guards hadn't stopped any to check their loads. They simply waved the tradesmen off and bowed respectfully to the carriages that carried ladies and gentlemen of the court away. There was shouting and well wishes, along with many complaining of aching heads and upset stomachs after so many days of drinking and overeating. Servants wandered to and fro, packing bags and boxes into the backs of carriages.

Amongst the crowd and shivering in the cold, Gwynnie stood facing her mother. Emlyn had adopted a servant's garb today, blending in with those around her. The warm woollen cloak at her shoulders was one Gwynnie had gifted to her. On her shoulder was her tapestry bag, and they both knew that tucked beneath her chemise was the jewelled cross Tombstone had pressed into her palm. Although they had already said their goodbyes, they still stood together, hands clasped, neither of them willing to walk away.

"Will you go to France?" Gwynnie asked, her voice muffled by the raucous noise around them.

It was the day after Twelfth Night. The fine evergreen boughs were being pulled off the cartwheels by serving boys running between them.

"Perhaps," Emlyn said, a soft smile on her lips. "I am not particularly good at walking far these days. A small village will suit me."

"You'll be bored."

“Of that, I have no doubt.” She laughed, but Gwynnie did not. It was her greatest fear that if Emlyn grew bored, she would fall back into her old ways. “I’ll find a way of letting you know where I am, miting. I promise.”

Gwynnie nodded and moved to hug her mother. They held each other close, until Emlyn stepped back.

“I hope that lawyer looks after you,” she said, with something like judgement in her tone. “I don’t trust his intentions.”

“This from the woman who just tried to blackmail —”

“I know what I did.” Emlyn cut her off. “Temptation comes to us all, sometimes.” She glanced over her shoulder at the open gate. “It is time to depart.”

“Life seems full of partings,” Gwynnie whispered, thinking of Devlin, whom she had said goodbye to just a couple of weeks ago.

“That’s what life is, dearest. Meetings and partings. And a chance to smile in between.” Her eyes were drawn by something, and she looked over Gwynnie’s head. Gwynnie turned to see Tombstone, who watched from a distance, his arms folded. “I hope your friend knows what he’s doing,” Emlyn murmured. “I’m not convinced the palace is a safe place to be.”

“It’s not about being safe,” Gwynnie replied. She could have told her it was about doing something good, about striving to protect people from killers in these very walls, killers who wore a crown and sat on the throne, but she had a strong feeling Emlyn wouldn’t understand. “Be well, Ma.”

“And you, miting.” Emlyn bent forward and kissed Gwynnie on the forehead, then she turned and left, melting into the crowd that was passing through the gate. Under the portcullis, she turned and raised her hand to wave. Gwynnie waved back, her chest aching, as her mother disappeared from sight.

"Come away," a voice urged in her ear. It was Tombstone. He'd come to take her arm.

"What is it?"

"Come, quickly." He nodded across the yard. "Fitzroy is taking his leave. I don't want him or his men to see you." Gwynnie walked in Tombstone's shadow as they passed by Fitzroy's carriage. He was being waved off by his father, King Henry, as Amaro and Humphrey hassled the coachman to hurry with the horses.

Together, Gwynnie and Tombstone passed through the tiltyard and into the lawyer's chambers in the southern wall of the palace. In Tombstone's office, the two crates still rested on the table.

"You haven't turned them in yet?" Gwynnie asked in surprise.

"I shall, later today." Tombstone shrugged off his cloak and laid it across the back of the chair behind his desk. "I didn't want to raise Cromwell's suspicions while Emlyn was still in the palace." He poured out two glasses of port and passed one to Gwynnie. "You are certain of this? You did not wish to go with her?"

"If you ask such foolish questions, expect no answers from me," she replied wryly, taking a big gulp of the port.

He smiled encouragingly and sat down in his chair. "I am glad, Gwynnie."

"Why?"

"Because you deserve a better life than the one your mother was offering you."

Gwynnie said nothing, but she moved toward the carafe and hurriedly topped up her port. She filled it all the way to the brim and was rather relieved when Tombstone didn't admonish her for it. He merely chuckled under his breath.

"Do you think she'll do it?" he asked. "Give up thieving?"

Gwynnie lowered the port from her lips. "No. I know what she means. It's all too easy to steal, as easy as breathing. I do it every day."

"You steal small things. Like port." He nodded at her glass.

"Even when she had all the jewels she could ever want, she still took that necklace from the woman at the Frost Fair, did she not?" Gwynnie stared down at her glass. "No. I do not think she's capable of giving it up."

Tombstone slowly nodded. "There is one more matter we must discuss." He reached into his doublet and pulled out the letter from the assassin, along with the jewel. "It shall not be returned along with the rest to the king."

Gwynnie nearly dropped her glass. "Why not?"

"Because it strikes me, that you and I may one day need to have our own bargaining tool. Fitzroy may be leaving for now, but he'll be back someday. Assuring him that we could make trouble for his father may prove a very good way to ensure he leaves you alone."

"That's blackmail."

"It's bargaining." Tombstone was firm. "We keep it, Gwynnie. There may be a day when we have need of it. What do you say?"

She stood on the other side of the desk and raised her glass. "Well, I suppose I should make a toast then. To blackmailing the son of a king!"

Tombstone laughed, then he shook his head. "No, Gwynnie. Let us toast to surviving."

She clinked her glass against his, understanding exactly what he meant. Living in the palace was just as dangerous as living beyond the palace walls. "To surviving."

HISTORICAL NOTES

Though elements of this book are inspired by true events, please note that *The King's Stolen Jewels* is a work of fiction. I have taken facts and used them to inspire a story meant for entertainment. I truly hope you have enjoyed the creative aspects of this novel.

This story takes place across the Christmas period of 1536. It shortly follows the Pilgrimage of Grace, when Robert Aske was invited to spend Christmas at Greenwich Palace with King Henry and the court. Although flattered much at court, unrest broke out again in 1537 and Aske was soon executed in July of that year.

In December 1536, the Thames froze over. King Henry and Queen Jane were seen on a royal parade down the river, along with a Frost Fayre, with stallholders lining the ice like a busy London street.

Key to the novels in this series are the chosen settings. Greenwich Palace, as mentioned in previous books, no longer exists. It was known to be a beloved palace of Henry VIII, and we know that he and Queen Jane enjoyed Christmas of 1536 there. Multiple phases of archaeological digs have taken place at Greenwich to try to discover more about the original palace. One of the most recent digs took place in 2017 on the site of the Old Royal Naval College in Greenwich. If you're interested in the archaeology, I'd recommend reading some of the resources on the **Old Royal Naval College** website and **The Archaeology Magazine** website.

I hope you have enjoyed the historical references in this tale.

A NOTE TO THE READER

Dear Reader,

Thank you for taking the time to read *The King's Stolen Jewels.* I truly hope that you have enjoyed reading it as much as I have enjoyed writing it. Gwynnie will be back in a new adventure soon.

Reviews by readers these days are integral to a book's success, so if you enjoyed *The King's Stolen Jewels* I would be very grateful if you could spare a minute to post a review on **Amazon** and **Goodreads**. I love hearing from readers, and you can talk with me through **my website** or **on X** and follow my author page **on Facebook**.

I hope we'll meet again in the next adventure.

Adele Jordan

Printed in Dunstable, United Kingdom

80107937R10150